...ne 2023

Chasing the Heartland

Lieve Ben en Loes

Goede vrienden
zelfs met een zee
ertussen.

Let's promise to
always

pull out of here to win...
together

♡

Pauline
xxx

Chasing
the
Heartland

Paulina Vanderbilt

Chasing the Heartland

ISBN Paperback: 978-94-6247-314-0

Edited by Kristin in Holland

Cover (Art) by unknown. All effort has been made to find the artist of this limited-edition print; I was unable to identify them. If you are the artist and can prove it, please get in touch to discuss copyright. Design: Paulina Vanderbilt
Indesign edit: Mischa van den Brandhof.

Printed by bestelmijnboek.nl
First published in the Netherlands in 2023

My life flows on in endless song;
Above earth's lamentation,
I catch the sweet, tho' far-off hymn
That hails a new creation.
Thro' all the tumult and the strife
I hear the music ringing;
It finds an echo in my soul –
How can I keep from singing?

From: *How can I Keep from Singing*
Pauline T (trad.)

Everything is swept away

The scent of freedom clung to Wendy like a mouldy wedding dress. The boardwalk was lying in the heat of the day and the buzz of seaside holiday makers complemented the roll of gentle breakers, a soothing foundation for the jingle-jangle flash of the makeshift fair rides a little further along. The fourth of July, in Asbury Park – half a lifetime later than planned, but here now. This then, was little Eden, the place she had dreamt of visiting ever since, well, forever. Tonight, the fireworks would be hailing, but first she was going to kick off her shoes and feel the sand between her toes.

The sand was hot; the day was hotter. Wendy left her shoes and jeans close to the firm dark sand and waded into the ocean up to her knees. The water was hungry for her and pulled at her calves but she stood calm and firm. She had forgotten to bring her bathing suit. Secretly, she smiled at herself. Her mother would have been so upset to know she had not made a careful list, checked it twice and remembered to always pack a swimsuit. The gentle sea breeze raised some hairs on her forearms. She jumped up as a larger wave threatened to wet her pants, but then, in the spur of the moment, Wendy undid the scrunchie that kept her black, unruly curls in check, whooped and fell backwards into the sea.

The sea was warm and carefree. Wendy relaxed her breathing. She was not the only one in the water but the only one with her clothes on. They would dry. She looked at the sky as she floated on her back, aware that at any moment a wave could break on top of her and leave her gasping for air. It didn't though, and after twenty minutes she waded out of the water and retrieved her jeans. She looked about her, briefly hesitating. Then she pulled off her pants and stepped into her jeans commando.

'Hey, there are children around here!' an oversized sun-bright woman shouted. Wendy looked at the woman who was sporting an ill-fitting bikini that revealed much more than the few inches of flesh she had shown in the whole 10 seconds it took to wrench on her jeans. She put it down to cultural differences but decided to keep her wet top on after this. She sat down, pulled up her knees and hugged herself, still in disbelief she was finally here.

Wendy woke up with a jolt. Her first instinct was to check for her bag. It was still there, and her passport and purse were still safe too. She checked her watch and saw she had slept for more than an hour. It had gotten busier, but the atmosphere was still relaxed. Next to her a young couple was holding hands and murmuring into each other's ears, brushing each other's earlobe with their lips briefly after each exchange. It was clear that the blonde girl was absolutely smitten. Her caramel tan was a sharp contrast to the dark fudge of her lover's skin; the disobedient sea-salt blonde curls the opposite of the other's straight-jacketed corn-braids. Both wore a crop-top revealing tight tummies and pierced belly buttons.

'Excuse me, sorry for bothering you, may I ask a question?' Wendy took the smile as a yes and continued, 'Are there fireworks on tonight?'

'Sure, it is the fourth of July. You should probably move over to another section of the beach though, nearer the Casino.' The cornbraided girl lazily waved her hands to a bit further up the beach nearer a ram-shackled looking building. 'Not to worry, there's plenty of time before anything happens.'

Wendy took out an A4 sized publication. She had not prepared this trip much, but she had found this thing online a few months back as she had looked up Asbury Park and Bruce Springsteen: A Rock & Roll Tour of the Jersey Shore. She had read most of it on the plane, but it had been too much to take in. Yet, she knew the first thing she wanted to do was find Madam Marie and have her fortune told. She strolled back up to the boardwalk and walked towards the Convention Hall. Its copper green detailing gave it a real art nouveau feel; it looked grander than she had imagined it from the descriptions she had read.

The square stone booth was right there on her left, but like a lot on the shore, it was little more than a remnant of past glory. The third eye and white writing on the side of wall reminded Wendy of the fairgrounds of her youth: the thrill in those days was not rollercoasters loop-the-looping at break-neck speed but the willingness to go along with the seduction of imagination. That moment of suspended disbelief when the world was richer and more innocent, which both players implicitly agreed upon when a coin passed hands. Wendy sat down and took out a small notebook. She might as well do some journaling whilst she was here. It would be interesting, no doubt, to look back on these days in years to come. As no one was working the Temple of Knowledge, she entered the date and wrote her first entry in the voice of Madam Marie.

I see a fork in the road into the future. If you allow your doubts and fears to direct you, you'll find yourself stuck with those demons somewhere in the swamps of Jersey. Lift the veil of doubt off your heart, and let go of the expectations of others. It is then that you'll find your true path, and return to the essence of you.

Wendy gnawed her pen, and gazed out over the crowd. The laughter and shrieks of excited children reminded her that this was a day of celebration. Eighteen years ago on this day, a muscled man with a voice of a rusty nail had changed her fortunes. He had blown her teenage world right open, and she had had a brief taste of freedom before she had blown it all. Tonight, she'd celebrate her independence anew, with the crack and flash of fireworks. Tomorrow she'd start her pilgrimage. She ditched the notebook in her jute duffle bag, snapped the clasp to, and walk to the section of beach she had been directed to, dizzy with the niggling dread that her version of Madam Marie's fortune telling was not better than they do.

All the fun has been had

I never thought it would happen: thirty. When I was fifteen, thirty was two times too old, thirty was over the hill, thirty was five years older than I'd given myself to live. Thirty had as much to do with me as Long Johns with the Chippendales. It came, and it went, and I didn't like it one bit. Springsteen was my age when he wrote Dancing in the Dark; it hit a nerve when I was fifteen. Life took over but it came back to me. Thirty is this limbo, a suffocating trap. Too old for chasing dreams, too young for giving up on them. I'm surprised I didn't see the moment coming. It wasn't an overnight thing I'm sure, but it knocked me like a wrecking ball last year at Wembley Arena.

Rosie looked up from the bit of paper. She sighed as she pushed a stray lock back behind her ear. This was so typical of her mother. Always talking too much, analysing everything. She read on.

I'm thirty-four now and I feel old. Not just old, ancient. You're at the academy, ready to fend for yourself. It's quite obvious from your behaviour you don't need me around. So now it is my turn. I'm lumbered with a forty-year old husband on the couch, zombified and slippered, for whom the footie is the highlight of the evening. It's like your father is ready to sit out his time.

Rosie rolled her eyes. Whom! Who said whom these days? Only her mother! She could just imagine her mother and her freedom: a denim skirt at least ten centimetres too short, a tight Lycra top in neon colours, showing off all of her carefully cultivated middle-age spread, teetering heels like knitting needles, and a cowboy hat to finish it off. She never knew anyone who could get it so wrong.

Well, I'm not. I need to find out who I am. I am going back to my roots. Mum.

'What utter shite!' Rosie crumpled up the note and tossed it across the room. She was hungry and tired. Her period had started and the start of school was just weeks away. This was just about the last thing she needed: her mother in some sort of mid-life crisis, looking for her family history. She glanced at her watch. It didn't look like she'd be back tonight though. Great! She'd better look in the fridge and see what she could muster up.

Rosie got off the stool and moved over to the fridge. It was another hour before her dad would be home. For a moment she contemplated sending him a text to prepare him for an empty house but quickly dismissed the idea. Then she'd have to explain over the phone. Better not. Anyway, she wanted to meet up with Maria tonight. No time to be the broad shoulder her dad could cry on, the foundation he could build on, or any of that sentimental crap. Let them sort it out between themselves. This was no matter for a teenager. They should be old and wise enough.

She looked at the worktop: one red onion, a wrinkled potato with white shoots sprouting from it, half a green pepper, tomatoes, a courgette and a thingamabob. She held up the blob with the green leaves. Some sort of cabbage. It always seemed so easy on those cooking programmes. People plonk their shopping on the table and the chef goes: Ah, excellent! I will be making… and then rattle of some delicious sounding dish using exactly those ingredients. What would they make of this?

She turned to rummage in the cupboard. It was full of baked beans. She had stopped eating them for the past three years but her mum still bought a regular supply, oblivious to her change of diet. Like it had only taken a good five months before her mum finally realised, for good, for real, that she was no longer eating meat. Then there were the following three weeks in which she tried to coax Rosie back onto it, then the two weeks of sulk and anger, all your bones will collapse and you'll end up like the hunchback of the Notre Dame, with his crooked back and bowlegs and then there was the day the moaning finally stopped and the beans started to pile up.

Rosie found a jar of plum sauce hidden behind the Baked Beans. The green blob looked somewhat like Chinese cabbage, so perhaps she could do an oriental stir-fry. She'd do a Jamie Oliver: everything in one wok, in neat little pieces. At least it would look … green. Sure, Jamie would do a sauce from scratch but then, he had nothing better to do. She had a social life.

Rosie took a small knife from the drawer and started chopping up the onion. The juice stained her fingers. Gad, how she hated red onions for that. A double whammy: stink and stain. She switched on the radio with her elbow. Some geezer with a voice like an auctioneer on speed was raving on about a local band, that, according to him, was going to be the next big thing to come from Aberdeen. Like there had been that many great things from Aberdeen. Rosie thought about it. She thought about it hard. And drew a blank. Of course, there was the deep-fried Mars-bar but even that wasn't quite from Aberdeen. She took the courgette and began to chop it up.

She went over the letter in her head. It was a bit weird, to say the least. Her mum had never gone away on her own. Never that she could remember anyway. She'd shrink at the idea of having to drive more than an hour by herself. Got nervous even catching the bus into town. Going on holiday was a theatre production in itself. The preparations started at least three months before. She'd book some sort of Gîte or mountain hut or German Castle and then spend weeks emailing back and forth, seeking confirmation of every single detail, over and over again. But all that stress was nothing compared to what happened when her mother had to get onto a plane. Passports held in sweaty palms, arriving two hours early for even the earliest check-in time. Reading over bits of paper again, and again, and again, flapping them about like a demented flamingo. Hyperventilating in the sick bag during take-off and landing.

Where would this woman go? A friend maybe. A friend in Aberdeen, who could keep a secret. That pretty much ruled out all of her friends then. A B&B or hotel even, waiting for the phone call begging her to come home. It wouldn't come from her. She shifted the courgette along the cutting board. Her eyes fell on her mother's mobile phone. Ah well, she would not be calling then. She shrugged. She quite fancied a few days without mum. Dad never got onto her about anything, so it would be pretty chilled. She could do chilled. No problem.

Rosie finished the courgette and put the wok on the stove. She poured in the extra-virgin olive oil and stirred the spatula to keep the vegetables from burning. As she reached for the pepper grinder she heard the front door. It had taken exactly half a day for her mother to stay missing. What a record. When she turned around, she saw it was her dad. He was very early today. He wore a grey trilby hat and a tartan scarf tied loosely around his neck. He dropped his bag and sat on one of the stools.

'What are you cooking?' Not even a hint of surprise. It must have been the fourth time ever in her life that she was cooking (and two of them were pancakes on Shrove Tuesday), yet dad failed to notice the significance. She grunted and tipped the pan over so he could see.

'A stir-fry? He looked a little worried. Rosie nodded curtly.

'Okay that'll do. Where's your mother?'

Rosie shrugged her shoulders and continued stirring the shrivelled vegetables. Her dad tried again.

'Where's your mother?'

Rosie looked up, sighed, and walked over to the crumpled-up bit of paper. She unfolded it and planted it on the breakfast bar. Then she went back to her wok. Her dad read the note. She watched his face. She couldn't read anything off it. Blank as a corpse. She took the jar with plum sauce and tried to open it. The lid was stiff. She twisted with all her might, trying hard not to show her dad she was struggling. She tapped the side on the edge of the worktop, turning it in her hands so as to not miss one bit. She ran it under a hot tap. Still she could not open the jar. She glanced at her dad. He was just sitting there, with the note in his hands, with that same vacant stare. He coughed.

'Urgh, what time were you home? When did you find this note?' His voice was stale and pinched. He sounded like a young boy who's been sent to the headmaster's office and who's trying to make conversation before accepting the belt. Rosie shrugged.

'What time did you find this letter, ROSIE! Speak to me. For once!'

Rosie was taken aback by the sudden anger in his voice. Where did that come from? She faltered, 'Uh, dunno. About half an hour ago, I guess.' She knew her night at Maria's was slip-sliding away. A darkish smoke started to come from the wok. She turned the gas low. One stir-fry, well-done, please. She held her jar out to her dad.

Her dad stared at the jar with bewilderment. Rosie turned the gas off to save the last few slices of courgette and green pepper. Her dad took the jar, read the label and turned it over in his hand. He looked at her, then at the note, and turned his head away. Then he let out one almighty roar and threw the jar across the breakfast bar, past the fridge, against the kitchen door. It splattered into a million little pieces. Black sauce slimed down like a slow lava stream, the bits of glass the debris of the explosion.

'SHIT, SHIT, SHIT!' he cursed. Then he paced out of the kitchen into the living room, slamming the door, and switched on the TV. He'd taken it well then.

Rosie ripped some kitchen towel and cleaned up the biggest mess. He could do the rest. Then she took out her mobile phone and texted Maria. Not eaten yet. C u in 10. She left through the backdoor without glancing back.

The wind bit her cheeks and she wished now that she'd put a coat on. It had been warmer for a few weeks but there was no sign of summer in the air today. Rosie tucked her head as far as she could in the collar of her black hoodie. She walked her walk, her bad-ass attitude barely disguised by her nonchalant sway. She felt on edge and sharp.

Maria's house was another two blocks away. It used to be a cool place to hang out. There was always something happening. Maria's two older brothers played in a band and showed off all the time. According to Marco, all a bloke ever needed was a guitar. A guitar, Marco bragged, was synonymous with sex. It brings in the chicks, the chicks bring in the booze. Once the booze is in the chicks, the dick's in the chicks. Marco was a sleaze-bag. But Toni, now he was a different story all together. He flashed his guitar about too, but on him it looked like a gun. There was no promise of lust when he played, just a real sense of danger. That intrigued Rosie. Toni had a mean streak. First time she spoke to him he wanted to know about her dark eyeliner. The next time she saw him he had died his hair black, and circled his eyes so they sank with the bleakness of a dying junkie. He also had black lips and nails. Nineteen he was.

One night when Maria's parents were out, the boys had organised a garage-gig. Toni had slung his arms around Rosie and pulled her in tight and hard. He claimed her that night, period. She loved the jealous looks from the other girls — pretty blonde girls with blue eyes and dainty noses, who nibbled their way through at least three lettuces a week and not much else; brunettes with doe-eyes and gullible written on their foreheads. The school's prefects, the head-girl, they all wanted to be with Toni but instead, he claimed her. They smoked her first joint together that evening. She had her first ever kiss with him too. It had been urgent and rough. She had not liked it.

Maria had been furious with her. Rosie had ignored her.

Next day, Marco and Toni were gone. Toni didn't bother to tell her or anything. From Maria she knew he was squatting in a flat in North London. She got one text a week later saying she was a cool chick but that he had to move on. She hadn't heard from him since.

Then, about a month later, Mr Dante told his wife he no longer loved her, moved out soon after, and settled with a young employee of his firm in a council flat across town. Mrs Dante had shrivelled up and just about died. So too had the place. It was no longer cool, it was downright freezing without the family. Maria didn't seem to mind too much. She and her mum just about tolerated each other in best of times, so now there was no reason for forced jollity, so at least she could get on with her own life. Or so she said.

Rosie turned the last corner. Her mobile vibrated. It was Maria. *Be cool, all right? C u soon.*

Rosie frowned. What kind of message was that? She looked about her. The trees were full of promise, the air felt of change. She took another deep breath: definitely change. With a whiff of danger. Maria switched off whenever Rosie described the smell in the air. But often she was right. Rain, snow, they were easy to sniff, but she was right about other things too: change, sadness, loneliness. It was right there. You just needed to be open to it. In the window on her right, an old couple were snuggled up together. He was asleep, his body heavy against her shoulder. A trickle of spit sat on his lower lip. She was knitting. The electric fire gave off an orange glow.

She thought about her mother. She always believed her parents were destined for long-term familiarity like the couple on her right. Seventeen years is a long time to get to know the other inside out, and read them like the back of your hand. She couldn't get her head round the note she found this afternoon. It was so unbelievably unlike her mum. The only thing she seemed to fuss about was her family. Why would she suddenly leave it all behind? Surely she was too young for a mid-life crisis! She'd have half expected her dad to drive off on a motorbike, all in black leathers, hair razored to the skin, like Mr Dante. But her mum didn't just drop everything and disappear.

Rosie stopped. In front of Maria's house was a car she didn't recognise. It was a battered old Volkswagen van. Flowered curtains had been drawn across the small windows at the back. Someone had doodled very bad graffiti all along the sides. Rosie spotted a guitar weeping blood, a Harley Davidson driven by a skeleton. There was a huge dent above the back wheel. She thought about the text Maria sent her a few minutes ago. Puzzled but intrigued she walked along the house. She rapped the backdoor and walked straight in.

At the kitchen table sat Toni. Or what was left of him. He still wore the black eyeliner, but now it no longer gave off a hint of gutter-chic. His drawn face with its hollow cheeks now matched the persona he'd painted on two years ago. He'd shrivelled away to the image he'd wanted to imitate then. His arms were brittle sticks, and Rosie spotted sores and bruises on the inside of his elbow. He was dragging hard on his Marlboro as if he couldn't be bothered inhaling just the smoke but needed to suck the actual tobacco straight inside him. He looked up at her.

'Hey buttercup.' Then he looked down at the table and muttered something.

'What was that Toni?' Rosie tried to sound nonchalant. She tried not show how shocked she was to find Toni here in such a state. She was surprised at the anger that rose to her cheeks. She should feel relief, really.

'Nothing.' He took a deep drag. It brought on a fit of coughing. He sounded like a 75-year-old with cancerous lungs.

'No need to be shy, you're amongst family,' Rosie joked lightly. She slapped his shoulder but made sure she let the back of her hand rest very briefly on his cheek before she pulled back. Toni shivered slightly.

'Just saying how you are still a bonnie flower in this fucked up place.' There was a chill in his voice.

Rosie caught Maria's look. She shrugged sheepishly and pretended she didn't notice the dark warning in Maria's set mouth. Mrs Dante was flustering about with tea and biscuits. Toni ignored her.

'Come on Rosie, let's go up to my room.' Maria dragged Rosie by the arm, snatching up some biscuits and slices of toast. She dragged Rosie past the family portrait in the hall, taken four years ago and now gathering dust, and up the worn steps. She slammed the door after them and flopped onto the bed.

Neither spoke. They often laid on the bed, staring at the ceiling and being quiet. Such silence between them had never been awkward but tonight it was tinged with speculation. Maria broke the silence.

'He's fucked up, you hear. Just ignore him. He's just after some food and heat. He's not looking to stay. He's not sticking around for love.' She paused and looked straight at Rosie. 'As soon as he's got my mum to give him some money he'll be off.'

'Don't worry, I got that the last time round.' Rosie sighed. 'It looks like my mum has left too.'

'What?' Maria bolted upright. 'Your mum? You're joking, right?'

Rosie shook her head. 'I still think she'll be back tomorrow, maybe even tonight actually, but it's still weird. She left this note about finding out who she is. Like, what's that all about?'

Maria looked at Rosie in disbelief. 'Your mother? You're talking about your mother? The woman who gets heart palpitations trying to find a parking space at Asda's? The woman who sits waiting every day after school, with a cup of tea and a biscuit? The woman who sighs when you come home late and then makes you a cup of hot cocoa? That woman? That's the woman you are saying has just up and left?'

Rosie nodded. 'Uh huh.' Rosie remained quiet. She gnawed the sides of her thumb. Maria said it was a disgusting habit but Rosie didn't realise she was even doing it, most of the time. Now she stopped herself. She started to pluck Maria's Sherpa bedspread instead.

'Shit, what is it about all of them? It's like, they're the adults, aren't they? Like, they should know better. So why do they end up fucking everything up?' Maria used her pillow as a punch bag. Oh, I feel that there's so much more to life than this. Punch. I didn't know really what I got myself into when I married your mother. I was young and foolish. Punch. I have a right to a life too! Punch, punch. She stopped and glanced at Rosie. 'Sorry, Rose. It's not about me. Do you think your mum is serious? Like my dad? You think this is for real?'

'I don't know, and I don't care. All she ever does is nag, nag, nag. And if she's not nagging, she's fussing. Good riddance, I'd say.' Rosie pulled back her shoulders and sat up straight. C'mon. I've brought some henna for my hair.' Rosie took out a random CD from the large pile on the floor next to the bed. Christina. Ah well, better than Britney at least. Maria's taste still needed some education.

Seeing Toni had rattled Rosie. Not because of what she felt for him, but because of what she didn't feel. The anger rising on her cheeks when she saw him at that kitchen table was not of a broken heart but of wounded pride. The girls at school had been vicious, slut-shaming her at every opportunity possible. She hadn't even slept with Toni. That whole night had been nothing but awkward fumbling, with both of them being too high to pay attention to the other. It had left her cold. In fact, she had been relieved he hadn't pushed her head down into his crotch or attempted to get his hand inside her knickers. Not that she would ever admit that to any of those girls.

She was angry at Toni for buggering off, and letting her deal with the fall-out on her own. School was a dog-eat-dog institution at the best of times. Put a jealous gaggle of teen queens in there and it became positively toxic. And then she was confused too. Should she not have felt tingling all over when he first kissed her? Should she not have pined for him, fantasized about what could have been? Smelt the lingering breath of him on her clothes, and ached for more? Should she not have felt a bolt of excitement for seeing him tonight?

Rosie stuck her key in the front door and noticed the lights in the living room were still on. She checked to see if her dad had forgotten, but as she put her head around the door she saw him staring at the wall.

'Hey Dad, you're still up?'

He shrugged. There was no sign of dinner, just two empty bottles of wine and a random sales channel harping on about a pair of garden sheers that were truly revolutionary.

'You want something to eat? I'm making a marmite toastie.' He shrugged. She left him to it, and returned a few minutes later with her toast.

'She won't stay away for long. I mean, where would she go? I'm sure whatever friend she's gone to will have enough of her after a few days.'

'I phoned all of them. Nobody's heard from her. And I don't think they are lying either.'

'Did you know she was unhappy?' She had not seen much change in her mum, but she had observed her mum would not join her and her dad on the settee when they watched The Weakest Link. She had taken up running too. Every morning at seven she'd be out for an hour. But wanting to be fit surely isn't a sign of misery? 'Dad? Had Mum said she was unhappy?'

'Restless, maybe.'

'Restless about what? What do you mean? Since when?'

'You know how last year she went to Wembley Arena to see Bruce Springsteen?' Her dad looked up from the TV screen. 'Did you not notice she started playing his music in the house all the time? After work, when I'd come in, she'd be dancing in the kitchen with a glass of wine in her hand, record player on high.'

Rosie had not been aware. She had not really paid much attention to her mum lately. There was too much in her own life to get on with.

'She's been going on and on about the first time she saw Springsteen. When we met.'

Rosie choked on her toast. 'You met at a Springsteen concert? Mum, I mean MY mum, went to rock concerts? How come you guys never told me?'

'You never asked.' Her dad opened another bottle of red. 'I first met your mother on the fourth of July 1985, Wembley Stadium. She had hiked her way down, despite your grandma and grandda trying to stop her. '

'My mother? Hitchhiked all the way from Aberdeen to Wembley?'

'No, she lived in Oxford at the time. But yes, she did hitchhike. Her dad had torn up the train ticket, and confiscated her concert ticket. She still went.'

Rosie looked at the TV screen. A man with Clooney-white teeth and a Jagger-smile was taking a vacuum cleaner apart, presenting each part as a miracle of technological innovation. Her mother had been a rebel. And her dad had been a gigging-guy, who picked up girls at concerts?

'How do you even meet the girl you are going to marry in a crowd of 80,000?'

Her dad chuckled. It was catching. Rosie felt a little jolt of carelessness lift some of the heavy curtains that seemed to enclose most of her thoughts these days.

'You know how I said that your grandda had taken her ticket too? Well, I'm sitting on the pavement outside Wembley with my mates. The gates opened at four that day, but we had come early to see if we could get to the front.'

'Since when do you go to concerts Dad?'

'I don't. Didn't really, but Springsteen was THE biggest thing at the time. Everyone and their uncle was going. We had taken a day off, the sun was out and the place was buzzing in anticipation. We were minding our own beers, and playing some tunes on this cheap guitar one of my mates had taken with him. I had just gone into the opening chords of Dancing in the Dark, when this firecracker of a girl with a cardboard sign walks by: one ticket to see the Boss. I remember thinking Good luck with that! She didn't look as if she had the money to buy it off any of the touts out there that day. She glanced over when she heard the tune, but never stopped walking. Anyhow, four pm arrives, we are all a little worse for wear, and it transpires that we are at the wrong turnstile. So we trundled over to turnstile C – I think it was C – obviously pissed that we'd be nowhere near the front now … and who should we see but the firecracker? I asked her where she'd found the ticket.

'I haven't. Not at those prices.'

'So how are you going to get in?'

'With you lot.'

'She figured that being quite late in the queue the security would be keen to get people in. So she flashed a random piece of paper in front of my eyes and said that she'd just squeeze in through the same turnstile as me. She told the rest of the gang to really crowd around me when I showed my ticket. I asked her why she thought I would agree.'

'You've got a button of The Clash on your jacket. Or are you only fashionably punk, to look cool?'

'What do you know about the Clash? Aren't you too young for that? How old are you anyhow?'

'Listen, my dad stole my ticket. I had saved up, and moved heaven and earth to get one. And then he goes all concerned over me, saying that London isn't a place for a 16-year-old girl on her own.'

'Really, just like that?'

'Well I had skived off school one too many times I suppose. Normally, I'd cover my tracks, but this time around I'd left some loose ends, and got caught. My dad is never home before eight at night, but now he suddenly decided to show me who's boss.'

'And let me guess, you reckon Bruce is Boss?'

'Got it in one strummer boy.'

Her dad had sat up a bit. 'And that's what we did. She squeezed in with me, waving about that empty piece of paper and smiling her pretty innocent smile. She hung around with us most of the concert, and afterwards we exchanged phone numbers. The rest …'

'… is history,' Rosie added.

In bed that night, staring at the ceiling, Rosie went over what she had just learned about her mother. Come to think of it, Rosie had been surprised last year when her mother decided to go to London alone. She had not really spoken about the trip with her. Rosie had assumed that it had something to do with work. Her mother had not said she was going to see Springsteen, and her father had not commented much at all. He had not liked it much – that much was clear – when her mother went away on her own, but besides being neurotic, her mother was also the most pig-headed woman Rosie knew.

Two years ago, her mother had made up her mind that Rosie's English teacher was not doing his job: he was letting Rosie skive off reading. Rosie had been a good reader in primary six, but really had other things on her mind when she got to secondary school. Mr Dannyston was not pushing her to read anything substantial, so she settled for Why the Whales Came to fulfil the course criteria, although she had already devoured the first three Harry Potters and Noughts and Crosses by the end of primary six. Her mother had asked, yes asked, for a parent-teacher consultation. And had told Mr Dannyston exactly what she thought of his lack of interest in her daughter and her slovenly book choice. He had retorted that perhaps a pushy mum was not what Rosie needed at that moment – he was absolutely right there – but Rosie had kept her mouth shut, looking down at the red, badly bitten rims around her nails in embarrassment. She had never witnessed a volcano erupt, but she reckoned if it was only half as frightening, smoking and fiery as her mother's hand on the table, it was sure something to stay away from in future. Three weeks later Rosie was moved to another class, and Mr Dannyston put in charge of outdoor activities, in a quiet 'career move'.

Sleep was not coming, so Rosie decided she'd listen to some Springsteen. What was it about that man that made her mum up and leave in the most un-mum-like move ever? She tiptoed to the living room. Her dad had fallen asleep on the sofa, clutching an empty wine glass that lay askew on his stomach. The TV was still on. Carefully she moved towards the CD player. A bunch of CDs were on top of the speaker. Rosie reached for the remote control and switched off the TV. The room was instantly clad in deep black-dog darkness, the way she liked her shed in the afternoons. She fumbled past the sofa but caught her small toe on the low table. For FUCKKKKK sake she inhaled. Her dad was oblivious in his drunken stupor. When she got to her bedroom, she switched on the light. The nail of her little toe was bleeding. She cursed again. At least she felt that! She took the CD out of the box and fast forwarded to the penultimate track. She laid down again and closed her eyes.

Last year, her mother had gone to London on her own, just like she had done almost seventeen years ago. It now seemed that was a return to a man called the future of rock and roll, a nostalgic attempt to recapture a past long forgotten. Listening to her dad, Rosie figured the trip had made her feel young again, and wanting to change her clothes, her face and, so it seemed, her life. Although Rosie could not really fathom what her mother was hoping to find away from her suburban middle-class life that had everything – a husband, a child, a house, a job, a yearly holiday – she began to understand the power of those words. And she fell asleep with exactly those words on the tip of her tongue, and a spark in the ember of her heart.

Shutting off the risk and pain

Cruising around Asbury was a reality check. Those early Springsteen records that had been set so firmly in this landscape had clearly romanticised the poverty Wendy encountered when she went looking for a car rental. Last night the shore had been lit up in beautiful whites, purples and golds but in the early-morning light of the town, she saw another side: faded jeans, torn and stained shirts, threadbare shoes, people bunched up in alleyways with hunger in their eyes. Not the hunger for the dreams Springsteen sang about, just the grovelling rumble in stomachs that hadn't been fed with much more than hard liquor and cheap fast food. She felt their eyes creep all over her, but other than lazy smirks, she didn't encounter much destitute animosity that prevented her from exploring the south side with the eye of a tourist. She felt guilty for bargaining so hard for the car.

'Yes, can I help you?' Everything behind the sly smile betrayed he had observed her and had decided she was easy pickings.

'I hope so. I want to drive around the area for three days. Would you have a car available?'

'You going far?' the man leant against the doorpost, his left foot without flip-flop, scratching his right shin.

Wendy had no idea. Maybe buying a map should have been the first thing. 'Don't think so, Asbury, Freehold, bit of the coast, Redbank.'

'You come all the way to the US of A and you're gonna cruise the dumps of Jersey? How come?'

‘Springsteen.’

The man sucked in through his teeth. ‘Uh-huh, middle-class white girl, chasing the myth of a working-class singer who is singlehandedly saving my hometown. Sounds about right. I guess it is how heroes are made.’

Wendy decided to ignore the sneer, and instead started to back off. ‘It’s okay if you don’t have a car, I’m sure I can find one somewhere else.’ She couldn’t help the sharp note to her voice. The truth always stung, but she’d liked the romanticism with which she had set off on her adventure. Living it for a little longer surely wouldn’t harm.

‘Easy now, no offence meant. Come ‘round the back. There’s a few cars to choose from.’

Wendy had chosen a beat-up silver Mazda, and got the store owner down to $30 for the three days, pointing out the scratches, the chip in the front window, and the dubious smell of the interior. She had paid in cash, careful to shield the contents of her purse from him. All prejudice on her side – she knew – but she also knew she was in his territory and vulnerable. Now she rolled down the window as she cruised through Asbury. The guide was on her lap and she made sure to stop at the facade of the Student Prince, where the big man or the wind, had ripped the door off its hinges. Whatever the truth – probably neither – show business needed big stories. Call it fate, the thing of legends, a carefully managed exaggeration, it was all rock and roll. She had had no idea, really, about the deep-rooted respect and love of the two men, when years later, in 1985, the Big man and Scooter met in an embrace that challenged her upbringing, and opened a chasm of doubt. No speech, no controversy, just the knee slide and a mouth-on-mouth promise. It was where her search had begun. And now, on an empty morning, she realised once again how one fateful moment can change everything; it clearly did, so the urban myth goes, for the two musicians. Maybe those butchered chords on an untuned guitar in front of Wembley arena had been fate too, for her. So why was she here, still seeking?

She took out the map of New Jersey and wrestled it open. Then she looked at the streets signs in order to note down the iconic place, knocking her rear-view mirror, and tearing the bottom of the map in the process. Goddamnit, who had invented these monstrosities? Obviously the person who had never had to consult them in a car on their own. With her best origami skills and grumpy impatience, she managed to somehow fold the map into a bulky A3-sized view. She dove into her bag to scrounge for a ballpoint pen, hitting her elbow off the gear stick. The electric shock briefly paralysed her fingers.

A polite knock rattled her passenger window. Now what? Wendy rolled it down and looked out. A pair of kind spectacles leaned in and their owner asked, 'Are you lost? Do you need any help?' Wendy was about to say thanks but no thanks, when the man pointed at the Rock and Roll tour of New Jersey that she had opened up on the front seat and the scrunched-up map in her hands.

'Well, well. Seems to me it's your lucky day.'

Wendy threw a quizzical look at this complete stranger.

'My name is Kyle, and I have a sneaky suspicion you will be at the Stone Pony before too long. Only to find it shut at the moment, in preparation for tonight's Ricky Springfield show.'

Wendy sighed. Why did people keep confusing Springsteen with Springfield? How hard could it be? But the man obviously meant no harm.

'You are right, I am on my way to the Stone Pony. I'm a Springsteen fan.'

The man chuckled. 'Got ya. I can get you into the bar for a quick peek, if you like. Show some of Bruce's legacy. If you want.'

'There are a few other spots I was going to find first,' Wendy answered after a brief hesitation. Was this a moment of fate too? Was she to take it as it was thrown in her lap or follow her own plans? Who even was this man?

'That's okay, I'm from here, I can direct you better than any old map can.'

Wendy looked at the man again. He looked so typically American: Bermuda shorts, a T-shirt under a sleeveless, unbuttoned shirt. His face was kind. Was he chatting her up?

'I'd love to show you around. I'm a big believer in the local scene, and anyone who takes the trouble to come visit when New York is beckoning just across the water, is a good guy in my book. Or girl,' he added hastily. 'It'd be easier than negotiating that map of yours.'

Wendy threw all caution in the wind; fate it was. 'Okay then, hop in.' She leant over and took her bag off the front seat and dumped it in the back. 'My name is Wendy, I'm from Scotland, and if you try any funny business I will scream.'

Kyle ducked into the front seat, and pushed the chair backwards. 'No worries Wendy, pleased to meet you. So, I am Kyle and I'm a sound technician at the Stone Pony. I'm on foot, so as long as you promise to drop me off later, we're good to go.'

Not only did Kyle know all the hotspots, and a lot of insider detail, he was also an excellent navigator and a breath of fresh air. He clearly cared for this town, and knew his music. He tuned into a local radio station that played a lot of the old R&B, and told Wendy all about the times the Asbury Jukes had performed in the Stone Pony.

'I love the Jukes.' Wendy thumped Kyle on his arm in excitement, harder than she had intended. He winced but didn't seem to mind. 'Oh sorry, Kyle,' she apologised. 'I was ranting and raving about Springsteen when this boy two years up from me slammed a tape in my hand. According to him, a band without horns was not a band. Modern synth pop-shite, he called Bruce's success in the 80s.' Wendy smiled at the memory of Robby. Robby had hinted at listening to romantic titles from obscure soul bands by sticking them on her locker for about four months until she had broken his heart by snogging Amy from two doors down.

It was only an experiment, but in Robby's universe that kind of self-discovery did not have a place. When Wendy saw him during a reunion some years ago, he was still wearing trousers that were an inch too short, and woolly jumpers with sleeves that were an inch too long. He had found a better hairdresser though, and true to form was still a walking encyclopaedia on anything Soul. 'Perhaps if I had seen them live before Bruce, who knows.'

Kyle agreed. 'They both came up from the same tradition. Bruce took a distinctly different path, but I don't think the Blues and Soul ever really left his songwriting. Whenever he joins the Jukes on the Pony stage, those shared origins resurface in the way he plays. The coolest thing is that most people here let him be, when he gets on that stage. There's an unwritten mutual respect. I like how he hasn't forgotten the old days. Just turn left here, and pull over beside that door.'

Wendy got out of the car surprised to see a small queue of women outside the building, sitting with their backs against the white brick wall.

'Hoping to be the IGE girl tonight, no doubt,' Kyle nodded at them. 'You have anything on tonight? If not, just come along; not quite your man,' he winked, 'I do know the difference between *steen* and *field*, but he does a more than decent Rock and Roll show. And you'll be able to brag you were at The Pony.'

Wendy had no idea what an IGE girl was, but was loathe to let a free gig pass her by. She followed Kyle in through the back door. Three youngsters were setting up the stage. Kyle walked to the bar and pulled out a coke. He handed it over to her, and showed her the wall with guitars and drum skins, most of them signed; the pictures showing Bruce, a mural of the Greetings from Asbury Park. There was nobody else around because of the show later on; she couldn't believe her luck. She sipped the coke and tried to take in the interior as best as she could in the dim light. She imagined being able to see Springsteen on the small stage, literally less than half a meter high, and no barrier. Insane.

Kyle handed her a pink shirt with the Stone Pony image on it. 'To remember the place. On the house. So here you have it Wendy, the inner sanctum.' Kyle smiled and motioned her over to an oval bar across from the stage. He pulled out a barstool, and sat down. 'So … you reckon that keeping a promise to yourself is going to help you make the right decision about your future?'

Wendy shrugged. 'I'm not sure it will make the future easier. But it will settle the past. In a way. If I stop blaming past decisions I made.' She studied the band announcement posters and tickets that were stuck under the Perspex on top of the bar.

'Maybe the music won't let you though.' Kyle looked at her. 'I mean, music gets under my skin, and no matter how I try, I can't divorce it from the moment I first heard it, or the feelings I had then.'

Wendy thought about it. 'No, I think I'll be all right. Despite my life turning out different from what I had promised myself, I wouldn't want to undo it. The past is not a regret. This trip is no more than a recalibration. Back then, visiting would have been chasing a romantic pipe-dream of reinvention. Now, visiting is seeking affirmation of who I was and still am.'

Kyle was quiet for a bit. He went behind the bar and got himself another beer. He notched the beer cap on the edge and slammed down on it with his left hand. The cap went flying. Kyle quickly brought the beer to his mouth to avoid the foam spilling all over the floor.

'Like, if you'd come back then you would have tried on a new skin, whereas now it is new jeans, different look but not a different you?'

Wendy smiled. 'Yeah, kinda. So, how about you? Did you ever want to run away from this place?'

Kyle shook his head. 'When I was thirteen, like any boy at the time, I wanted to play in a band. And I wanted to make it big. Truth be told, I played bass and hid behind my fringe most of the set. When I saw the Beatles land in America and those screaming girls, it scared the shit out of me. That frenzied adoration.'

Wendy held up her hand. 'Hang on, you saw the Beatles land? Here, in America? How old are you?'

Kyle shook his head. 'No no, not the first time round. I'm not that old!' He puffed up his chest like a belligerent cockerel. 'I watched a documentary on them somewhere in the 70s. Two months after seeing it on TV, I was invited behind the sound desk here at the Pony. A friend of a friend, whose sister, who had a friend … You know how it goes. I realised that nobody notices the sound engineer but that without one, even the best of artists would only be mediocre. A sliver of the glory of their success rubbed off on me, but I didn't have to sacrifice my sanity for it. I have had so many personal conversations with the best of them, I feel quite a star myself.'

Wendy raised an eyebrow.

'Yes, Bruce too. I learned quick that I had a good ear. I know about getting a mix that allows each musician to shine at the right moment. I found a Jersey girl who loved me, and left me. I live with my three dogs, and still have friends from high school. My life is comfortable. I'm good.'

'I wanna get to I'm good.'

Kyle looked at his watch. 'I reckon that's not too much to ask. Right, you'd better see some more of the shore. There's Belmar, Monmouth, Ocean Grove. The band will be here soon, and I gotta get to work. Why don't I put you on the guest list, and you can decide how you feel later on? I'd love for you to witness me being awesome. You can even hang out with me. Best sound is always where the sound guy sits.' He winked.

Wendy laughed. 'Okay. I'll come. After I have followed the star to where that hero of mine arrived on this earth.' She high-fived Kyle and he led her to the front door. He nipped into the box office and asked, 'What will I write? Wendy … from Scotland?'

'Aye, that will do.'

He opened the door to let her slip out. 'See you later Wendy from the bonnie bens.'

Standing on the crossroads of 10th Avenue and E Street was surreal. Wendy turned up her iPod, and did an E-street shuffle round the white post, well-aware that any passer-by would scratch their head at the silent dancer. Not that there were many. She'd just keep dancing until she could ask someone, anyone, to take a photo of her at this iconic spot. She had danced for almost half an hour before a Hispanic woman turned the corner. Hers was a tired shuffle on broken shoes, her plastic shopping bag making the waddle more pronounced. Her head heavy and her gaze inward. Wendy hesitated. This woman clearly had other things on her mind, but she had been patient; no way could she leave without the obligatory picture with the giant Fender. She took a step towards the woman but before she could ask the question the woman put down her heavy bag and held her hands up apologetically: no Ingles. Wendy had to rely on her best miming but in the end the woman understood what she was hinting at.

Wendy was driving by the medical centre where Springsteen was born when it hit her how insanely creepy this whole endeavour was. My god, the hospital was just a hospital. People were born there, people got sick there, and got better, some people died; Springsteen was just like any other. She looked at herself in the rear-view mirror. A thirty-four-year-old woman swooning over the birthplace of some dude who didn't have the foggiest she even existed. Still, when she got to Long Branch and stood in front of the house where Springsteen had written most of Born to Run, she felt the hairs on her arms rise. She sat down.

That whole album was full of dreamers, who may have been beaten by the harshness and meanness of the world, but somehow they could see a better place. A way out, a way forward. They had such hope for life. Just like her when she first heard the record. She heard a car door slam. She looked up. Nobody. Then a voice.

You thought you could get away by relegating me to the backseat, did you? You thought if you'd take over the steering wheel, ban me from driving shotgun, I'd be gone? Right? Well, we've always been on this ride together. In fact, the car is getting rather full with the past-selves you've pushed away all these years.

Wendy looked around. The street was empty. She looked at her car. Nothing.

Come on then Wendy, you know who I am. Remember I took that train to Wembley and nothing could stop me then. Why stop now? What is it that you are chasing so hard? Step on it. Why hesitate? I was hungry for the empty road to find out if love is real. Forget what's been. Pull out, if you dare.

Wendy closed her eyes, hands over her ears.

Not easy, is it, to take responsibility for your own choices? Much safer to blame others for what you did or didn't do. You thought I had left. Silly. I was always in the car, but you chose to follow the white lines signposted by others. There's a guy waiting for you in Asbury, hoping to meet up. His car too is full of ghosts and passengers. He might sound like he's got it made – he certainly tries to present himself that way – but the woman that left him is still riding shotgun every single night, her hands on his as he manoeuvres the gearstick, and sighs himself to sleep. Remember the ride ain't free. Who's at the wheel tonight then?

Wendy bit the side of her thumb. She had said yes to tonight's show on impulse. But now she realised that she might have been a little naïve. If the invite was more than just that, she'd have to decide not for her, but for him. There would be no glory in chasing her own needs and kicking someone else in the teeth in the process; ultimately it would be a short-lived, hollow thrill at most. After all, she only existed within the realities of others, equally precious. But rather than sacrificing her own dreams for other people's like she'd done all those years – she knew all the other faces squashed against her car window even without looking for them – maybe she should try to have them co-exist. Should she get on a plane and work it out back home? She shook her head. Too early. So yes, she would claim her free ticket tonight but she'd not be a fool.

The gig was fun. Her exasperation at people poking fun at her love for Springsteen by purposely getting the name wrong, had stopped her from ever properly listening to Springfield. It transpired he was very much a rocker like Springsteen, albeit a little too poppy for her liking. From the same era too. She heard a lot of 80s references, saw a dedicated artist with charisma and passion. To her it felt he got stuck in the same mould all these years though. She loved how Springsteen kept evolving his sound. This guy was a little more predictable, but clearly, for those in the Pony that night, he meant as much as Springsteen did to her. She had spoken to some of them and they had all 'found' him when they were teenagers in 1985. For many he had been their first concert. That tracked. Funny how that high of your first concert seems to determine the rest of your musical path. At least, if the music got into your veins at that precise moment. So much so that all your nerve endings tingle. That you feel the whole world fade into the background. Nothing is focused but one thing: the artist on the stage, and the energy of both of you that collides, dances a dance of seduction, appraisal, questions. Your pulse starts to race, and you can't sit still, because you know you will burst out of your skin if you do. All that is inside wants to come out and lay itself bare. To be prodded, massaged, shifted. Your voice becomes this independent creature that roars, thrills, and whispers words that settle in your capillaries like loess in the banks of meandering rivers. Danny loved music, but she never had the impression his world changed when he listened. More so when he played. When he strummed his guitar is when he communicated best. That is where he got lost and unknowingly showed his true colours. Had she wanted too much from him? Demanding he'd talk to her once in a while? Maybe he had been speaking all this time – and she just hadn't heard.

Kyle really was as good at his job as he had so modestly professed. Wendy had enjoyed his dedication to his trade and the way he ignored her during the gig to focus on the job at hand. Best of all, being his guest meant that she had the best vantage point too. For once her 5'2" was not an issue. Kyle had turned an empty crate upside down, and Wendy had been able to look over the heads of all of the fans. For a solid two hours, the Pony was humming with sweat, music, and beer. And Springfield's IGE moment was nothing short of the 'Dancing in the Dark' dream that she had secretly held all those years. The lucky woman who got to be inside that guitar strap was so excited, her dark curls bounced right in Springfield's face. He just took it in his stride.

After the gig she and Kyle had had a few drinks. She had asked him what the idea was with the dollar bills people left on the bar, and Kyle explained about the low wages in the service industry and the American way of tipping. Wendy felt extremely embarrassed, as she had put the change in her pocket before. So next round, she had paid and made sure to leave enough of a tip to make up for her ignorance before. Kyle was clearly buzzing, but the bar was too loud to discuss the inner workings of the heart. They agreed to meet up next day for lunch in Redbank. There was one vegetarian restaurant there, Angelica's Kitchen, Kyle had said, so hard to miss. They hugged and both went their own way.

Now she was cruising Redbank for a parking space. A few landmarks to tick off here. Count Basie and of course Jack's Music Shop. What would she have given to have been at the midnight album release in 2001, only for Springsteen to walk in. She guessed there were a few benefits to living in 'exit' state – the place Springsteen had been so keen to leave. And yet, he was back in New Jersey now. In fact, he now lived very close to his hometown. Returning home would feel like a defeat to her. She wasn't sure where she wanted to be, but she didn't kick up all this fuss if she was just going to go straight back. But maybe if enough shit had shifted it could equally be a triumph.

Kyle held her a little longer than recent friends do. She took note. Careful. She ordered a salad; he stuck to the chili sin carne.

'How long did it take you to come down and get to sleep after last night's show?' Wendy asked him after the waitress had plonked down their plates.

Kyle smiled, hanging in his chair. 'I ran around the house for a few hours. I find tidying up is the only thing that waters down the kick of adrenaline. After, I slept like a baby, dreaming of you.'

Wendy cringed. Who's at the wheel tonight? Kyle shovelled another spoonful of beans into his mouth, leaning on his left forearm. Wendy heard her dad's voice you're not a farmer and felt the slap of his flat knife on her wrist. She would not judge a man on his manners. Manners were nothing but a means to keep class division in its place.

'And you?'

'I was thinking about New York. I'm on my way there after two days in Freehold.'

'New York has changed. It is still reeling and smoking. I mean it is probably safer than ever … if you are white. But since 9/11 there's a veil of fear over people's lives. The grief hangs like a menacing teardrop above the town. Hard rain might fall at any time. It's like the city is tiptoeing through the day.'

'Are people afraid?'

'Not so much of another attack. More of the people next door – who to trust? The attacks ripped the feeble foundations of community right from under them. There's lingering mistrust behind eyelashes, hateful words on the tips of people's tongues, only held in place by the gratification of our government at least doing something to revenge those bastards.'

'So,' Wendy hesitated, 'you support the war?' She put her fork down and looked Kyle in the eye. Her jaw tightened. Kyle looked straight back. 'I joined the protests against the Iraq invasion in February. There were over a million people in London. That was a bloody huge stomp if you ask me. It made no difference; they still went to war on the basis of nothing. So sickening.'

'Over nothing? They flew planes into the Twin Towers, ripped the heart out of America. They flew planes to the ground outside Washington. Over nothing?' Kyle put his fork down and straightened his back, his nice-boy lethargy sliding off him. 'Easy for you to be anti-war. The planes didn't kill your folks. That Saddam Hussein is a threat to our entire world!'

People round about them looked up from their meals. The sun shone brightly into the window, not only warming the place but shrining everything in a golden sheen. Wendy wished she had kept her mouth shut. When would she learn politics are to be avoided on first dates, during dinner (or lunch as it may be), actually pretty much during anything social really. Still, she couldn't let this slide.

'These days there are two superpowers: the USA and public opinion. Public opinion was very clear: there is no evidence nor grounds to start a war against Iraq. Surely, politics should be a reflection of public opinion.' She skewered a piece of cucumber.

'As if you can measure public opinion by the number of people turning up at demonstrations,' Kyle retorted. For a moment it looked as if he was going to say more. Then he sighed and picked up his fork. 'You didn't stand on the other side of the water, seeing the smoke and ash blocking all light. Ash of buildings and of people who had simply gone to work that day. You weren't here Wendy.'

Wendy thought about the morning she had stood frozen in her living room, watching the towers fall again and again, knowing without a shadow of a doubt that the world had been forever altered. And she had cried for the loss of the innocence and peace in Rosie's time. For the first time in years she had been genuinely scared. Not for herself, but for the world her Rosie would live her adult life in. She understood Kyle, but didn't agree.

'Let's not fight. Tell me about you being a vegetarian. I don't meet many men who'd pass on a tasty morsel of red meat.'

Kyle dropped his tight shoulders, and relaxed the grip on his fork. 'Okay, clumsy segue lady, but fair enough. This is not the place nor time to let politics ruin a perfectly fine date.' He sipped his giant coke, and looked at his plate. 'My dad used to hunt. He'd bring home the game and prepare it in the shed behind the house. In a way, I was desensitized to dead things by the time I was four. We didn't have a lot, but we did have five hungry mouths to feed. A man takes his chances. Then one day – I think I was eight – the loot hadn't been quite dead. One of the rabbits was still squirming in his hands. I had run out to meet him on the path. My dad took out his gun and shot the creature point blank, in the head. Right in front of my eyes. He blew the head clean off. I puked over my socks. I haven't touched a piece of meat since.'

Wendy felt tempted to make a comment about killing and war, but they had agreed on a truce, so instead she touched his hand. 'It must have left a lasting impression. Sorry you had to see that.'

'It's okay. My dad was being practical; he did what needed done. I loved him until he died a few years back. It doesn't even bother me much to see meat on a plate. It's just when I eat red meat my stomach gets all tight. What about you?'

'My daughter topped eating meat. I tried to fight her over it, but in the end I gave up. Then I did some research and saw where she was coming from. I never much liked meat when I was younger, so I decided I could give it up too.'

They finished their meal with Kyle telling fisherman's tales about all the stars he'd crossed paths with. It was light-hearted, never a moment's bragging. She watched his cheeks get flushed as he remembered particularly bad nights, when managers had thrown every insult and 'body part' at him; the twinkle in his eyes when he'd managed to meet up with the 'left-over groupies' at stage doors. She felt the ex-lover hover about him though. Clearly in the front seat still, no matter what Kyle made himself believe.

'So, you want to go past Springsteen's house?'

Wendy sat up. 'You know where he lives?'

'Baby, everyone around here knows that. Let's get into my car and I'll take you there. No, here let me pay that bill.'

The house was surrounded by high trees. No fence. A big gate on two sides. A grass curb. Didn't look like a rock star mansion. The town itself was unremarkable too. They got out. Wendy pried through the green branches to see if anybody was about. She couldn't see a car. She contemplated running through the hedge of trees. Then, she spotted a bell. Would she ring it? Slowly she brought her hand to the bell.

'People don't usually bother him. It's why there is no fence. Don't be mistaken though; there are dogs.'

'I'm not usual people. It is now or never.'

'What will you tell him? Many people believe it is better never to meet your hero.'

'I am not many people either.' Still, Wendy stopped momentarily. She had no idea what she would say. She hadn't thought this through. But she was here now. Some chances only come once in life. She pushed the button, her heart in her throat. A metallic voice asked who was there.

'Wendy, I was hoping to speak to Bruce.'

'I'm afraid that won't be possible.'

'I travelled all the way from Scotland. Brought him a small sample of whisky from near my home town. I thought I'd give it to him personally. It's a twelve-year-old malt.' She wanted to bite her tongue for sounding like the morose teenager swooning over posters and postcards that covered all the walls of her tiny bedroom. She was thirty-four, what was she thinking!

A pause.

'I'm afraid that won't be possible.'

Now what? A police car rounded the corner and slowed down. Then stopped. A policeman stepped out. Kyle took her arm gently but urgently.

'I'll leave it just inside the fence for him then.' She rummaged through her bag and found the miniature and a sharpie. She scribbled *with 17 years of love, Wendy* on the label and pushed it through the fence leaving it against the pillar. The cop asked what she thought she was doing.

'Move on lady, unless you want me to take you in.' He had his hand on his holster. Wendy nodded apologetically and backed off. So near, yet so far. They got back in Kyle's car. He chuckled.

'You came prepared then.'

'I feel stupid!' She dove into her bag again and held up a shallow silver cup with two handles. 'I even brought this. It's a Quaich, a cup of friendship to drink the whiskey from. I mean, stupid.'

'Not stupid, hopeful. You came all this way, you might as well dream big.'

Wendy checked to see if Kyle was mocking her. He looked sincere, eyes on the road. He twirled the dial of the radio, keeping his eyes on the bendy road lined with high trees. This is where the well-to-do lived; definitely. Kyle stopped messing with the radio when he hit the right frequency. Percy Sledge lamented about the strain of a man loving a woman.

'I'll take you to a spot I like the best around here. It's where I dream big.'

Soon, they got out of the car, and started to climb. When they got to the top of the hill, Wendy could see why Kyle came there. They could look out over the whole area. Dreams could fly away on the wind here, reaching far yet equally getting no foothold ever. She looked down on Redbank and the Navesink River that lay glistening calmly in the summer breeze, the bustle a distant murmur on this windy outcrop.

'I do this as often as I can. Sit somewhere and wait for the sun to go down. It slows down time. Suddenly you become aware of the quiet beauty that goes unnoticed every day. It is the best moment of my day. You should try it.'

Wendy liked the idea. She was glad she had taken a chance on this stranger.

'What's your big dream then? Yesterday you said you were good. You sounded like you had it all made, with the three dogs.' Kyle didn't answer straightaway. He looked out over the water. Somewhere a bird was singing its heart out.

Kyle pointed at some shrubs on their right. 'See the little red bird hopping about?' He pointed to a plump red feather ball, its tail a downward anchor. 'That's a northern cardinal. Look carefully, it's a male. See that Zorro bandana over his eyes? He could be singing because he is content, or somewhere we cannot see, there's another male that he's trying to scare off.'

Wendy squinted her eyes to see the small bird. Hearing it was definitely easier. Kyle continued, 'He's a funny fella. Look at him prancing about in his red robes. Impressing the ladies, also when no other males are around. He attacks anything that is red to get rid of competitors, so he even chases away his own reflection in the mirror.'

Wendy nodded. 'And sometimes you feel like what others see is nothing more than a disguise, the truth hidden behind that black mask?'

'More that I look at myself in the mirror sometimes, and all I wanna do is chase away the reflection.'

Both remained still for a moment or so, watching the small bird busying itself amongst the branches, listening to its excited song. Kyle sighed, 'I am mostly happy, truly. I love my dogs. I am good. But there are moments I wish someone would leave the light on in the house, so that when I get back in the middle of the night the house welcomes me in, and I can quietly slip into bed next to a familiar body. The unspoken comfort of little gestures like a cold beer in the fridge, my favourite shirt ironed without having to ask. But when I recognise that picture of need in my reflection I know nothing better than to chase it away. To let it into my territory of ache is too much. After all, alone is but alone.'

Wendy took his hand and squeezed it. 'Gosh, if a little of that human touch is you dreaming big, you are a modest guy indeed.' Kyle turned and kissed her on the mouth. It was rough and unapologetic. Wendy pulled back. 'Kyle, I'm sorry if I gave you the wrong impression. I'm married.'

Kyle sat back. 'You are? But you don't wear a wedding ring?'

'I am; it is on the other hand.' Wendy held up her right hand. She became very conscious of the gold band and all it stood for. Was she still married? She had walked out, pulled closed a door. Yet she still wore the ring. If feelings of doubt and loneliness overshadow the earlier bliss of infatuation, if days of silence outnumber the minutes of laughter, can you still call the legal bond a marriage? Or had marriage morphed into an agreement of restriction only, ruled by the many 'thou shalt nots' that are expected from the day of the vows onwards? Was the wedding band no more than an empty token of her marriage? 'I am not sure, actually what I am anymore,' Wendy stumbled. 'I guess you look in the mirror and chase away what you see. I don't even see anything much when I look. Maybe me coming here is an act of divorce, but whatever it is, it is too early for someone else's needs.'

Kyle looked crestfallen for a moment but recovered quickly. He took Wendy's hand. 'Whatever you say, you are an energy that fizzed through town. It jolted me from the haze of quietly settling for less. When you looked at me with those hazel eyes of yours, you shot right through my armour. Momentarily I felt alive, this connection. Can we hold on to each other, Wendy? We lay no plans for the future, we just enjoy the moment where neither of us has to look in the mirror. Can we dance to the song of the northern cardinal and linger a bit in this slow-motion moment in time?' He stood up and held out his hand.

Wendy hesitated. It wouldn't be the first time that her kindness was mistaken for flirting. The river below was a silver bowl glistening in the early afternoon glow. The song of the cardinal changed. Wendy spied a tan bird in the undergrowth, moving her body towards the male's wing, which twitched like an outstretched hand. He spread his tail. Offered a seed. She scuttled about, first ignoring him but in the end answering with a brief dance of her own.

Wendy took Kyle's hand. He pulled her up and close to his body. His hoodie smelled like dog. He trembled as he wrapped his arms around her. 'Just allow me to hold you. It's been too long since I felt someone else's body fit mine.'

Even if Kyle might just be the best Don Juan in the neighbourhood and this all an Oscar-worthy act, Wendy realised how badly she needed to be held too. She curved her head into Kyle's neck and so they stood, embracing in an almost imperceptible sway. After a few minutes the awkward stiffness eased out of Wendy's body, and she felt the nudge of Kyle's steady hand on her lower back, holding her up. Kyle was crying with his eyes closed but at the same time he would not let her crumble. She was settling in the dust of someone else's past relationship, unsure of her own status but comforted nonetheless.

Someone had to pay the price

What had she been thinking? Why on earth had she decided that signing up to summer school was a good way to spend these short weeks of light and warmth? The sports fields lazed in the sun, green and inviting, but here she was, stuck behind the window working on her 4th year physics. Mrs Andersson had presented these weeks as a different approach to last year's content. To solidify understanding for those who had grasped the basics but lacked the depth to build on in the coming year. She should have known teachers are compulsive liars. Fair enough, Andersson started each morning with a fun riddle about something physics that always had a cringe-worthy wordplay solution to it, but other than that it was just doing the same old sums.

She was hot. She twirled her pencil between her fingers like Finn had taught her before they broke up for summer. Her mind drifted to her mum. She had noticed her mum's passport was missing from the drawer in the study, so possibly her mother had left the UK. If she was finding out about herself, did they have some hidden family somewhere on the continent? Why else did she need to take a passport? The second thought that had immediately followed was that her mum might have left for more than just a few days. No word so far, it had been over three weeks now.

She kicked Maria's chair and yawned. Maria yawned back. She was sweating over her French.

Ça va? Maria mouthed.

Non, très boooooring, Rosie mimed back, rolling her eyes. She pointed at the door and then at her watch, flashing three fingers at Maria. She raised her hand and asked if she could possibly go to the toilet. Yes, she knew it was only ten minutes into the class, and that she should have gone during break, but any-old-how, could she please be excused? Mrs Andersson sighed and agreed. Rosie knocked against Maria's table on purpose, stuck up three fingers again and scuttled out of the door.

The toilets were cool as ever. In winter time it meant you froze your arse off, but in summer it was a welcome change from the poorly ventilated rooms in the south wing. She chose the 2nd last cubicle and took out her sharpie. Time for some education of the masses: *school – if you are forced into learning, you are not in it.* Let them chew on that one. Funny how Joey effectively said much the same thing as Springsteen who claimed he learned more from a record than from school. Yet one was considered trash punk to be avoided by mainstream DJs, and the other clean-safe rock & roll suitable for nostalgic airplay. Same message, different attitude. Anyhow, to balance it all out she'd scribbled Springsteen on the 1st cubicle of the 2nd floor toilets, after her mother had stood up to Mr Barnes who had proclaimed Rosie 'stupid and a waste of school's time' after she'd missed the English mocks by oversleeping after a particularly booze-heavy gig on a Wednesday night. So much for Mr Barnes being a role model as a school principal, with a comment like that. Her mother, on the other hand, had done good that day. It had been embarrassing but she had at least rocked the boat. So far nobody had yet removed the graffiti. Her earlier quote about punk in the boys' toilet had led the janitors straight to her, despite the gender confusion she had tried to create.

The door slammed open. Rosie jumped up and turned to see her friend in the backlight that streamed in from the hall.

'Bonjour, mon amie. Nous allons acheter some fags?'

Rosie laughed. 'Nah, just wanted to run something by you and physics isn't doing it for me today.' She moved over to the window.

'Ah well, you decided to be all clever clogs and that. Should've taken business administration. Walk in the park. Or French, oh lala! What's on your mind, chieftain of the punk race?'

Rosie opened the window and let the sun fall on her face. The fields on this side were all set up for the summer camp of the small kiddies, with bouncy castles and miniature football goals. 'I discovered my mum left with her passport. So I reckon she's no longer in Scotland. What do you say?'

'Oh, Rosie P.I. has done some digging has she? Fair enough, but where on earth would your mother go?' Maria hopped on the ledge next to Rosie and dangled her feet out of the window. It always made Rosie a little nauseous but there was no point trying to explain that to Maria.

'She wrote that thing about finding out who she is, looking for her roots. So I am thinking, do I have any family abroad? A history my mother is trying to work out?'

'Like doing a sort of family tree research thing? Finding out if you are descendants of Napoleon? Or some Viking warlord?' Maria paused. 'To be honest, no I can't see that. I think your mum might be more punk than you give her credit for. I mean, I hate my dad for leaving and all that shit, but I think it was a similar thing. It's more like what that punk dude said, what's his name?'

'Sid Vicious?'

'No, the American one with the 70s bad hair do. The one that got you expelled last year, for writing in the boys' toilet.'

'Joey Ramone?'

'Yeah, that thing about punk being about what really matters, passion, the heart and the soul. I reckon she is looking for her passion in one way or another. Like, who she is, instead of a mum, or a taxi driver. The note was crystal clear to me. Not sure why she needs a passport for that though.'

Rosie gave it a moment to sink in. Blinded by her short-sighted opinion of her mum, she'd overlooked interpreting finding herself metaphorically. Duh, of course. 'So what was your dad looking for then? Did he find it?'

Maria lit the last cigarette from the pack and took a drag. She was careful to hold it outside the window. She exhaled. 'Not sure, but I do know that the motorbike was a passion he had to give up on when Toni came along. It was traded in for a car for practical reasons.'

'How does that work with the young redhead? Is she a more adventurous version than the practicality of your mum?'

'Nah, I reckon he loved the flattery. My mum, well you know her. She can be a moody cow at times. Not really a fairy tale princess with a cutesy smile and almond eyes, now is she?'

'More like a bull in a china store who's been speared one too many times by the matador.'

Maria grinned. 'What's in your mum's past that she kinda gave up on?

Rosie took a deep breath. It was staring her right in the face. She glanced at Maria.

'Springsteen,' she and Maria mumbled in unison.

A reason to believe

Freehold: Main Street, a diner and a railway dissecting the town in two. Wendy lingered at the tracks. She started to hum 'My Hometown' in some sort of musical Pavlovian reaction. She imagined the black youngsters in the backseat Springsteen sang about, the shots being fired and the moral, more than physical wounds, the act must have left. She had reads somewhere that a year later the violence would spread to Asbury and Redbank but here in Freehold, the literal division between two sides was where Springsteen's song reminded her to take heed of her roots. Belonging somewhere was a funny old thing. She had seen the houses Bruce had grown up in, leant against that one tree and crossed her arms, gone by the school that failed to keep him; all these were place markers in her unashamed hero-worshipping. She was touching the ghosts of someone else's life to find milestones in her own. Bruce had been desperate to leave the confines of his small town that must have felt like the death of dreams when he was 15. He had stepped beyond the suffocation of his upbringing. But today he lived not even 30 minutes away from all of his past. The sirens of familiarity had been stronger than the silt lure of a fresh start. She didn't really miss Aberdeen, but the act of pulling the door shut behind her did give her a sense of homelessness. Maybe her home was basking in Danny's silence, or swimming in Rosie's chagrin. She winced at the thought.

A truck honked. She stepped off the road and closer to the tracks. She looked over her shoulder as the yellow fire truck turned the corner. She'd follow it back into town. She was peckish and was determined to experience a real American diner. She'd seen the silver railroad car when she had parked her car and taken a mental note. It was about an hour and a half before closing time. It unnerved her how wide the street was and how singular each house. The front porch that she had always found such a romantic concept in Springsteen songs was common place here. Wooden houses, each with their own driveway, front lawns and hanging baskets. Judging by the houses she expected these people to be well-off, yet she knew the economic struggle many Americans lived simply to afford a car, let alone a house. Compared to Aberdeen's bleak housing estate with street after narrow street of the same terraced houses and grey, harled façades, concrete front patches lacking any colour from grass or flowers – gardens would be too big a word here – Wendy experienced a sense of luxury and freedom walking past these houses that looked like individuals. They were all connected by the wires hanging off wooden electricity poles like slacklines. The neat and tidy fenced-off houses were a sharp contrast to the black Gordian knot of thick cables above the streets. She turned onto Main Street. She saw the diner on her left. A few motorbikes in front, helmets left on the seat, a sure token of familiarity with the community frequenting the place. Carefully she pushed open the door.

The interior did not disappoint. The booths with orange faux-leather seats and the Formica tables were just like she'd remembered from Grease. Obviously, they were all taken by young lovers tentatively tipping their toes in the others' lives. And by old couples that would take longer to settle down than to eat their burger. The clatter of the cutlery in the open kitchen punctuated the sizzle of eggs and bacon. She decided to sit on one of the high barstools rather than waiting for a booth. She was alone anyhow, so this way she wouldn't take up someone else's space.

On her right sat a man in overalls who busied himself with a newspaper. Every now and then he'd sigh, or mumble indistinguishable words under his breath, but he appeared content rather than grumpy or upset. The rims of his nails were black, and despite visible signs of scrubbing, the hands turning the newspaper page were grease-dirty. He picked up his coffee without glancing up from the paper. He scribbled furiously in the margins. Then she noticed the date on the paper. Yesterday's news.

'Excuse me, but I notice you are notetaking on yesterday's paper. Are you aware?'

The man didn't react at first, but as Wendy let her gaze rest upon him for longer than was comfortable, he grunted, 'I collect typos and misprints.'

That shut her up for a bit. Where do you store typos and misprints? In a jar? What do you do with them? This was the oddest idea of a collection she'd ever encountered. 'Do you keep them somewhere?'

'No, I find them and send the newspaper an update every month.'

'Really, why?'

The man looked up and let his eyes wander all over her. She could see the cogs of his judgment turn. His face was too expressive to hide that he considered her a busybody of the highest order and wanted to be left alone. He appeared to give her the benefit of the doubt though, when he sighed, 'I left school at fourteen. Took a manual job in the auto trade. Been there for over forty years. I'm just a car mechanic, but that doesn't mean I'm any less than folks like you that went to college. So I find the errors in the paper and send them back to the editor.'

'Ready to order?' A middle-aged man leant towards her over the counter. 'My name is Tony, I'm the boss here. I can afford to buy a newspaper every day.' His voice sounded like a hacksaw.

Wendy was taken aback. 'No offence meant. I was just curious. I thought he was studying the wrong paper by accident.'

'Lady, I have no time nor money to study. These 15 minutes is all the time I can take off work. You from England?'

'Scotland. But if you went to college wouldn't you get a better job?'

'I like my job, nothing wrong with it. Not all of us are fortunate enough to have money or time to travel to the other side of the world. I have one kid and he needs food on the table. Education is for the rich. Make no mistake there. Doesn't mean I can't educate myself.'

Tony came round again. 'You ready to order?'

Wendy ordered a fried egg, fries, and a milkshake. She'd do without the coffee, having spotted an Italian along the way and figuring their coffee might a tastier option later on.

'Scotland not the same island as England then?'

Wendy looked to the side and smiled. 'No, yes, it's a long history, we are protective of our independent spirits. I reckon it's a bit like the NY - New Jersey thing. I heard NYC folk look down on you guys sometimes. We get that with the English.'

The man nodded. 'Fair enough. So what brings you here to Freehold, apart from a feeling of solidarity?' He winked. Tony put her eggs in front of her.

'I'm doing this Springsteen thing. Visiting places from his life, places he mentions in his songs.'

'This being the place he was born. I see. What's the big deal?'

'Dunno, trying to recapture feeling fifteen maybe. I mean, I used to sit and listen to his songs and always wanted to see the things he sang about with my own eyes. Then life got in the way and I thought I could easily do without. Then the Twin Towers came down and something in the world shifted.'

'Back in Scotland too?' The man sat up now, folding his paper. He clicked his pen and put it in the back pocket of his overalls along with his paper.

'Yes. I don't know if I can come close even to understanding your hurt, but it made me aware of the fine wire we walk. And I started to think about my place in the world. I looked at my life and didn't like it. I lost some of my hope, I guess.'

'Well, if you are lost, you'd better find out where home is. The world might be falling apart at the seams, but I know where I belong, and that gives me a reason to believe. I get up every morning, feeling alive and home. A satisfied life is in the roots of belonging. No, I don't know you lady, and I don't know how far you've strayed, it might be a long walk home for you, but there's nothing else to it: you gotta find out where or what home is.'

Wendy looked at the modest man next to her. His eyes had softened, his brow relaxed. Was she chasing the wrong home? She came here drawn by the homes and lives described by Springsteen. Lives of others, far removed from her own. Yet, at home was very much what she felt when she immersed herself into the lyrics, let the narratives take her by the hand and lead her through the Badlands, the backstreets, the alleyways. She had always believed she knew what they looked like from Springsteen's descriptions, and this trip had started out from her curiosity to see if her image matched reality. 'Dorothy learns that home is where the heart is, and she only has to click her heels three times to get there. My silver slippers didn't work. So I came here to see with my own eyes what Springsteen sang about.'

The man said nothing. Wendy heard herself, stopped and reflected what she had just said and added, 'homes of others …'

Nothing.

'… right, okay, I get it.' She fell silent. But this trip was something else too. It was the promise to herself that she was keeping. A naïve and perhaps childish promise from when she was 15, but still. That was something. 'Loneliness,' she said instead, 'they spelt loneliness wrong in the heading of the article in the 3rd column. It's not a 'y' but an I – beginner's error.'

The man took his paper out, checked it and scribbled the correction in the margin. 'You got kids?', and when Wendy nodded, 'I found a lot of my home is in my child's eyes. Enjoy your trip. I hope you find what you came for.' And with that he slid off the bar stool, raised his hand briefly at Tony and out of the door he went.

'He's the first philosophical car mechanic I ever met. Everything okay?' Tony wiped the place next to Wendy with a damp cloth.

'Yeah, I'd better start on this breakfast. Can't think and eat at the same time, it seems.' She settled into the warmth of the buzz of conversation around her, the clattering of knives and forks, the hum of the airco. In this comforting soundtrack of people's daily business, she started on her fry-up. So if it wasn't the places but the atmosphere evoked by them that felt like home, she just had to find what created that mood. Tomorrow she'd return her car, and somehow catch a ferry from Atlantic Heights to New York, passing by Lady Liberty.

Wendy looked through the gap in the green plastic. Below street level, men in fluorescent orange vests and bright yellow hard hats bustled their way through the worksite. A German on her right was telling his children the gruesome lowdown of what had transpired here, his sound effects resembling action hero movies. The pneumatic drills were hammering away at some of the remaining concrete. In the background a building that looked like a torn overcoat blocked the midday sun. A big truck laden with metal bars reversed into the main gate. People took photographs. It was tourist season in New York City.

Somewhere in the noise a bird sang. A siren turned the corner, raising the hair on Wendy's arms. An overwhelming sadness enveloped her. She thought back to Kyle's flushed cheeks a few days ago, and she now began to understand. A little. The reality of the dust and that gaping wound were a whole different story from the political rhetoric that had inspired her anti-war protest back home. She felt the weight of the country's grief here, standing in the chaos and noise where one single bird defied recent history. Tourists were snapping pictures of the men tasked with rebuilding the impossible: the unscathed confidence of America pre 9/11.

But Wendy still couldn't shake the deep-rooted conviction that war was never the answer. The threat of a Russian nuclear war had been a heavy blanket over her teen years. The first Iran-Iraq war the start of her pacifism. Before that she had been saving the whales, protesting about coal mines, climbing the barricades for women's rights, and petitioning against Apartheid. Now she watched rockets actually destroying buildings, tanks rolling into the broken bones of cities surrounded by desert, listened to high-pitched wails of mothers with bloodied children in their arms. Like many, she had gotten lulled into a false sense of peace: Glasnost was real; it should only have been a matter of months before the Berlin Wall would come down, and James Bond villains would become has-been tropes. But then Iraq invaded Iran. Not much later, Springsteen released Born in the USA, and the cover 'War' in the string of hits that accompanied it. She read the newspapers daily, her anger grew, and her denim jacket became a laden canvass for anti-war and pacifism buttons. It's when she first started listening to punk too. The radio was a beacon of anti-war music, a luxury easily afforded when terrorists were shedding blood mainly on a different continent, and Towers of Capitalism were boldly reaching for the skies.

Until they fell. In an act so hideously over-the-top Hollywood that not even the worst scriptwriter would have dreamt of suggesting it to any director or producer. Or if they did, that disaster movie would never have taken place on American soil, the land of the free, the keepers of the world. Here she was, witnessing a city being dumbstruck in the aftermath. Still, even the heart-wrenching farewells outside and inside Paul's Chapel could not change her conviction. War really was no good for anything. Hitting back hard would never be the solution. It would be nothing but a spiralling staircase of violence and destruction where there would only ever be one loser: the bystanders on the ground.

She took a last look at the gaping hole. It was still. The bird had gone. Wendy was acutely aware it would take much more time for New York to adjust to a new reality. And so must she. She had a job interview in an hour. Time to freshen up and get focussed on her own survival and reinvention.

She let her go; the sun, earth and moon

Rosie strummed her guitar. She wasn't inspired to write, again. One song a month, she'd promised herself. An album in a year. The stupidity of it all only increased her chagrin. As if she had the talent. And taking twelve months to write and record twelve songs? Sloths were fast compared to her. The shed, at least, was a forgiving space. Her dad had moaned and protested when Rosie first suggested she'd move her instruments in and his tools out, but it only took a few sessions of hardcore-punk songwriting for the neighbours to complain and for her dad to relent.

She had transformed the tool board with its grid of holes into a handy guitar and microphone cable holder. The opposite wall was painted completely black. She'd bought random picture frames, the most hideous and old-fashioned she could find from Oxfam, spray-painted them in purples and golds, and made collages of her favourite artists: the Ramones, Hendrix, Siouxsie, the Slits, Blondie, The Clash. Records she had found in her parents' dusty collection in the loft. The record player underneath the records had needed a little love and tenderness, but she was glad she spent the money on it. Playing the old stuff on vinyl gave it that extra grit and depth. The sheer act of having to get up and flip over the record, the care when dropping the needle, made the whole musical moment something she experienced rather than underwent. It still wasn't as good as live at The Tunnels, but it certainly elevated the intensity, even if the sound would benefit from better speakers. She had also discovered Tom Waits. Her parents had put his albums in frames in the living room as decoration. She had taken down the frames, taken out the vinyl and listened to them. She was blown away. God, how she loved Tom Waits. The combination of sheer poetry and cacophony of unusual instruments was irresistible, and inspired. And as for the art: every photo of him so very punk – maybe punk was better defined as unglamorous black and white reality. From the 90s and 00s era she had collected Pussy Riot, Nirvana, and Elastica on CD. Plenty of art work to go around too. A few of the trashy frames held the punkiest of all: Dolly. The over-the-top feminine persona she had created couldn't be farther off how Rosie presented herself to the world – but if Dolly's career and attitude weren't punk, then punk was dead.

Rosie had collected stacks of posters and magazine pictures of her punk heroes. Then she'd taken the original images and torn them up, and reassembled them to imitate Picasso's multi-angled perspectives. It was yet another one of the projects that her art teacher had managed to not understand. Fragmentation and distortion and punk; what was so complicated about the idea? In the 80s they had held themselves together with safety pins; she'd used the Japanese philosophy of Kintsugi. But more than putting things back together and restoring it to beautify, she had created a new reality through the purposeful mis-assembly. Rosie's teacher had stated that her work was derivative and didn't showcase her skills. Bollocks. Fine art wasn't going to cut it with her anyway, ever. The wall with the door and small window, she had covered with egg cartons. She was still contemplating how to pretty them up.

The sofa came from a skip from Rosemount. She'd sewn together random band shirts she had bought in charity shops, to form a quilt that covered the worst stains. A potato crate served as side table. On it balanced an ashtray – full – her incense burners and two dirty plates. It was comfortable. But she was restless.

It had been three weeks now and not a peep from her mother. No phone number like she had promised. No postcard or dramatic ransom note. Nothing. The house was a racket of unwashed clothes on the landing, dusty bookshelves, spiderwebbed ceilings and under-sofas, and bland, uninspired meals. She'd been listening to her mum's Springsteen albums a lot. There was so much Waits-ness to the lyrics in his early records, the underbelly of youths on the boardwalk on *Greetings*, the simmering oppression and weight of life's harshness on *Nebraska*. Compared to these earlier works, *Born in the USA* seemed almost simplistic. Still, the desperation of a train whistle, shattered illusions, relationships grinding down over the years, longing for a glorious past — was that what her mum was feeling now? Musically, she found the record flawed, very 80s non-committal pop-rock. So it was easy to overlook the lyrical gnash of the teeth. In that sense, it really didn't stray miles away from the precursors that Rosie found so spellbinding.

Rosie shifted from position. Suddenly she missed her mother. It surprised her, this acute sense of longing. She realised she didn't know who her mother was any longer. They hadn't really talked much these last two years. Ever since Toni, Rosie had felt a looming blackness. It came in waves of self-loathing and despair. The last person she wanted to speak to was her mum. She wouldn't understand anyway. What did her mum know about the bleak nothingness that hung like a shroud round many of Rosie's days? Maria had been the voice of reason and kind optimism, but wouldn't delve deeper than absolutely necessary. And even to Maria, Rosie wasn't ready to confess. Maria was a born optimist, and far more with the in-crowd than she was. It wasn't that Rosie was jealous, but when she saw Maria smoking, and laughing, she just wished she knew what it felt like, to feel; feel connected, or part of something bigger, without having to … Rosie shook her head. No longer, she had promised herself. No longer the quick-fix. She glanced at the chest of drawers. There, in the bottom drawer, she had hidden her stash. It would only take two steps to reach the shimmering solution. No. She slapped her wrist. No more.

She picked up her guitar and played a simple chord progression without any distortion. Maybe that was it, lightweight music – not the aggressive gritty guitar slamming she was so used to playing. Same chords, different texture. Worth a try. She hummed a tune. Abandoned the melody, tried again, working her way through a number of chord progressions in C, changed to G, and found a melody. She turned on her recorder.

Her dad rattled on the window in the shed door. Rosie saw his puzzled face haloed in the outside light. She closed her notebook and waved him in.

'Are we doing dinner?'

He could do with a shave, but otherwise looked as though he had made an effort today. Rosie shrugged. She didn't feel much like cooking. Last time she had looked, the fridge had been pretty empty apart from some shrivelled-up carrots, and half a green pepper. She probably could rustle up an omelette.

'We could order in pizza,' her dad suggested. Rosie noticed the droop in his shoulders, and how he held his hands in his pockets because he didn't seem to know where else to keep them. He was looking around. 'Not a very cheery place this, is it?'

'I like it here.'

'What is it about it that you like?' Rosie was taken aback by her dad's sudden interest. She considered sending him away to order pizza with the promise she'd be in the house soon. 'Why don't you sit down?' She pointed at the empty spot on the sofa next to her. Her dad reached for the light switch, and then sat down.

'You still playing on that piece of wood?' He pointed at her fourth-hand Fender.

'Does the job.'

'You do know Springsteen plays a Fender too, don't you? A Telecaster. Rumour is it's actually two guitars – Telecaster body and Esquire neck.'

'There you go then. Two pieces of wood is better than one – but I'm not quite Springsteen.' Rosie glanced at her dad, who was looking around the shed. 'You wanna play some?' She held her guitar out to her dad. Danny took it and strapped it on.

'Here's some culture for you. Not like them shouty sods you fill your head with.' With that he started Get Back. Rosie and Danny harmonised on the chorus and it was like a weight fell off both of them.

'I wish she'd come back.'

'Me too, do you think she will?'

'Don't know, your mum is not easy to gauge.'

'Did you, ever try, you know, gauge? You guys didn't seem to talk all that much.'

'Your mum, not talking?'

'Ay, but you, did you say much back?'

'Didn't know what to say. I was content. I can't fathom the edge she is searching for. It's like she thinks she's only alive when she's on some sort of edge of disaster and safety. I mean, we have it good, haven't we? Why leave? I can't see what she's hoping to find on the crumbling rock face skirting the abyss.'

Rosie was quiet. That was more than her dad had said in weeks. And actually quite uncharacteristically poetic. He clearly understood more of what had been brewing in her mum's inner world. Maybe the jovial and oh-so-irritating energy that mum presented to the world was only a front. A thought struck her.

'Didn't Mum keep a diary?'

Her dad's eyes narrowed. 'Why?'

'Maybe we can find some clues as to whether she'll be back.'

Danny put the guitar down, and looked into Rosie's eyes. 'Do you? Keep a diary?'

'Sure, doesn't every teenage punk?'

'Right. Well then, there you go.'

'What do you mean, there you go?'

'Don't you see Rosie? How would you like it if I read your diaries? Pissed off, right? Your mother …'

Rosie broke in, 'I'd be furious! You'd better never, ever ...'

Danny put his finger to his lips. 'Rosie, don't fret. I won't, ever. Because of your mum.' He strummed a couple of chords on the guitar, then continued, 'There's one golden rule your mother got me to swear to when we first got together. I was NEVER to read her diaries or yours. In return, she would never open my letters. Or sit behind a door to listen to my telephone conversations. Your mum was very adamant about that. I think it had something to do with her own family.' He got up and placed the guitar on the hook. He turned back to Rosie. 'So I am not about to rummage through anything your mum has written. She left a note with what she wanted to share, and that is it.'

Her dad's comment was like a nippy slap on the wrist but Rosie was not convinced. These were special times, and special times allowed for special measures.

'So you were never curious what is was that Mum scribbled down?'

'Sure, but I always figured that what she wanted to share came out anyway. The rest would probably only hurt me. She might be fickle, and gone right now, but I don't think she set out to hurt me. She needs to get things out of her system.'

'Aren't you scared she won't come back?'

'Every single minute of the day.' Danny stood up. 'But that is part of the deal. Anyhow, enough, let's get some pizza in. Uno pizza quattro formaggi with extra artichoke, I'll light some candles. We'll watch a DVD.'

'A candle. Such a Mum-thing to say Dad!'

'Ah well, gives us the idea she is still here, a little.'

When all was quiet, and Rosie was certain her dad was fast asleep, she squirreled her way up to the attic. Behind the rucksacks and blow-up mattress was a small cabinet with a few boxes. One held the Christmas stuff. Then there was a box full of negatives. So like her mum not to chuck those after the prints were developed. Not that you'd ever find your way to any particular photograph, as it was one almighty mess of acetate. At some point someone had tried to label the photo envelopes, but most were unidentifiable. Then there was a box labelled 'Rosie'. It showcased the same good intention executed terribly. Rosie opened the top: there were drawings, bits of art, photographs, school jotters … but none of it sensibly categorized. She picked up a drawing of a girl: red braids, huge grin, knee-high boots, and a very short skirt. The head was way too big for the body. The emerald green eyes had small hearts as pupils. And there was a big purple heart with stars around it on the T-shirt. She turned over the drawing. In wobbly letters was the word mum. In a firmer hand was written a date and a place. Rosie did the maths: she was six when she drew this. Were the hearts a sign of her mum's love for her, or her love for her mum? Rosie put the drawing back. This was no time to be all sentimental about her own youth.

Finally, behind the three boxes of 80s vinyl, she found the box she was looking for: Wendy personal. She dragged the box forward. Do not open. Well don't up and leave without a trace, was all Rosie could think. She took the lid off. Another box. On the lid: Danny, respect the deal. Rosie shrugged her shoulders and opened the box she found inside. Another box. Or rather suitcase. Rosie! Do not open. I promise you! You do not want to know. Rosie couldn't help smiling. Her mum did know her better than she figured. She saw the number locks. She grimaced; her mum clearly had trusted her husband more than her daughter.

A long time ago in primary five, Rosie had read about random not being random. There's a certain predictability to people's choices in significant information. If the numbers were completely random, they'd be much harder to actually remember. People gravitated to patterns, dates. Rosie felt secure that her mum would be exactly like the average Jane. So she tried her mum's date of birth, her dad's, their wedding day – which did take a bit of maths – and her own date of birth but nothing worked. She snapped at the lock, tried her pocket knife, but could not prize it open. Brainwave! Of course. She tried Springsteen's birthday but no, not even that. The date of that first concert? 040785? No movement. Rosie sighed. She knew she should take this as a hint. But at the same time, she could not help but wondering what was so secret that it needed this kind of security measure.

'Rosie? What are you doing up there?'

She glanced around in a panic. 'Nothing Dad. Just remembered I'd seen some records I wanted to listen to.'

'At two in the morning?' His head peeped out of the stairwell. He looked rough. 'Come down, and leave your mother's stuff alone.'

Rosie made a lunge for the record collection and grabbed the first things in her reach. She showed her dad as she came down. He grinned.

'Bizet's Carmen? Well well, the miracles … at least your film choice is a little more in keeping.'

Rosie looked at her hands. Opera indeed. And a DVD of a random Black and White cult movie. She shrugged her shoulders sheepishly and went back into her room.

Next morning her head was a fizzing ball of fire. Her temples throbbed, and the daylight streaming into her room did nothing to ease the hurt. Rosie pulled her pillow over her head. She heard the front door close, then the pic-tac of her dad's wonky bike pedal as he set out to work. For a moment she thought she would throw up. Next thing she knew it was noon. The stars and nausea had dramatically calmed down. She thought about her mum, the suitcase. She sighed. Turned over, and knocked a glass off the bedside table. Shit! She lunged to straighten the glass and plucked the vinyl and DVD from the puddle. She wiped them on the duvet. She looked closer at the DVD box. Only now did she see the film was called Thunder Road. It piqued her interest. Her mum had highlighted the lyrics sheet of Born to Run, exactly for the song with the same title. Had drawn fat exclamation marks. This film couldn't be a coincidence. She studied the cover. She recognised the face on it – but could not come up with a name. Old-fashioned cowboy and western chin, dimple, no-good eyes with a burning – masculine – glare, half hidden in the shadows of a car's interior. She turned the DVD over in her hand and read the back. Some random moonshining dude who gets killed whilst being chased by the cops. Ah, a "modern" Western. Cars, cops versus underdog, not at all like a movie her mum would watch. Although, it looked very much like the type of Film Noir B-movies her mum labelled classic. Rosie read the credits. Robert Mitchum – that's the one. She opened the case and saw a few newspaper clippings, mainly on a miniseries in the 80s called The Winds of War. It also featured Robert Mitchum, much older now. Underlined was the mention of this film called Thunder Road. There was an interview too, with Mitchum, who claimed that the role of the son in the movie had been written especially for Elvis Presley. But Elvis's then-manager asked for too much money. Her mother had scribbled like Springsteen – Fire in the margin. The credits stated Mitchum's own son was cast in the end.

Rosie decided she would stick it in the player downstairs, and make this a cinema afternoon. Might as well. For some reason her mum had bought and kept the DVD. Must be a good film. Or it must be something else. She pulled on her joggers, a long-sleeved shirt, and her toe socks and went downstairs. Her dad hadn't bothered to open the curtains, so the living room was all set. She opened the DVD player and inserted the disc. She took some plain biscuits from the pantry, filled a pint glass with water and installed herself on the sofa. She pressed play, and was prepared for the worst. The Ballad of Thunder Road opened the movie. Not quite the uplifting anthem Springsteen had written. Rosie sipped her lemon-water observing the dialogue in Tennessee drawl and the car chases, jumps out of windows, and explosions with mild amusement. Mitchum playing the tough underdog, in what now looked a fairly stilted manner. Rosie didn't much like the plot or the hot-rod action, apart from the cars. They didn't make them like that anymore. Even in black and white that Ford with those tail fins, epic. Suddenly, she had a flash of inspiration. She walked to the shed and checked the date on the album. Born to Run was released 25 08 75. She climbed into the loft, and tried the number lock. Bingo!

The suitcase was filled with notebooks. Not one was the same, but all were labelled. She noticed they seemed to cover certain periods rather than being one continuous and complete record. There were even school diaries. Her mum must have had little homework, because the one of her fifth year wasn't much larger than a credit card. It was bulbous though. Her mum had been a scrapbook artist too then, in her time. Most pages were plastered with magazine pictures of Springsteen; there were handwritten lyrics, and every now and then, brief instructions for homework, grades listed at the back. Rosie also noted lots of hearts. Times next to them. Dates with her dad? Important events? In December she found one page without any pictures. Just one word on the double spread for the 3rd week that simply stated FUCK! in capitals. And then in February a double spread on which every inch was filled with the word fuck over and over again. Rosie was confused. She thumbed through to the end of the school year. There on the 23rd of May was a page that Wendy had painted black. Rosie new that date. It was the day her grandmother died of cancer. What had happened on those other days? Weeks? Rosie also spotted a lot of drawings of a ball and chain with times next to them: 7:30 am, 4:10 pm – 5:30 pm. Babysitting? No, not in the morning. Paper rounds? Detentions? Not her mum, surely.

Rosie rummaged through the other notebooks. She reached for a slim A4 moleskin one, deep moss-green; an unsent letter slipped out. Rosie picked it up. It just said mum. Would she? Her grandmother wasn't here to mind; her mother wasn't there to stop her.

Mum,
I don't want to keep it. I am too young. I have a full life ahead of me. How can I bind myself to someone I barely know? Sure, life is precious, but this isn't life. Not mine anyway. Mum, I am sixteen years old. I'm gonna change the world. I can't, this way.

Rosie held her breath. There was no date. But she could do the maths. Yet here she was. Ten toes, ten fingers, a full mouth of teeth. What had happened? She stared at the letter in her hands, the suitcase full of notebooks, the lock her mother had told her not to crack. She felt stupid. And numb. The musty smell of the attic muffled her thoughts. Should she stop here? Then again, why stop here? It couldn't get much worse than knowing you weren't exactly received with whoops of delight and jubilant fanfare. And in that one split second, finding out what had motivated her mum to leave became a quest for what had motivated her to stay, and to keep. Rosie rummaged through the notebooks. Just cheapo random blocks of paper without any inkling of taste. She felt a sharp pain. Her blood rushed through her head and neck, heating up her cheeks and leaving her momentarily suspended in anticipation of the drop. Lightheaded, and slightly nauseous now, she stared at the crook of her left thumb and pointer finger and saw a massive paper cut. Her blood was actually dripping onto the immaculate white of a linen tote bag. She sucked the cut, enjoying the familiar metallic melted-butter taste. Then she opened the bag and saw what was in it: scans. She guessed at the nature of them: echo scans, x-ray scan, PET scans. She turned them upside down a few times, unable to distinguish what she was looking at. Then she noticed a small scribble at the bottom of one: terminal 9 Feb. Terminal – Rosie whistled into her throat. Was her mother ill? My god, was she dying?

Rosie stared at the scans. Her hands were trembling. But then, why leave? Why be alone? She felt the prick of tears behind her eyes. Her dad, was he in on this? Is that why he lost it before? Was the greasy stain on the kitchen wall his helpless anger and fear? She looked at the scans again, and noticed the date. 1986. The penny dropped. It was a clunky drop in the slow-turning cogs of her panicked brain. These were some of her grandma's medical records. She let out a single sob of relief. Then she picked up a square scan on a flimsy paper – this she did recognise immediately. An echo. And on it in blue: 12 weeks – is a dream a lie? In the same handwriting, joined up and sloping backwards – her grandma must have been a leftie. Rosie realised she was staring at the beginnings of herself almost sixteen years ago. And it seemed her grandmother had swayed her daughter with the only words she thought her daughter might listen to.

Rosie's breath and the tightness around her throat eased. She considered the notebooks: grey-blue floppy classroom jotters with wide margins for teacher feedback, a flowery ringed softcover, many flip-over notelets, black hardcovers with the red lines of a label, a few see-through ringed ones, A4-sized, A5-sized, A6-sized even. No logic in this madness that was her mother's notetaking administration. No number to indicate an order, many without years, although flipping them open, she did clock the dates. At the bottom was a stack of postcards bound together by a ribbon her mother had saved from a bouquet of flowers. She turned the pile over.

I miss your smell, and the softness of your fingers. The way you hum when you are happy and the way your tongue sticks out when you are drawing. Are you sure? S xx

Rosie hesitated before loosening the ribbon; she took another postcard. A stunning Grace Kelly looked at her, in black-and-white suave and sophistication. She flicked it over. I still remember. Be the queen. You're worth it. Miss you. S xx These declarations of … what exactly? Love? Was it mutual? Addressed to her mum and dated! Dec 2002? Was her mother having an affair? And here she was thinking her mother was depressed and alone, and needed looking after. This S, was her mum staying at theirs? Where and who was this S?

She heard her dad's key in the door. Better lock this all back up. She managed to make it look like nothing had been moved, quickly scuttled down the ladder, and closed the hatch behind her. She smudged some of her mascara to fake a sleepy look, and went downstairs.

After an unremarkable dinner – potato, two veg and no meat – Rosie and her dad sat down for a game of University Challenge. Why being made to feel completely inadequate was part of her upbringing Rosie never quite got, but there it was.

'Dad, how was Mum when grandma died?'

Her dad took a swig from his Carlsberg, and peeled at the label. 'Alone.'

Rosie looked at her dad. 'Alone?'

Her dad nodded. He stared at the TV. Paxman was rattling off questions at the speed of light, in that monotonous drone of his. That was the first challenge, keeping up with the question. Before you could even contemplate thinking about the answer, you first had to get the question, or at least some keywords. No such luck today.

'When her mum fell away, her dad retreated into himself. And from then on your mum was alone'.

'But she had you? Right? At the time? You were an item?'

Danny didn't look at Rosie when he mumbled, 'Not quite.'

Rosie took the zapper from her dad's hand and shut up Paxman. 'What do you mean, not quite?' In the pool of silence that followed, Rosie heard the drip of the kitchen tap. The refrigerator's temperature regulator clicked on. The oven clock ticked heavy, lazy minutes. Rosie wanted to shake her dad.

He put his beer bottle on the low table and looked at Rosie. 'I had chickened out. Lived with my brother for a while, not seeing your mum. I left your mother to carry all the weight of her mother's treatments, her bad days that weighed like ten thousand tons. And I left her to the morphine deliriums, the paranoia and her morose father.'

Rosie was stunned. Her dad hadn't wanted her either. She couldn't let on she read her mum's notes. 'But wasn't mum pregnant at the time? Of me?'

Her dad sank deeper into the sofa. He switched on the sound of the TV. Paxman made a snide remark, as if he was rightly tired that one wouldn't have the atomic weight for zinc at the ready. 'Dad?'

'I'll get another beer first. You want anything?'

Rosie shook her head. Answers is what she wanted. She switched off the TV as the blue sheen distracted her, and she had had enough of the arrogant superiority of Paxman anyway. She stood up, and closed the curtains. Switched on the standing lamp in the corner and the salt lamp in the bookcase. She turned down the big ceiling lamp. Now, at least, it looked more like a living room, rather than an interrogation cell. When her dad returned, he put his hand on Rosie's shoulder. He sighed.

'You gotta understand the context. She was sixteen, I was twenty-two. I had a job but my wages were not enough to take care of three people. And we had only been going out for five months or so, when I found out.

'Well what was your dick doing unprotected then?'

Her dad cringed. 'It sounds so crude coming out of your mouth … We actually hadn't done ... I think it was the third time. Anyhow, we used protection.' He took a sip, then let go of a hop-filled burp. 'In December we had found out that grandma had a tumour.'

Rosie mentally checked the first fuck in her mother's diary.

'Tests were done. It was all very nerve-wracking. I supported your mum as well as I could. I hate ill people. Can't stand hospitals, at the best of times. But your mum was so distraught. I took days off to help her cope. She bombarded me with all the research she could get her hands on. She was a bluebottle fly in a spider's web. I guess your mum wasn't paying much attention to her periods. And I was blissfully unaware. Anyhow, in February your mum started to be worried and bought a test. By that time, she was about twelve weeks pregnant. On the same day, we got the results for grandma, and they were very grim.'

Check two: *fuckfuckfuck*, over and over.

'I said no, when she found out. She agreed. Obviously, it was way too late for the morning-after pill, so we had to make an appointment at the GP. He refused to help, saying he was a conscientious objector. Your mum asked her mum for help. In a way, you have your grandmother to thank. I don't know how, but she convinced your mum to keep you. And when she did, I broke up with your mum.'

His shoulders slumped as his voice whimpered off. Rosie had never seen her dad this crestfallen. Rosie swallowed her wounded pride – in the end they had kept her, and her dad had stuck it out with her mum too. Nearly twenty years. She tried to make him feel better.

'It's okay Dad, I mean here I am – and there you are, my dad.' She hoped by now she was the expert at lying she had herself down for; her dad seemed to brighten up a little. Inside Rosie was scurrying around for clues. She tried to add the dates together. Wendy must have written the note somewhere in February, made the decision somewhere in March all those years ago.

'A few days before your grandmother died, she phoned me. Danny, come over. I remember thinking how small she was. A bone-white sparrow, no hair left. She wore a golden turban with style. I was sitting in the garden room – the sun was just heating up early morning dew. Somewhere a starling was singing. Your grandma was in the window seat letting the sun caress her skin. 'My daughter,' she said, 'is young, is fickle, and rebellious. But most of all she is scared shitless. How would you describe yourself?'

I replied we barely knew each other, that I had not wanted the child, and that she made the decision to keep you on her own. Surely, I had something to say in matters of life-changing proportions.' Danny peeled at the beer label. 'Your grandma said something quite similar to what you said, actually. And then she said her life insurance would leave enough money for a down-payment to a small apartment – probably not London, or Oxford – somewhere to set us up. Your mum was applying for jobs, and would not finish school. It wouldn't be a rich life, but it would be a responsible life. Your grandma held a hand mirror up to me and asked me to look in it. When I did, she said: Seriously, you can look yourself in the eyes? Truly? And I knew there was only one way I could.'

Rosie didn't say anything, for a long time. Seemed to her she existed despite her two parents. The tap still dripped. The fridge still hummed. Her dad put his hand on her leg.

'It was the best decision I could have made. I never regretted it.'

Rosie swallowed hard and decided she needed some time alone. She stood up and smiled weakly at her dad. She walked through the kitchen, to her shed, switched on the fairy lights and took Born to Run from its sleeve. She dropped the needle and slumped into the sofa. She looked at the lyrics sheet and the harmonica whined into her soul. The piano took her heart, and before the screen door slammed, she broke out into uncontrollable sobs.

Rosie woke up with a crooked neck. The black dog was howling in the corner of her mind, and her limbs moved slowly and heavily. She shifted on the sofa, and heard something tear. She looked down; she'd accidentally ripped the folded lyrics sheet. She felt bad, because in the end these were her mother's records. She got up, moved the arm back to its hold, and switched off the record player and amplifier. No point staying at home today. She might as well make it to school. She and Maria could have a smoke behind the bike shed. Maria would listen at least.

As she sauntered onto the schoolgrounds Rosie felt a strange vibe. She was used to being one of Hazlehead's outcasts, but she had always felt the mistrust was because her peers had a hard time placing her otherness – your uniqueness her mother would argue – and so they'd stay aloof so as not to have to fake interest or mild acceptance. For a few months after the incident with Toni, the aloofness had been particularly spiteful, but as he had faded, so had the memory of the ugly duckling ruling the roost. Today, she felt stares piercing her back, heard pointed whispers, and she had no idea what sparked it. She spotted Maria near the bike sheds. They made eye contact and Maria hurriedly gathered her bags and moved towards her.

Before Maria got near though, Jamie fell in step with her. 'Well well, so it is genes after all then. Like daughter like mother. Apples and trees and all that.'

Rosie shoved him away from her. 'Personal space Razorboy, never heard of it?' They called Jamie Razorboy ever after his older brother had shaved off Jamie's eyebrow during a night of drunken boasting. It had taken forever for a thin stripe to grow back.

Melanie and Tanisha walked by whispering, just ever so loud enough. 'I'd be sooo embarrassed, imagine. Your mum … '

Maria got to Rosie and dragged her aside, shooting angry looks at the sniggering pair who clinched arms and disappeared through the main entrance with swooshing pony tails. 'Okay, Rose, you'd better know something. The boys found something on the internet.'

Rosie wasn't surprised the boys had found something on the internet. The days of trading cards with filthy pictures had been behind them for some time now. Filthy magazines probably still found their way under the mattresses of some horny boys, but on the whole the internet was a lot livelier and interactive these days. The bell rang. The throng of pungent deodorant, greasy pimples and smoke-stained sweaters swarmed slowly towards the main entrance. The janitors opened both doors in order to speed up the lazy procession of resistance and boredom. Maria held Rosie back.

'Do you know what a blog is?'

Rosie shrugged her shoulders. 'Some new sort of upper?'

'No. It's a computer thing. Like a diary, that is on the computer.'

'Eh, come again? Bit pervie right? I mean who'd want to hang their dirty laundry out for everyone to read?'

'Your mum – apparently.'

Rosie looked at Maria incredulously. 'My mum? What do you mean, my mum? My mum is somewhere God-knows-where. She's left to find herself – like some midlife crisis thing. She is not writing diaries on the computer. She wouldn't know where to start. She writes all right – that came as a surprise to me too – but she writes on paper, I tell ya. Yesterday …'

Rosie was about to explain to Maria about all the notebooks she had found in the loft, the scans, the revelation her dad had dropped on her, but before she had the chance, Sharon – Goat's Teeth – spat on Rosie's Docs. She sneered, 'It takes a slut to raise one.'

Rosie shrugged off Maria and stepped right up to Sharon and brought her face real close. 'You looking for a Glasgow kiss, bitch?'

'Rose,' Maria tried.

Sharon smirked. 'Depends, is the alternative a hicky 'n a pricky? No wonder Toni tried it on with you – he knew you were easy meat.'

Rosie grabbed Sharon by the collar and smacked her with a flat palm. Sharon shrieked and lashed out. Her gel nails caught Rosie's cheek. She could feel her skin burn. All dams were broken. Rosie shoved Sharon on the ground and started pounding her body with her fists. 'Say that again, slag! I'll thump you in your mouth.'

Rosie felt four hands on her shoulders pulling her back.

'Easy meat, and your ma is a hoore; Your ma's a hoore!'

'Rosie let go. She's not worth it.'

Rosie looked up and saw Lea from 6C tugging at her sleeve. She was looking at Maria and signalling that the two of them should drag Rosie away from the bloody nose squirming under Rosie's weight.

'Hey, yous!' the janitor came running out.

'Rose, come on, let go!'

To avoid the long arm of school rules and regulations, Maria and Lea pulled Rosie away and ran out of the school gates, dragging Rosie with them. After fifty meters or so, they sat down on a bench near the school wall.

'Rose,' Maria began.

'Listen to us, Rosie,' Lea continued. She grabbed Rosie by the wrists to calm her down. She looked into Rosie's eyes. Rosie saw what Lea had felt and had understood. It was right there in the mirror of her eyes. Lea squeezed her wrists a little tighter, and whispered, 'Horizontal – thank fuck. But that's for later. Listen to us Rosie. Calm down and listen to us.'

Blow away the imprisoning dreams at night

Wendy felt her pocket for the hundredth time. Burning away inside it was her pit ticket to the show at the Giants Stadium. Sofia had been right when she told her that tickets would be available if she ever decided to go to the States. Wendy had met her in the queue at Wembley last year. As the fans were huddled up together, seeking shelter from the biting wind, she had been surprised to hear an Italian accent and had started up the conversation. Sofia had seen Springsteen in 1985 at San Siro Stadium, the first time he had played Italy. Now, two husbands and seven kids later, she was a single woman and determined to live life to the max. Hearing such an American expression with an Italian lilt had made Wendy giggle, but she turned serious when Sofia rattled off the shows she'd been too, all over Europe. And now, she had said, she would also go to the USA. Wendy had been taken aback. She'd never considered people were going to more than one show in one tour, let alone abroad for one. Sofia assured her that every show was different and a completely novel experience. It sounded somehow extravagant and indulgent, but the spark in Sofia's eyes was infectious. She had flapped her hands, emphatically underlining her words, like a football player protesting his innocence with the ref. They had found each other after the show, and spent most of the night in London pubs, reeling with the magic that they had just witnessed. Sofia had told Wendy more about her travels without ever boasting. Something had shifted within her then, a seed had been planted. She stored away the idea for a while. Yet when they'd struck up a correspondence, that seed of an idea had started to grow. But when Sofia had bought tickets in March the next year, Wendy had chickened out. Sofia had threatened to come over and force her. Be the queen you are! she'd written. It was only after she'd found herself hyperventilating, pacing a deserted house when The Rising was playing on the radio one sorry morning in April, that she'd made the promise to herself.

And here she was, on the 164 bus, about to attend her first concert outside of the UK, her third show ever. This ticket was the first big purchase she'd made with her first US wages. She'd asked around in the hostel, then talked to Brendan, and of course he knew exactly where to go. The ticket had cost her a fortune; she'd paid about $200, which was still cheaper than her Wembley ticket last year so she counted herself lucky. It was Bruce after all. Sometimes, money had to flow. This was sometimes. She wondered about the American audiences. The day was balmy with a gentle breeze, the lost wages from the slow Tuesday night were a sacrifice made without regrets.

When she got off the bus, her own excitement was matched by the throngs of people all headed in the same direction. Many were carrying cool boxes, and shopping bags. Wendy couldn't understand why you'd bring those things to a concert. Where would you keep them once the doors opened? But as soon as they got to the car parks she understood. It looked like the carboot sales in old town squares. People had driven their cars in, and were now setting up for a comfortable afternoon with friends. Chairs came out. She even saw barbeques. Flags were waving and Bruce was blasting from boom boxes. Others had brought guitars. Wendy stood agape. Nobody seemed to be rushing or queueing. When she got even closer she saw they had recreated a boardwalk in front of the stadium with a carnival attraction including a Ferris Wheel. Only in America, she smiled. And when in America do as the Americans, she decided. She walked around, taking her time to drink up the atmosphere.

'You look lost dear,' a woman with long sleek hair held out a can of beer, 'here, have one.'

'Not lost, merely surprised. I've never seen anything like this before.' Wendy accepted the beer, tapped the top a few times with her nails, popped it open and took a swig.

'Come join our party over there. See the white van with the flag? That's where we're hanging out.'

Wendy looked around and saw at least ten white vans. And at least as many flags. 'Ehh,' she began but before she could ask the question the woman had linked arms and was dragging her over.

'Haha, I see the problem. Here, I'll take you. My name is Marty, and I am sure I'm the biggest Bruce fan in New Jersey. I've seen over 100 shows, so you are in good hands.' Marty smelled of sea breeze and open-fires Wendy noticed.

'I'm Wendy, I'm here to find out if love is real.'

Marty cocked her head, then let out a burpy laugh. 'Well Wendy, not sure about love but this is where we keep it real.' She waved frantically to the folks hanging around the white van. 'Hey here guys, this is Wendy, she's joining us for some beers.'

It took only a few minutes of bragging rights before she had to admit that this was only going to be her third concert. These past few months she had discovered the Backstreets website, lurking on the BTX forum. She had pored over the concert reports, argued over song meanings, and their importance in the grand scheme of things. She had been part of the setlist watching. Via SPL she had downloaded bootlegs of the holy grails of concerts. So this would only be her third concert, but in her understanding of the lyrics, and everything they stood for, how they paved the modest road she walked yet defined her moral compass, she was just as committed as Marty. And the gang certainly did not think any less of her; in fact it seemed they were mighty impressed.

'It's easy for us, remember. We live just around the block. You've come all the way from Scotland That's commitment right there!' There was not an inkling of cynicism in the eyes of Andrew with the cauliflower-haircut. 'The question of course of fandom comes down to just one thing: sways or waves?'

Wendy hesitated. *Sways or waves?*

'Does Mary's dress sway or wave?' Andrew took a roasted chicken leg from the barbecue and started munching.

'Oh, ha! What? Never thought about it really.' She quickly went over the lyrics in her head. 'Waves,' she decided after trying both options numerous times. A howl went up.

'Oh no, Marty, how could you!! You allowed a traitor into our midst!' Andrew raised his chicken leg to salute Wendy. 'But at least you're honest.'

'Well really whatever the lyrics, this must be the most important song ever written, right? Whether the dress sways or waves, aren't we all pulling out to win?'

Wendy's remark was welcomed with a lot of high fives and nods of agreement. She had vindicated herself.

'So did you come over especially for this concert then?' Marty asked. She was scooping sauerkraut into the buns, squishing mustard on them too before passing them to Robert who added the barbequed sausages.

'No, I came to follow Bruce's early footsteps; I've been to his childhood home, the bars he used to play, the Stone Pony, that sort of thing. I did hope to make a show, but I didn't have a ticket when I got to New York.'

Marty laughed. 'You probably saw more about the Boss in your time here than I ever took the effort to. I hope Jersey treated you well. I hope you're keeping a diary.'

'It's been amazing so far. And actually, I am keeping a diary. I have just started a blog diary thing to keep track of my personal journey. The website is called Blogger. I am Poet Down Here. It's more about what moves me than the Bruce stuff though.'

Marty shot to the front of the car. Wendy could hear her opening and closing various compartments before she appeared again, waving about a piece of paper and a black marker pen. What was it again? Blogger?'

'Poet Down Here.'

'Excellent moniker. I'll have a look tomorrow.'

Despite the warm welcome, Wendy decided to go for another wander after the third beer. The tall tales of friendships and epic previous concerts shared, made her acutely aware she was here by herself, unable to share this momentous moment with a loved one. Wasn't it the sharing that made relationships worthwhile? She was destined to forget most of the details if she couldn't test her memory against that of loved ones who had been there at the same time. The collective memory – a powerful reason to have a partner at a later age. She'd read that somewhere. And here she was alone amongst strangers.

'I gotta go. I want to figure out where to enter the stadium, maybe take a ride in the Ferris wheel. Thanks for these. Have a great one!' Wendy hugged Marty.

'Hey Poet don't forget to swing by the karaoke tent. A buddy of ours runs it,' Andrew shouted. He laughed sheepishly. 'Being a Bruce fan in New Jersey is a little bit like being in a cult. We all know each other. But, honest, he's a great guy. Sing your heart out poet. Tell Mike that Andrew sent you!'

Wendy promised she would look for him, then set off. She wandered through the yellow and white gazebo stands, ending up at the official merch table. She didn't have much cash left over but wanted a token to remember this moment. She tried on a raspberry T-shirt with the boardwalk scene on the front. On the back it had a massive number 1 and the date written, wrong-way-round American style. It left her with barely enough to buy any food; a pretzel and some water, but she didn't care.

For forty-five minutes she watched amazing singers get up to belt out their favourite Springsteen anthems on the small stage. No way was she going to make a fool of herself up there. Mike looked like a 70s pimp in his purple Hawaiian shirt, reminding her of Little Steven's outfits when he played with The Disciples in the 80s. He took the microphone off a young boy who had given a raw rendition of Backstreets.

'And the next one up has come a long way. I have it on good authority she flew in all the way from Scotland!'

Wendy sat up. Oh sweet, someone from home. She'd sit this one out and then head over to the gate. She marvelled how much she enjoyed the whole paraphernalia of this make-believe boardwalk.

'So Poet Down Here, please come to the stage and gives us your best!'

Wendy's heart stopped. She looked around. Nobody was moving.

'Go on Poet, knock 'm out!' Wendy turned to see Marty waving her beer about. Andrew wolf-whistled, 'She's right over there Mike! The one with the fanny pack.' Wendy shook her head, frantically making a cut sign with her right hand along her throat. Mike jumped off the stage and took her by the hand. 'Come on girl, you are amongst friends here.'

Her mind went blank when she scrolled through Bruce's enormous back catalogue. In the end, she went for the song that expressed so well why she was here. Mike started up the track, handed her the mic and she started.

'I get up in the morning …'

Afterwards she had a mock-fight with Marty and Andrew. Secretly, she felt elated. She had given a rendition that most seemed to have enjoyed. She was drunk on her three minutes of fame. This is how Bruce must feel, she thought, only 1000 times over. The day had turned out much richer than she had even dared to wish for. And it would only get better once she was inside, she was sure.

Around seven she went to the gate indicated on her ticket. Pre-gig nerves started to fizz. Would she get close to the stage? She had no idea what to expect once she got in. She showed her ticket to the attendant. He took a good look and was about to rip the stub off when he took a closer look.

'You bought this yourself?'

Well, erhm yes. I handed it over didn't I?' Wendy said with a slight tremor in her voice.

'I mean, you bought this when they first came out? At a Ticketmaster outlet?'

'No,' she hesitated, then said, figuring she had nothing to lose, 'I got it off a guy in New York. He couldn't make it, so passed it on to me.'

The security guard sighed. 'I'm so sorry lady, but this is a fake.'

Wendy's breath stopped. 'What do you mean a fake? It looks fine to me. Same as hers?' She pointed at the girl behind her. The tickets looked identical. Same blue and white, and typewriter lettering. Ugly as sin really, but it's all about the music not the ticket.

'You can go to the box office to get it verified, but the price isn't right, see? There are general admission tickets but they do not cost $85. It's a very good fake, but a fake it is. If you don't believe me go check the barcode at the box office.'

Wendy's world stopped spinning. She had just forked out all her wages for a ticket that wouldn't let her in. The girl behind her started to shuffle impatiently. There was little point staying in the queue.

The box office confirmed that her ticket was a counterfeit. The $20 she had left, and a brand-new T wouldn't buy her another. The boardwalk was emptying as people started to find their way in. She saw a few people mulling about with signs that they too were looking for tickets. She sat down near the strongman game. The guy running it came over to her.

'You wanna have a shot?'

'No, thanks,' Wendy sighed.

'You don't sound too happy. Aren't you excited about the show?'

‘I am, I was. When I got to the gate, I was told my ticket is a fake, after I had just blown my money on a pretzel and T-shirt, as well as all my wages for the last weeks.’

‘There’s plenty folk trying to offload tickets I think. How much have you got?’

‘I only see people looking for tickets, I’ve about $20, but that includes my bus fare back.’

The guy whistled through his teeth. ‘Them folk trying to “buy tickets”, they aren’t looking to buy. They are selling. But you’ll struggle for that money. Opening night and all.’

Wendy looked up. Since when did wanted tickets, mean here I’ve got some! The guy glanced about, then walked away carrying a few beers. It seemed a lifetime before he returned. An almighty roar came from the stadium. Bruce had just walked on stage. When the guy finally returned he had a big grin on his face.

‘Here you go. You give me a tenner, and we’ll call it all squared. It’s not much of a seat but it will get you in. You’d better get going. You’ve missed too much already.’

Wendy looked at the bloke in disbelief. He tapped his NY Yankees cap, and smiled. ‘Hey, it happens to the best of us. Welcome to the swamp of Jersey. Now listen, if ever you buy another ticket from someone, first get a feel for the person you’re dealing with and if you can, always check out the offered ticket next to a real one, looking for tell-tale signs of it being a fake: different colour, type of paper.’ He stuck his hands in the back pockets of his jeans that hung off his butt like an empty potato sack.

‘Checking the price too, it seems,’ Wendy added sheepishly. ‘But listen, I can’t accept a gift like this from you.’

‘Don’t worry, I got it cheap and did good business here today. I’ve got another nine shows to earn back the few bucks I handed over just now.’

Wendy shook his hand. It was warm and limp. But that didn't matter. She was going to see Springsteen on his home turf. 'Thank you …'

'Joey.'

'Joey, you're a life saver.' She sprinted towards the gate, praying that this time the ticket would pass. In the distance, she heard Springsteen's harmonica, followed by the sax. She ran faster, ignoring the stitch in her side. *Third Tier, how would that be?* Both times at Wembley she had been standing, finding her way forward as the concert progressed. She had been so chuffed that this time was going to be the same again. Now, she would have to settle for an ants' eye view, no doubt. She finally reached the gate and held out her ticket. Typically, security didn't even rip the counterfoil this time, but let her straight through. By the time she found her seat, way up in the gods, tiny Bruce was roaring that his *love would not let her down*.

Punk Soldier

Lyrics Paulina Vanderbilt Music Otto de Koning

I

Punk Soldier

Lyrics Paulina Vanderbilt Music Otto de Koning

2

to listen / download
scan – open link – click on image – enjoy!

POET DOWN HERE

making an honest stand

THURSDAY, 10 JULY 2003

Disappearing in the darkness

I don't regret one moment. Not the moment I first laid eyes on him, not the moment we first kissed, not the shaky, but oh so careful and tender first intimate moments, not the moments of doubt, of joy, of anger, of that miracle that is my daughter Rosie. As a matter of fact, I regret not one of the moments I shared with him the past 18 years.

Nor do I regret the moment I finally left.

It's been just over a week now since I left my husband. Some may call it selfish, what with a fifteen-year-old fire cracker waiting for the results of her 4th year exams. Some may call it foolish; a husband with a comfortable job, a home, at the age of 33 is not such a bad thing, I hear you think. Maybe that's so, but had I not gone, I'd have disappeared anyhow. Crumpled up, shrunk away, Trojan-Horsed out. The shell would be walking and talking all right, smiling the smile, faking the fakes but the girl inside would have gone without even a sigh or a whiff. I had to hold on to her. She is me and I used to like her. She's worth another shot at it.

I've never written a weblog. Until I met Brendan I didn't even know what it was. Brendan is the guy who manages the hostel I'm staying in just now. He saw me furiously working my way through wads of dead forests and suggested I write a weblog instead. Less paper to carry around, internet cafés a-plenty and a willing ear worldwide, he says. He says it's going to be a BIG thing, this weblogging. I'm not too sure about that. Still, I decided to give it a go after some Spanish chick spilled coffee all over my notebook (accidentally of course; it's easily done after 7 tequilas and 4 vodka-cokes).

So I'm not too sure how to go about this. I guess I'll just tell you my life as it is, like a diary.

Previous Posts

I Power Blogger

POET DOWN HERE

making an honest stand

THURSDAY, 10 JULY 2003

Disappearing in the darkness

I know there's so many of you who are in the same boat. You sit there in front of your screen, in the dark hours when the house is quiet, the wine tastes sweet and the night is a gentle lover. Maybe this diary will give you courage. I hope it gives you strength to do what's right for you. I'm not saying you should all leave your husbands, boyfriends or partners. I don't say men are heinous monsters. I am not a man-hater. I do believe in the institution of marriage, even after walking away from it. I just think, sometimes separation is the only way to build a bridge. For me it was all that was left. I'm scared shitless, but all I can say to you is: don't be.

I came here to New York and the Promised Land to find out what love is – stick around if you are looking *to prove it all night* too.

posted by poetdownhere@ July 10, 2003 comments

POET DOWN HERE

making an honest stand

FRIDAY, 11 JULY 2003

Not settling for a hard edge

So I came to the USA to find out if love was wild. But first I'd better start by telling you something about the people I left.

My husband is a gentle man. He is kind and loyal and I'm pretty sure he loves me. He's got a steady job that pays the mortgage, and leaves us money for a two-week holiday abroad each year. He's into darts, which I can forgive him for; he could have been into fishing or snooker.

My fifteen-year-old daughter Rosie is angry. With me, the world, herself. I don't know if she loves me. I hope she does. At the moment any tender feelings are hidden away, as with most girls her age it seems, behind a long black fringe drawn across her eyes on a permanent basis. She's a volcano of mixed emotions: hatred, self-pity, and self-loathing, self-doubt, anger, extreme confidence and dismal lows. A teenager.

So what's all so horrible about that, eh? Might seem a pretty contented family portrait to most of you. On the outside anyhow. But tell me, do you ever look in the mirror and don't like what you see? Yeah, I know: all the time. Especially when you finally get into Marks & Sparks and try on new trousers two days before your period is due. But I mean, apart from that. Does that feeling ring a bell? Or worse, do you look in the mirror and you don't recognise who you see? Well, one day I looked in the mirror and I saw nothing. And all I could think was: it's better than seeing me. That's when I realised I had to leave.

So here I am: alone in New York, where nobody knows me, behind a computer. It's three am and I can't sleep. My hair's a mess. The neon lights show every crease and the dark bags under my eyes when I glance at myself in the chrome side panels. It's not a pretty picture, but at least I can see me again.

Previous Posts

Disappearing in the darkness

I Power Blogger

POET DOWN HERE

making an honest stand

FRIDAY, 11 JULY 2003

Not settling for a hard edge

All I need to do now is work on making it a reflection to be proud of again.

Brendan says, the secret to a good weblog is witty, short pieces. Not too sure about the witty. And actually I think I am failing on the short bit too. So I guess I'd better sign off.

posted by poetdownhere@ July 11, 2003 comments

POET DOWN HERE

making an honest stand

SATURDAY, 12 JULY 2003

Wondering what I am getting into

The staff in this hostel are great. I don't exactly class as their target customer but none of them blinked an eyelid when I followed my yellow suitcase through the door, huffing and puffing like a hippo after a 200-metre fly.

I had booked a bed in an eight-bed dorm to save money. I'm not sure how long the little funds I gathered over the years with my freelance garden design jobs will last. So I took a job too, in a bar on West 49th Street. I work late and am rarely in my bed before 2:00 am anyway, so a bed is all I need, just like the hip and trendy students this hostel wants to cater to. I just don't have their stamina. They get up at eleven and don't come back in until the early hours of the morning. I can't heave my limbs from the mattress till the afternoon, 1:00 pm, sometimes even 2:00 pm.

Last night I sat down with Brendan. Yeah, that's right, the manager of this place. He's a ginger PhD student from Perth (Australia) who has taken a year out. To refresh his brains, he says. Working in this backpackers' place allows him to forget the abstract calculations of maths (apart from when he's tallying up the week's total takings of course). He says he wants to see the world with an emotional eye and restless heart. I was once full of youthful idealism too.

Anyhow, he took out some beers. I had been on my feet for a nine-hour shift without anything to eat since the free breakfast bagel. It only took a beer and a half to get my tongue loser than a Jimmie Hendrix guitar lick. As usual the alcohol in my blood fermented into a song of lament and self-pity and I plunged my heart on the kitchen table with a ceremonial thud.

Or maybe it was just the insomnia. Rosie never used to make it home much before 1:00 am, despite the tearful threats and punishments and me lying awake like the undead, body rigid and eyes wide open until the click of the door would allow me to shut them, but that was only

Previous Posts

- Not settling for a hard edge
- Disappearing in the darkness

I Power Blogger

POET DOWN HERE

making an honest stand

SATURDAY 12 JULY 2003

Wondering what I am getting into

Fridays and Saturdays. And maybe an occasional Thursday. I'm out till 2:00 am every night now. My body sure is struggling.

I'm up when the rhythm of the city's breath slows and fragments of conversations between lovers seep from subway vents and apologies slip free down the fire escapes. I haven't gone daft, in case you're wondering. I don't hear voices. But I can feel them. Danny reckons I'm slightly deranged when I talk about feeling conversations around me. I feel the weight of words linger in the air like an unconscious echo; every night when I walk home from work (not safe, I know, but limited choice makes you brave). Maybe it was the pining in the air that got me talking.

Or maybe of course, it's because Brendan is gorgeous – ginger, but dark and rusty, with green eyes and a strong jaw – and I needed a young unattainable male to fix his eyes on me for a bit. I'm sure Brendan does not understand but he's the type of boy who'd always sympathise with a woman old enough to be his mother, if only out of politeness.

I guess it doesn't matter why I opened up. All I know is I did and I ended up in a private room for the same rate as a dorm bed. ON MY OWN! In case your mind is racing. I am a married woman. Brendan says it is not yet high season anyway, and that it is easier to have me in there on my own, than change sheets every night to accommodate impromptu shags from horny guests. I promised I'd wash my own sheets and clean my own bathroom. He agreed to let me stay two weeks at least.

It's funny. I've stayed in a few four-star hotels where they leave complimentary chocolates on your pillow and potpourri in the bathroom, with staff that bow at immaculate angles and a restaurant to die for.

Tonight I shall sleep without dreams.

posted by poetdownhere@ July 12, 2003 comments

POET DOWN HERE

making an honest stand

SUNDAY, 13 JULY 2003

Having a heart that is hungry

A man walked into the bar tonight around nine. He looked around 45, clean-shaven, tie, suit, leather laptop bag; obviously successful. He looked a bit like George Clooney: same square face and brooding eyes. A babe-magnet. Normally it is the young girls that bring the men in but this here man had the girls flitting around him like butterflies. All nervous and shy they were. Eager to feel his hand brush against their thighs. It was as if his beauty was breathing new hope into their existence. He reeked of money, even I could not help but be drawn. The intriguing bit was that he did not seem to notice the effect he had on these girls. While they were falling over each other to be near him, and searching his gaze from under their eyelashes, he just looked into his glass and drank.

He didn't say much for two hours. He drank steadily but the alcohol didn't seem to affect him much. I could see his shoulders slouch a little after the 5th whiskey, and his hand tremble. No more. That's when he accidentally looked up, while I was having a good look at him, trying to figure what it was he was "drinking away".

I like doing that, assessing the customers and guessing what they are in for. For most of them it is pretty easy. They come to wind down from work, needing a little me-time before going back to domestic bliss. The students come to loosen their tongues and discuss their course, the latest gossip, conquests, flings and things. Nothing too deep. Those who do, go to the bar on the Lower east side. Others come to forget, often something they can't remember. This man didn't fit any of these categories. It seemed he drank without any intention. He was just there, gazing at a point I could not detect. Until he caught me looking.

It was like one of those cartoons. The minute he caught me staring, his eyes switched on, suddenly ablaze with jet-black depth and I

Previous Posts

Wondering what I am getting into

Not settling for a hard edge

Disappearing in the darkness

I Power Blogger

SUNDAY, 13 JULY 2003

Having a heart that is hungry

could feel myself blush. I can't remember what I muttered, but I know it was lame. Very unprofessional too. He ordered another Jack Daniels, but I reached for Lagavulin instead.

I had noticed the bottle a couple of days before, but it was obviously kept for special occasions, stacked away right at the back of all the other liquor. Since arriving in New York, every minute of the day, these voices have been talking in my head. Voices asking questions, non-stop, reminding me of Danny and Rosie. Forcing me to think about them. Voices nagging away about my selfishness. Voices confusing me by piling on the guilt and at the same time cheering me for the freedom regained. Voices, incessant, obnoxious and so loud sometimes that I find it hard to concentrate on customers' orders. I have checked in the mirror to ascertain whether the voices are visible, in my eyes maybe. I swear to God nobody would know, yet my head feels like exploding with them. The few hours sleep I do manage to get are an oasis of calm that evaporates like a fata morgana far too quickly. Despite, or maybe because of the voices, I haven't thought about Scotland as such. I haven't missed the granite, the river, the seagulls and salt. When I clocked the Lagavulin, I felt an unexpected pang of utter desolation and longing for the North-East.

I recognized a similar desert-island feeling in George's eyes when he rested them on me. The void was so limitless I had to grasp the edge of the bar to steady myself. I can only guess what caused it, but I recognised the ache. So I decided to pour him the Lagavulin instead. The boss wouldn't ever know. I reckoned the peaty barley would warm George up and maybe remind him of a blazing hearth and home comforts. A childhood memory perhaps but one that would help him find safe shores. I slid the glass to him without a word.

posted by poetdownhere@ July 13, 2003 comments

POET DOWN HERE

making an honest stand

SUNDAY, 13 JULY 2003

Having a heart that is hungry

He lingered his index finger on my hand and gently brushed my skin. The gesture lasted only a nanosecond and was completely undetectable to the naked eye. Then he took the glass and brought it up to his mouth. I turned away but watched him in the mirrored tiles. He didn't drink the whiskey. He looked across the bar and found my mirrored stare. His eyes smiled and he nodded. Only then, did he lift his glass and drink it slowly, his gaze never leaving me.

By this time, most of the girls in the bar had given up on him. A gaggle of students had just come in, which offered a much easier prospect, with far fewer potential complications. They turned their backs on the aura of George's mystery for the instant gratification on offer with those young boys. They were calling orders from the far corner of the bar, so I turned away from the tiles and went back to work.

I never saw him leave. He settled his bill with Aimee but left a tip specifically for me. A $20 note.

For the first time in years, I was hungry for sex.

posted by poetdownhere@ July 13, 2003 comments

POET DOWN HERE

making an honest stand

MONDAY, 14 JULY 2003

Being on fire

George was back again tonight. I was so rushed off my feet that I didn't even notice until Aimee tugged my arm and told me Spencer wanted only me to serve him. I was utterly confused. I had no idea who Spencer was. So she pointed out George, then gave me a wicked smile. Told me to remember the boss's rule: no fraternising with the patrons. I told her I had dubbed him George yesterday and she giggled at that. A lot manlier than Spencer, she agreed and then she told me to get working for my tip.

I have to admit I was flattered by the attention. I have noticed people's heads turning to look at me, but I think that's more because I often wander home crying my eyes out. I try not to but I get bowled over at really unpredictable moments by these tears: a sneer about a dirty glass, a trailing thumb as a tip is pressed into my palm, one wink of the eye as the young girl puts a dime in the jukebox and the train rhythm of *I'm on Fire* rolls into the bar. I don't even mind that much, because when I cry the voices stop. The knot in my stomach also stops me from eating much. For the first time in a long while nothing bulges when I bend over. I am elated at the unexpected bonus. With my hair up, my cheekbones are high and my collarbones straight like a coat hanger my body hangs on. I know I can compete with twenty-five-year-olds; at a first glance, not many men would guess I had borne a child and was nearing thirty-five. Was it as simple as that? A bit of recognition of the superficial outer shell, and all is well? I never thought I'd be that shallow.

Spencer called me over and asked when the last time was that I had been home. I didn't want to tell this man my whole sob story; after all it's the patrons that need to empty their aching hearts; we behind the bar, simply help to fill it up again with copious amounts of alcohol. It's my job to open their flood gates, not the other way round.

Previous Posts

POET DOWN HERE

making an honest stand

MONDAY 14 JULY 2003

Being on fire

He was not perturbed by my round-about noncommittal answer and asked for two Lagavulin. When I returned with the glasses, he gently pushed one over to me, did this I'm-sexy-and-I-know-it thing with his eyebrows and waited for me to raise my glass. A brief Slàinte mhath sealed the evening.

It was my night to lock up, and once I had booted everyone out, I cleaned away the last few things, and sorted the till. There was a soft knock on the delivery door round the back. This is New York so I knew better than to be careless at two o'clock in the morning. But the Slàinte mhath confirmed that I had understood Spencer's earlier reference to stocking up correctly. I opened the door carefully, and let him in.

I will spare you the details: what happens on a bar's pool table, shall stay there. Let's just say I hadn't reached the top of four Munros in less than an hour, for a long time. His hands knew exactly where to roam. My body knew exactly how to respond.

I know I should feel awful. I am a married woman after all, but I feel liberated in a way I hadn't even known I was seeking. Spencer warned me about the steel shield of protection around my pain. Said the shield was holding things at bay, but was also stopping me from giving and sharing. And *that*, he said, makes for a poor life.

We kissed goodnight, locked the door behind us, and Spencer headed off. I walked back to the hostel with a lightness of heart and step I hadn't felt for years.

posted by poetdownhere@ July 14, 2003 comments

POET DOWN HERE

making an honest stand

WEDNESDAY, 16 JULY 2003

Being stuck in the swamps of New Jersey

You know that thing when you have dreamt about the moment for weeks, and then when it's finally time, it is the most epic adventure ever? Yesterday was epic but not at all in the way I would have ever predicted. You see, I was going to see the Boss at the Giants' stadium but the ticket I had got on the corner of Madison Square Gardens ended up being a fake. So last night turned into a life lesson in improvisation.

Being at Meadowlands – the Swamp as it apparently is called endearingly – was epic in itself. They had actually shipped in sand and planks to create a boardwalk which included seaside-resort rides. I mean, where else but in America? I had expected to queue up from the moment I arrived, like I did in London but everyone was so chill and enjoying the carnival atmosphere I decided to follow suit. I met up with fans that have seen so many shows I almost felt ashamed I ever dared to call myself a fan at all. I didn't meet them in a queue though but drinking beers from the back of their cars. Tailgating they call it. Wow what an invention.

Nice as all this was, I had come for Bruce Springsteen and had spent all my earnings on a ticket that would give me entry to the front part of the field. So I was nervously excited when I finally did go into the queue, only to be turned back from the gate. Fake? What do you mean, fake! I felt the ground swallowing me whole. But would you believe it, in stepped another kind American who went out to find me a ticket right there and then. I ended up so high up and far back from the stage that Springsteen was no more than a tiny speck. I ended up watching most of the concert on the large screens. Still, I was there, in New Jersey watching the Garden States' favourite son ...

Previous Posts

I Power Blogger

POET DOWN HERE

making an honest stand

WEDNESDAY, 16 JULY 2003

Being stuck in the swamps of New Jersey

The audiences are weird over here. People kept getting up to buy food and drink, right throughout the show. Seriously, a conveyer belt of comings and goings, non-stop. Yet I was asked to sit down when I got up to dance and whoop, celebrate life, Bruce, the Land of the Free. All I was thinking was: *but this is a Bruce show. Nobody sits down.* Apparently, they do in the USA. So I moved over to the aisle where I didn't bother as many folk, dancing my socks off. Hey, if they won't join, improvise.

Bruce was no bigger than a pin prick from where I was sat but he still got through right where it hurts. I came to be liberated, and Bruce sure is the man to do it. He played loose, the band played tight and the night was balmy and perfect. I thought the concert last night would be the cherry on the top of the fantastic days I had before I started this blog, and visited all the Bruce spots in Jersey that I had been picturing in my head, sitting on my bedroom floor with his album on the turntable and the others fanned around me. I found I have so much further to travel yet. Last night I was reminded of the fickle ways of life. Control is only an illusion. Surfing the waves of unpredictability is a skill I have started to learn; this concert experience was another opportunity to practice.

My one-word wish to anyone reading this: TRUST! And you shall be found.

posted by poetdownhere@ July 16, 2003 comments

POET DOWN HERE

making an honest stand

TUESDAY, 22 JULY 2003

Getting a redheaded man to do the dirty job

Glory Hallelujah for kitchen stoves and midnight feasts.

After 'playing pool' George stayed away long enough for me to get the hint, and be slightly frustrated. Every brush on my skin – opening the curtain, the towel after a shower, the bed sheet after work, walking too close to someone in the kitchen – triggers an instant reaction. I feel the blood rushing, saliva wetting my mouth. And sorting myself out is all dandy but a little tedious after a while.

Enter Ryan and a game of cards in the kitchen. Ryan's your typical fuck-boy: jeans, not too tight, a hole here and there in the right place; classic All Stars; surf T; sea-salted peaks over his right eye. Ryan was scooping up all the poker chips when I walked in to prepare an early dinner. I put the lettuce, tomatoes and noodles on the sink after I had made some space. Sometimes I wondered if these youngsters realized that the cutlery and plates in The Beauty and the Beast are not an accurate depiction of reality. Of course they don't sing, AND they also don't tidy themselves away, do they?! I asked Ryan and the 4 others what they were playing: a game of Fan Tan.

Fan Tan does not need a whole lot of brain, but plenty of verbal brawn. As all chairs were taken, Ryan invited me onto his knee, promising to show me the way to play. He smelled of coconut and cigarettes. I pressed my body into his chest as he explained the rules of the game. My skin was jubilant! His tongue piercing gave him a slight lisp. He assured me that it wasn't vanity but respect for the ladies that made him get one. When I asked him to explain himself a little further, the other boys made some obscene grunts, and Ryan just whispered in my ear to meet him after work, right here in the kitchen.

POET DOWN HERE

making an honest stand

TUESDAY, 22 JULY 2003

Getting a redheaded man to do the dirty job

I got in around 1:30 am and quickly changed out of my work clothes. I slipped on a long T-shirt, and some clean pants. I washed my face and brushed my teeth. I slinked down to the kitchen, and found Ryan reading D.H. Lawrence. He had closed the shutters. The floor was swept and mopped, though it still felt student-slimy-slippery. He grinned when I teased the book out of his hand.

There was not a spare gram of fat on his stomach. His chest was smooth, his hands purposeful, the kitchen empty. He closed the door behind me and turned the lock. He did not bother with much sweet talk, but cupped my arse and hoisted me onto the kitchen stove in one practiced move. He leaned into me and started kissing me. The piercing made me giggle. His hands slid underneath the T-shirt and he squeezed carefully. I arched my back, feeling the grease on the cooking rings as I supported myself. He shifted me forward, opened my legs and pushed aside my pants. Then he lowered himself and let his piercing do the talking. Who'd have thought it was all this easy in the end?

posted by poetdownhere@ July 22, 2003 comments

POET DOWN HERE

making an honest stand

SUNDAY, 03 AUGUST 2003

Swearing to give everything for one kiss

OMG how did the stars align? I can't believe my luck. After working solidly for weeks, I finally had a day off. Time to sample some of NYC's famed museums. On top of that, I might have just found my lift to Atlantic City. Let me tell you what happened.

I decided to go to the Guggenheim. Modern art is not really my thing but after I complained about being out of good things to read, Ryan had pointed out a book on architecture in the hostel's swap library. On the cover was a picture of the Guggenheim and I knew I had to go.

I marvelled at the dizzy stairs serpenting up and up. I fell quiet by the infiniteness the central hall invoked. Dante's staircase sprung to mind but this slow spiral was like a whirling dervish meditation, rather than a descent into hell, or jolly up into paradise. Round and round, up and up it went. The ribbon was interspersed with clumps of thin, stretched-out statuettes. The black wiry forms breathed such desolation, I felt the urge to reach out, to connect with the cold metal, infuse it with warmth somehow.

I don't know if it was the estrangement that the cold bleak statues evoked, or the dizzy disorientation as I wound up the central spiral but I felt I had to veer off the main circuit for a bit. I picked a random arch on the 2nd floor and walked through into a subsidiary exhibition space: work by Picasso. I guess he's considered modern. I wandered around without purpose. And then all of a sudden, I found myself face to face such grief, such worn-out hopelessness. Remember me saying that at one point I couldn't see myself any longer? Well, I felt like I was staring directly at the inside of myself. Just that devastating hollow echo of being so wrung out, you can no longer feel anything but lead-heavy tired.

Previous Posts

- Getting a redheaded man to do the dirty job
- Being stuck in the swamps of Jersey
- Being on fire
- Having a heart that's hungry
- Wondering what I am getting into
- Not settling for a hard edge
- Disappearing in the darkness

I Power Blogger

POET DOWN HERE

making an honest stand

SUNDAY, 03 AUGUST 2003

Swearing to give everything for one kiss

I couldn't stop the tears, and in a way, didn't want to stop them. It was a relief also to feel real.

When I stepped outside moments later, I decided I'd be in Central Park with myself, my thoughts, and the acceptance that I was hurt, alone, but still here. I found a beautiful spot on a stony plateau half in the shade. For an hour I was minding my own business – the view of NYC is so calming when you are in this vacuum bubble in the middle of the park and you hear very little of the craziness beyond Central Park's gate. The breeze uncreased my loose-fitting skin, and I felt genuinely grounded for the first time in a long while, on the bedrock foundation of this crazy busy city. I closed my eyes, but before I could drift off a group of singers joined me on the rock. Guitars and joints came out; bottles of beer were popped.

Somebody touched my foot and apologized. I opened my eyes and told them not to worry. Right next to me was the hottest man ever. He looked at me, and I looked at him.

'Hey I'm Dwayne,' he said. And I melted.

posted by poetdownhere@ August 03, 2003 comments

POET DOWN HERE

making an honest stand

MONDAY, 04 AUGUST 2003

Loving again with that broken heart of mine

So Dwayne has this sky-blue, beat-up old Camaro Z28 from the 70s, that he had been thinking of taking on a road trip somewhere. I told him about my love for Springsteen and how I had lost so much money on the Meadowland ticket. I showed him pictures from my trip to Asbury that I had developed at Duane Reade's and how I followed in Bruce's footsteps, and went to as many iconic places as I could. After he heard my story he asked if I also considered visiting iconic references beyond Asbury and NYC. This was excuse enough to get a Starbuck's and make a list: Baltimore, Graceland, Cadillac Ranch – it is a real thing, I had no idea, in Amarillo – Nebraska, Philadelphia, Atlantic City …

After a second coffee and a shared lemon poppy seed cake, the list was endless. I was surprised how much Dwayne had been able to add. He admitted he doesn't like Springsteen that much. I suspect he might be a Republican, but he could really place the references that had been magical realism to me up to that point. I stared at the 4 napkins full of scribbles. We agreed that it was ambitious, too ambitious for now. Dwayne then said, why not stay on the East coast, and that he would love to help me out, where he could. Atlantic City, he said, he would really enjoy.

Atlantic City – the chicken man song – I looked it up on the map. It was not even that far away. And I could easily get a train, but a car ride was hard to resist. If only because, well he drove a Camaro, had to be fate right? Dwayne promised to take me to Philadelphia on the way back to look for where the Chicken man was shot.

I came to the USA to discover. Bruce extended far beyond Asbury and New York, it seemed silly to tie myself down to this area. I could always rebook my flight.

Previous Posts

- Swearing to give everything for one kiss
- Getting a redheaded man to do the dirty job
- Being stuck in the swamps of Jersey
- Being on fire
- Having a heart that's hungry
- Wondering what I am getting into
- Not settling for a hard edge
- Disappearing in the darkness

I Power Blogger

POET DOWN HERE

making an honest stand

MONDAY, 04 AUGUST 2003

Loving again with that broken heart of mine

I looked at the map once more, and made up my mind. Time to get going!

I handed in my notice, and the boss told me the job would be waiting if ever I made it back. She knew full well that reliable, undemanding staff willing to work for scraps was a godsend. She also knew that my sensitive ear had significantly influenced the number of new regulars – dreamers that were stuck in a rat-race because of choices made, consequences unforeseen. They didn't come to share regrets necessarily, but a drink or two or three, they could go home with a re-energized appetite for the long haul. Sometimes the best conversationalists are the ones who say little.

I handed in my keys to the hostel – Brendan warned me to trust nobody in Monopoly City. *They're not there to make you money Wendy! Remember the one-armed bandit always wins.* I didn't admit I had never gambled in my life. In fact, I was planning to lose so as not to feel anxious about wasting money. I had told a few of my regulars about my impending adventure and they had all come on my last shift. Let's say the tips they left collectively were enough to have a great night out and not be any the poorer for it.

I have no idea how easy it will be to find a computer. Brendan promised me internet cafés were littering the strip these days, and made me promise to continue writing. I do find my mumblings mildly therapeutic so it's a promise easily made. Right now, I'm in an empty kitchen, feet on my backpack – my whole life in forty-five litres – waiting for a dude to drive this little girl away.

posted by poetdownhere@ August 04, 2003 comments

Friday's the day to be in love

Rosie stared at the screen. There was no way she could share this with her dad. In an effort to get him out of the house, she had suggested he go out with the boys that night. Maybe a shared beer or two would lift his moroseness. Stewart had just separated from his wife and would be a supportive mate to her dad. Luckily, he followed her suggestion, and she had the house to herself. It had given her a chance to look up the blog Razorboy had mentioned and read what was going on with her mum. The doorbell rang. Rosie glanced at herself in the mirror at the top of the stairs, ruffled her hair, and bounced down the steps two by two. When she got to the front door, she exhaled, and tried to stop the pounding of her heart. One last breath and she opened the door. 'Hey Lea, come in.'

Rosie led Lea into the kitchen and opened the fridge: a lost lettuce browning on the edges; a slice of cheese crusting up at the edges; Dijon mustard, ketchup and HP sauce; a single gherkin floating in vinegar. No melt-in-the-middles, home-made jams and jellies, freshly squeezed orange juice, French cheeses. She sighed.

'Want anything to drink? I have beer, coke, or coffee.'

'Just some tea if you don't mind.'

Rosie put on the kettle and glanced at Lea. She was wearing jeans and a crop top under her leather jacket. She wore very little make-up, if any at all. Her nails were a feast of bright colours though. She looked at her own; bitten down and the rims red. Her dad complained all the time about her disgusting habit. *A real guitar player keeps his right-hand nails long*. Rosie used a pick instead.

When they got to the study Lea snuggled onto the fauteuil in the corner. She patted the space next to her. 'I've read the blog, so you don't have to show me. Come cuddle up and tell me what is on your mind.'

Rosie felt awkward. The chair was oversized but this felt more intimate than she'd even be with Maria, and they had shared many crises and gossip over the years. And Maria didn't make her go all short-breathy like. But to remain at the desk was also weird. She had not much to lose. She tucked her sleeves over her hands and gingerly sat on the edge of the chair.

'It's quite something, eh? Your mum. It's like too much information already!'

Rosie chuckled. 'Yeah, I sincerely do not want to contemplate my mother having it off with all those guys. My dad is bad enough, but this …'

'Apart from grossing you out, do you feel, I dunno, betrayed by your mum?'

Rosie shook her head. 'No, not betrayed. If anything, I betrayed my mum first.' Lea raised an eyebrow and Rosie continued, 'I found my mum's notebooks in the attic. The box said not to read any of it. To destroy them without reading.'

'And you read them anyway?'

'I know it sounds bad, I feel bad.' Rosie paused. 'But I was genuinely worried about my mum. And my dad. I thought I would find some clues, maybe.'

'Did you?'

Again Rosie shook her head. 'No, not really. I did find out my grandmother knew about Springsteen, and understood my mum better than I thought she did. And that I wasn't exactly a wanted child.'

Lea pulled Rosie closer onto the chair. 'Don't be silly, who would not want you? Such a ray of optimism, quiet, demure – such a good little girl!'

Rosie let herself be drawn in. 'Haha very funny.' She took a sip of her beer. Then she squared with Lea. 'You know what's weird? I feel more of a peeping Tom seeing all this stuff online, than I did reading those hidden notes. Even though my mum clearly meant for the blog to be read. Why else would someone who has protected her own thoughts for so long suddenly blurt out the most revealing things for the whole world to read?'

'Why would anyone so gifted, funny and beautiful cut angry permanent markers in their innocent skin?' Lea took Rosie's right arm and pushed up the jumper. She looked Rosie in the eye. Rosie did not detect any scorn or mockery. Just warmth and kindness. Then Lea let go and dropped her leather jacket off her shoulders. There was no missing it, there on the inside of her left upper arm was a long vertical scar. 'Maybe you and your mum are not that different. A cry for help can take many forms.'

Rosie felt her head spin. She had been so careful to conceal the scars. She had been wearing long-sleeved shirts most of the time; on the rare occasions she chose a short-sleeved T, she made sure to wear her leather wristbands. Then she remembered the slow rub of Lea's fingers when she had held her back, pulled her off Sharon. Her cheeks flushed. Who was this person next to her, so calm and yet offering her own past so uncannily and unashamedly?

'Do you mean to hurt yourself? Like really?'

'Did you?'

'Yes, but I am glad my mother didn't knock first that morning. Because if she had, I wouldn't be here, on this comfy chair with you. And that would have been a real waste.'

'Why did you do it?' Rosie whispered, not sure she wanted to know, really. This was scarily personal. And real.

'I was "told" to do it. I used to do a lot of drugs, you name it I used it. It was great to escape from the boredom and small dreams of my parents. The highs were magnificent, but the downs got worse and worse. At one point I got into this weird psychotic state, and started hearing voices. One of them was a little nasty.' Lea winced. 'It started to talk me down all the time, saying how I was a dirty slag, a rancid trout sniffer. Said nobody needed me, why would anyone miss me. I was such a waste. That last thing, actually, I get a lot from men too these days.'

Rosie felt a jolt in her limbs as Lea spoke. 'Why do men tell you that you are a waste?'

Lea gently tucked one of Rosie's locks behind her ear, and placed her palms on Rosie's cheeks. 'Come on. Look at me.' Rosie did. The flaming red locks and the green eyes, the freckles. The downy hairs on her cheeks as the light fell on her skin. Lea was gorgeous.

'And then consider this: have you ever seen me with a boy? In the corridors, on the benches outside school? In the clubs?'

'I don't think we go to the same clubs,' Rosie said. 'But what do you mean? What does that have to do with anything?'

'Knock knock,' Lea rapped Rosie's skull, 'anybody home? Hello! Earth to Rosie! I know I am considered beautiful Rosie, and I have had many a boy who wanted to get their hands or dick in my knickers. Or both. But that is not what turns me on.'

Rosie hesitated. 'So what turns you on,' she swallowed, 'is ...'

'Other girls. Yes, Rosie, I like girls.'

Rosie felt a slight flutter. Right, so Lea fell for girls. 'How did you know?'

Lea was still for a moment. 'I think you know the answer to that one,' she replied. 'But maybe you want to know how I felt about it? How I told other people? What it meant for my friendships?'

'Yes, I guess,' Rosie stammered. 'All of those questions.'

'Well the first thing that I knew was that I had to stop listening to those voices. Stop the drugs. And definitely stop the self-harm. Why do you cut Rosie?'

Rosie was taken aback by the directness of the question. She had hoped that focussing on Lea would let her off the hook. But Lea was sharp and determined to dig deeper, it seemed. She might as well give in. 'I feel numb, most of the time. I don't hear voices. In fact, a lot of the time I hear nothing, as if my head is filled with soft cotton balls. Everything is muffled. It lifts sometimes when I play the guitar. There's a clarity when my fingers feel the steel of the strings. The vibration goes through my nerves. But there are times that not even the music can find its way through. That's when I get anxious and I cut, to feel my body, alert and alive.'

'So, are you not feeling anything, or feeling too much and don't know how to deal with it?'

Rosie shrugged. 'Same difference.' She was ashamed that she should feel better after hurting herself. But worse was that she kept going back to it. She knew it would floor her father should he know. She daren't think what her mother would say.

Lea shifted her legs from underneath her. She planted them firmly on the floor and looked Rosie in the eye. 'The first time I took the scissors was when I failed a French test. I hadn't studied for it, so I really should not have expected to pass. I didn't, I just wanted to make sure I knew I was a failure, and that it was all my fault.' Lea touched her own scar almost tenderly. 'My mother has offered to treat the scar, but I'd rather keep it. It reminds me that I am worth something. That there is no shame in being gay either.'

'You sound almost proud. I feel miserable about it. I have been trying to stop, but then my mother left and …'

'Was it her though, your mother? When was the first time you cut?'

Rosie had to think. It had been such a long time, and since one day often blurred into another, she struggled to recollect the moment. It dawned slowly. It was the night after Toni and not feeling at all like the way she should feel. Or *how* she thought she should feel. And then he disappeared and she was so mad. 'Toni, after I had kissed Toni. And I didn't feel love, or excitement. I didn't even get wet.'

'I told you, you knew the answer to your question.'

They were quiet. The moon shone through the small Velux window. Rosie listened to the soft drip-drip of the summer rain. After what seemed an hour, Lea continued, 'Rosie, maybe you feel all mixed up right now, but things will fall into place, you'll see. Are you scared?'

Rosie thought. 'I don't know. I don't want to talk about it.'

Lea held up her hands. 'Hey that's okay.' She straightened up, reached for her jacket and slipped it back on. She patted Rosie on her knee and when she continued, her voice was soft. 'I'll be there if ever you should want to. I suppose we really need to figure out what to do about your mum. How do you feel about what she's been writing?'

Rosie hesitated. 'I feel,' she paused, 'I'm upset because I don't want to know about her frickin' sex epiphanies. But I'm worried too. She is getting into people's cars, roaming the streets way past midnight, in New York of all places. Goddamnit the times she has told me never to accept lifts from strangers! She could have got really hurt.' Rosie paused again. 'Silly maybe, but I feel proud too. She is living her life. She is making a stand for herself.'

'Is it like you get to know your mum as a person, for the first time?'

'Yes, I never knew she had this in her. I'm not even sure I would dare to travel to the USA alone'.

Lea shifted over and drew Rosie into her body. 'Close your eyes. Shhh, just do it. Just try to see yourself getting on a plane. Looking for your mum.'

After the first awkwardness, Rosie relaxed. It felt good to be held by someone. She became aware all of a sudden that wanting to sort things on her own, being her own person, had meant she had also deprived herself of the human touch. Maria was a great friend and Rosie could talk about anything with her, but now she realised, it wasn't enough. Words are only so much of a healer. Her skin was crying out for another skin. 'I mean, where do I even start. She could be anywhere. I checked the list she mentions in her blog, and have been hunting lyrics for place references too. Have you listened to Springsteen, looked at a map of America?'

Lea kissed Rosie lightly on her cheek. 'No I have not. To both.' She giggled. 'Springsteen seems a bit run-of-the-mill safe for you, isn't he?'

Rosie sat up. 'What do you mean?'

'Well he's a little square? Bit safe. Sings about the common guy, about his dad and cars. Where's the social injustice, the kicking against the regime? Changing the world? Isn't that what punk does?'

'Springsteen sings about people. He's a storyteller, a painter of portraits. He sings about hope.' Rosie took a moment to collect her thoughts, then continued. 'There's two ways of dealing with injustice. React against, rage against the machine. I listen to the Sex Pistols for that. The Clash. Their music gets blood boiling, limbs kicking, their music more than their lyrics is a call to revolution. Springsteen simply tells the human story, and that in itself is kicking up a fuss. Change never starts in the big companies or government; it is in the small acts of defiance of the seemingly insignificant people. Gather enough of them and change can be affected.'

'Fair point. I mean, I'm into dance tunes – a real waste of space, I know. But let's get back to your mother, isn't there a pattern? What would she still want to see? That is related to Springsteen?'

'Nebraska?'

'Ahh, well that is a lot of nothingness, am I right?'

'It's also an album full of criticizing the system.' Rosie paused to reflect. It seemed her mum was staying mostly on the east coast. Maybe she would still attempt to see Springsteen another time. 'Wait, let me see the dates of the tour.' She jumped up and sat behind the desk. She searched for Backstreets, a website she had discovered when she'd realised Springsteen was the missing link. She brought up the schedule. Pittsburgh was still to come, New Jersey, Philadelphia too. It all depended on when her mum was due to return. 'What we should find out is when she's coming back.'

'What if she booked an open return?'

'Not like my mum. Let me get into her bank account. Maybe I can trace where she bought her ticket.'

Lea got up and leant over Rosie to look at the screen. She rested her hands on Rosie's shoulders. Rosie could smell lavender soap. Lea whispered into Rosie's ear, 'Remind me never to get in your bad books. How do you even get into someone's bank account?'

'I guess I do have access to the account details from the statements. Then it is a matter of knowing the person's habits. My mum doesn't trust herself to remember. She has a little notebook. Hidden, but not well enough for young Sherlock here.' Rosie got up, ducked under the desk, lifted a bit of the carpet and found the loose plank. *"Art as an imitation of Life", my arse*. Life is one long series of clichés. Most people are predictable, and her mum was the best at being just that. 'Just keep your important information safe inside your head; that should keep me from raiding your fortunes,' she said to Lea. Rosie crawled back from under the desk. 'Promise you will never tell anyone about this.'

Lea swore on the holy cross and Christmas. That was enough for Rosie. It didn't take them long to figure out that Trailfinders would be the first phone call in the morning.

'Let me know if you find out anything else Rosie. I must head off now. Promise me though, tonight you leave that razor blade where you've hidden it. There's nothing wrong with you. In fact, there's a shitload incredibly good about you. And,' here Lea hesitated a little, 'if you need to feel something, take this.' And with that Lea kissed Rosie on the mouth softly. She stroked Rosie's scratched cheek lightly, and said, 'I'll give you a ring tomorrow afternoon. Better stay away from school for a bit. You won't be missed. By most. I know where to find you.' With that Lea walked out of the room, down the stairs, and out through the front door.

The odds are not in your favour

Wendy felt Dwayne's firm hand on her arm, guiding her through the lobby. Norah Jones was crooning in the background, smoothing them into the gambling arena. As soon they stepped onto the psychedelic floor where table games began, Wendy noticed Nora gave way to Bon Jovi. The carpet was a whirl of burgundy circles and orange victory wreaths, and clashing geometrical shapes. A man in a tank top and blazer was staring intently at the spinning pin on the roulette table. The bouncy pin skittered frantically like a cat on a hot tin roof. At the blackjack table the noise hushed a little. A woman with hair bound back tightly along her skull tapped her finger nervously on her cards before deciding to take a hit. It was at the periphery of the fruit machines that the noise played loudest. The visual overload of flashing lights, coupled with ringing wins and pinging reel spins made her head swerve. Everywhere, every square inch of the floor, was part of the gamblers' game. People were concentrating, and took whatever happened as part of the deal: don't brag or despair about what happens within these walls.

A warm orange glow from the large Pantheon eye in the ceiling looked down on them like a Roman God. The tactic here was like those of the conqueror's that the place had been named after. Caesar had been ruthless at the time, yet disguised his ambitions by appeasing those he conquered. Assimilate rather than suppress. At least, that is what Wendy had learned in school. The casino did a similar thing. The low, soft-glow ceilings in the lobby created a feeling of intimacy and belonging. Nowhere did the punter get the idea that there was a cynical money-grabbing system behind the welcoming faces and faux-antiquity. There was no money to be lost here, just chips. Time was invisible too, no clocks anywhere. Last night they had gambled until 2:00 am, but those hours had felt like minutes. Today, the lack of daylight made it seem like they had never left. But deep down she could feel the Roman soldier's sandal on her throat. The pressure enough for her to stay, not enough to end it all. A gambler's fate.

It was the third day of their visit. Almost unnoticeably, things had started to change. On the first night Dwayne had let her choose the stakes and the tables, encouraging her, whispering tactics in her ear. He had delighted in her wins by stroking her hand. Her losses, and boy there were many, he had smiled away. Tonight, though, his hand felt heavy on her arm. She had wanted to call it quits today after they had started to eat into her earnings but he had gone into a long tirade about odds and maths, and the science of beating the casino. Quitting now was giving in to them. It was those who persevered that came out on top in this game. She stared at the swirling carpet, and felt slightly nauseous. She had barely slept.

'I don't feel all too well Dwayne, can we skip today? Catch up on some sleep after last night?'

'Oh baby, did I exhaust you?' He winked and blew softly in her neck. 'You prefer to go back to our room? I would too, but a few hours here will make me go for much longer when we get back.'

Wendy felt a soft throbbing between her legs, her body's lusty betrayal rather than anything close to love. 'I'm not sure I have the energy for more.'

'Did I not delight you?' He bent over and slow-kissed her, sucking her bottom lip for an instant. 'From what you were moaning, and the way your body squirmed and bolted, I'd beg to differ.' Dwayne's hand moved in slow circles on her lower spine. 'Mmmm, I would let my hands wonder all over you, if there weren't all these decent people around us. A few hours baby, and I'll take you even higher.'

'Let me fix my make-up, Dwayne. I'll be right back.' Wendy looked around for the sign, as she blindly started to navigate the labyrinth deeper into the casino. Norah Jones questioned what would make her run. Wendy felt a sudden panic, but the toilets were roomy and refreshingly quiet. She sat down on the purple velvet sofa in the far corner. It smelled like cedar and lemongrass in here. Her head was throbbing so she rested it briefly against the marble wall. After a few deep breaths she pulled herself together. She turned the gold-plated tap and let the cold water run off her wrists. She looked at herself. The dark circles under her eyes almost looks shabby chic under these complimentary ceiling spots. She closed the tap. On her right, next to the potpourri was a carefully stacked column of white handtowels. She picked one up and delighted in its softness. At home Rosie always complained about their cardboard towels. She often compared Wendy's refusal to use fabric softener to the Spartan way. Mum, I don't need toughening up, seriously! Wendy smiled involuntarily, and bathed a little longer in the wealth of the ridiculously opulent ladies' before she moved towards the door. When she walked out, she bumped into a man wearing a blue Hugo Boss suit. She faltered but the man caught her by the elbow. Her lipstick and some tampons rolled onto the floor in front of them.

'Oh excuse me, I wasn't looking.' Wendy watched the tampons spinning around like the arrow on the wheel of fortune.

'Don't worry, it's my lucky day. I don't get run off my feet by beautiful women on a daily basis. Here, let me help you with that.' He bent down and swooped up the tampons and without making any remarks put them in her bag. 'I'd zip up my fanny pack in future, it would be a waste to lose this.' He picked up the lipstick and placed it in her hand. 'Your smile deserves to shimmer and shine.'

Wendy spotted Dwayne on the other side of the craps table, looking at her. He started to move towards them. She fumbled with the bag, in a hurry to ensure some distance between herself and this stranger. 'Thanks, please excuse me.' She moved away towards Dwayne.

'Too tired eh? Who is that man?'

'I have no idea Dwayne. Seriously, I accidentally bumped into him. He helped me get my things off the floor. Come on, let's go. You wanted to play, didn't you?' Wendy glanced back at Hugo Boss. He was still observing her, and raised his eyebrow slightly as he watched her manoeuvre Dwayne away from him.

'Who is that man? You've been seeing him before then? You went to the toilet five times yesterday. I thought you just had a weak bladder,' Dwayne hissed. His voice was paper-cut thin. His eyes were steel. 'I thought I could trust you!'

'Dwayne, I don't know him. Let's play.'

Dwayne held out the square of passport photos they'd made on the day they had arrived. They had squirmed into the small booth, squeezed onto the turning stool, and roared their way through the four flashes, high on the anticipation of adventure after their two-hour drive from New York. She saw herself draped around him like a cashmere shawl.

'You are with me, honey? Bonnie and Clyde!' Dwayne pulled her hair away from her cheeks carefully. 'Don't leave me on my own baby. We're in this together, remember.' He took her hands and guided her to the craps table.

When they got to the table Dwayne joked with the croupier, and when the marker was changed to black, Dwayne put his dollar bills on the table. They were exchanged for chips and then the player opposite him rolled the dice. Dwayne started shifting various chips about on the velvet mat. Wendy still didn't get what all the numbers meant. She had figured out that the simplest thing was to put chips on the pass line and just wait on the player to throw the dice. But Dwayne had big plans. This morning he had sat on the edge of the bed and excitedly explained how he was going to beat the odds. Wendy had only half listened. At the terms place bet, and field bet, casino's edge, and Dwayne's assurances he had been observing the dice and the odds the night before, she had simply zoned out and taken a shower. She had never understood chance during maths and wasn't about to start now. Also, she got no joy from the convoluted theories on how to beat the casino. All she knew was the one golden rule Brendan had imprinted in her brain: the casino always wins in the end. She was here for some fun. But Dwayne was seriously invested. She decided the easiest thing would be just to watch him. At least the drinks were free. She fell quiet and emptied glass after glass as Dwayne moved the chips around the green velvet. Tonight she'd tell him she was ready to move on.

Dwayne got so engrossed in his play he no longer attempted to engage in any conversation. Wendy observed the others around the table. There was laughter and carefree banter between a group of young men to their left. They looked like they were playing away their first pay cheque from their jobs at a second-hand car dealership. Their ties and suit jackets had a synthetic casual-smart look, dependable slate blue. Their faces still showed the scars of high school acne. Across from them sat a woman with grey dreadlocks. White skin, blue eyes. Wendy thought she sniffed a hint of white sage incense over the fresh orange and earthy geranium notes that seemed to belong to this particular table. Her bony fingers were loaded with rings showing off sparkly glass stones. Her earlobes were drooping dangerously close to her chin with the weight of the huge gold-plated teardrops. She was a solitary player. Their eyes met briefly. The old woman squinted her eyes and hardened her jaw. It seemed she was communicating an unspoken warning. Wendy kept the woman's gaze, but other than the tight mouth, she didn't gesture or give any other hints. She looked away at her own hands. Maybe she should varnish her nails; it might distract from the red rims. She heard Dwayne whoop and watched him receive a pile of chips in a different colour than what they had started with.

Dwayne had assured her that novices were a good thing to bet on and that he could smell them a mile away. Was he playing off the car sales boys? She straightened up.

'Could we try the fruit machines for once?'

'The slots, you mean? You Brits have a funny way with words. Have you ever tried them before?'

'What do you think? This is my first time in a casino, I told you.'

Dwayne began to smile. A seven was thrown, the stick man whisked away his chips, and Dwayne got up to leave the table. 'Let's go to the one over there, besides the one along the path. The three machines before it have all paid out, I reckon that one next to them is hot.' He scooped up a free glass of bubbles and pushed Wendy towards the noise of the machines that sat along the back wall like a flashy noose.

Wendy stood behind the machine and pressed buttons at random. She had no idea how to create combinations, or even how to freeze a reel. The spinning, the flashes, the American songbook hypnotised her. Dwayne was pushing the buttons and told her when to spin again. She was brought back to the here and now when the machine started to splutter: seven-seven-seven. A never-ending waterfall of rattling coins brought her back to the room. Dwayne slapped her on the back.

'Come on baby, keep coming!' He patted the machine. All around them people stopped and pointed. The noise wouldn't stop. On and on. Dwayne held a bucket under the tray and scooped the coins into it. 'See what a little faith can do?!'

They cashed in the coins for paper bills. A cool $230. Wayne slotted them into his own wallet. 'Let's celebrate. There's more wine and snacks in the bar. Afterwards we can drive back to the motel and order in some pizza if you're still hungry. This is what I call a good day's work. And do I have some treats for you planned. The night is wide open, butterfly of mine!

When she woke in the middle of the night, the light next to her pillow was dimmed low. Her head was pounding. On her nightstand was a yellow box of chocolates and that picture they had taken in the booth when they first arrived. She was beaming, he was handsome. They were a hot item. Anyone would believe they were in it to win. No one would believe the sore cheekbone and aching, raw neck that made swallowing hard. Dwayne had scribbled *morning gorgeous!* on it, replacing the o's with little hearts. Her mouth went dry. Apart from her head there were few signs of the struggle or the sex. The straps were gone, she was wearing clean pants, no sign of the ones he had ripped off. He had undressed her, and tucked her in tightly. Her jeans and top lay neatly folded on the broken chair next to the bed. She turned her head to her left.

Dwayne was snoring lightly. Not a persistent snore, more an occasional rattle followed by a wheeze almost like a soft whistle. She was tempted to stroke his head. He really was beautiful, and the smell of him sparked an involuntary reaction in her body. She checked herself though. What was she even thinking? Despite the past few intense days, this man was a complete stranger to her. Yet somehow, she had let him demean her, and here she was about to caress him?

Then, she heard a thump. Followed by a low moan. From the room next door. No drama, just a few seconds of deadly silence and another muffled punch; this time a voice whimpered. Wendy thought she heard a sob and a please stop, but she couldn't be sure. She tried to ignore the struggle next door by covering her head with her pillow. She struggled to breathe, and realised with a shock that what had happened in her own room tonight might be the start of something far more sinister. Nothing Dwayne did or said was accidental. Who would have the chocolate at the ready when staying in a random motel on the edge of Debauchery Downtown?

When the third thud came and Wendy heard something snap - a spine, an arm, a leg of a chair - she knew she needed to get away from Dwayne, without having to face him. He would find a way to sweet talk her into staying another day, and another. Staying this long in Atlantic City had never been part of the plan. His sexual appetite that had so excited her now frightened her. This was the worst place for her to be.

She slid from underneath the covers. The plastic floor was cold and she felt the sharp edges of nail clippings from a previous guest on her bare feet. She barely dared to breathe, let alone sit on the edge of the bed to wipe them clean. Dwayne turned around in his sleep, rolling over onto her side of the bed. Wendy pulled on her jeans, thanking Dwayne for his obsessive compulsion to fold clothes before sleep. She took no time to get dressed but couldn't find her trainers. Then she remembered she had left them next to the door, on the step. Outside the rain started to pelt. At least it drowned out the crying from the girl next door.

Her bag was standing in the corner. She checked it for her credit card and passport. Both were inside the secret compartment she had been careful to conceal from Dwayne. She lifted up the bag. Something fell out, clattering in the darkness. Wendy froze. When would she learn to always zip up? She could just leave it but what if it was her phone? She went down on her hands and knees and groped around. Soon enough she held her brush. So where was her phone? She checked the top pocket, the side pocket but it wasn't there. Goddamnit, she should just leave without it. She took another deep breath. If she had taken someone's phone, where would she keep it? Under her pillow, right? Like in a bad Hollywood thriller. She hoisted the bag onto her back and tiptoed to the other side of the bed. She reached under the pillow. Classic C-movie stuff.

Every move she made sounded like a thunder clap in the darkness of night, so when she turned the lock of the door she was convinced Dwayne would veer up and grab hold of her. He didn't stir though. Wendy sidled out, and closed the door softly. Her shoes were not there. Wendy cursed. No way was she going back in. She stepped out of the soft haze of the green emergency light. Within minutes the rain soaked through all her layers. She quickened her pace, turned left out of the car park praying left was the right direction.

After an hour she began to doubt the rash decision she had made. Okay, so Dwayne had missed her no, but maybe she should have been clearer. She had not said no before and had they not been moving towards that kind of intimacy over the past few days? Had Dwayne not explained tying up was the ultimate act of trust? Should she trust him now still? She shivered. Despite the mildness of the season, walking around in wet clothes for an hour was beginning to chill her bones. Her bare feet were sore. Why were there no cars? The casinos behind her beckoned, bright, shining in the night. Did nobody ever leave this place? She walked on. Then, when she had just about conceded that Dwayne would pick her off the hard shoulder within 20 minutes of him waking up, she heard the low drone of a heavy truck. The full beam emerged gradually like the end of a solar eclipse. She stopped on the spot and raised a hopeless thumb.

Didi threw a towel into the truck cabin, a pair of shorts and a Dodgers' sweater. 'Bloody tourists,' she mumbled as she hung Wendy's wet clothes on the backs of the seats, protecting the truck mattress behind them with some extra towels. 'First mistake, going to that hell hole in the first place. Wasting your hard-earned cash on any of these Indians. Suckers. There's nothing legal about it. It is all dodgy deals down there, no matter what the law says. Then, deciding to hitch a ride at three in the morning.' Didi turned to Wendy. 'You comfortable there?'

Wendy nodded. She was glad she had weathered Didi's initial downpour of curses: *What the Fuck are you doing out here? You desperate to get stabbed and raped?* The rape-bit had stung a little. *Idiot. Lunatic, freak! Hitchhiking in the dead of night, as a woman, in NJ. You do know it is illegal, right? Christ, you are easy pray for anyone having a shot at being a serial killer. Or just any old vagrant in search of some meat and bread.*

Didi had stopped shouting when she had reached Wendy and seen the wet t-shirt clinging to her naked breasts, and the swollen lip, the bare feet. Never mind, she had shrugged. Looks like I am your lucky streak tonight. No snake eyes. Come on, let's get you dry.

Wendy considered the stocky driver next to her, concentrating hard on the white lines as they sped by. She wore a checked flannel shirt over a black Motorhead T-shirt, jeans with a chain holding her wallet. What looked like steel-nosed workman's boots. Wendy felt stupid and started to speak.

'I know, all right, how foolish I was to get out without thinking. I panicked, but felt like it was safer than staying.'

Didi spoke to the swishing windshield wipers. 'Don't worry. You don't need to explain. You're okay now. Where are you travelling to?'

Wendy shrugged. 'I didn't leave with a plan. But I have a list. Maybe I'll do Graceland. Was hoping to get to Amarillo too at some point. But I'm grateful for the lift, so anywhere is good.'

'I'm going to Baltimore, should be there in a few hours.'

Wendy laughed softly, despite the cocked-up situation she found herself in. Didi briefly glanced at her. Wendy explained. 'Long story short, I am doing this Springsteen pilgrimage thing – and now you are going to Baltimore.'

'I'm not following you. I know Springsteen, but what has he got to do with Baltimore? He's from the Jersey shore, isn't he?'

'Yeah, but – okay, wait, let me go back a little. You got time for a bit of a story?'

Didi slapped the steering wheel and roared, 'Right, so you literally took a wrong turn when you ended up with this creep in Atlantic City, and now I am taking you to Baltimore – and you are trying to still your hungry heart? Man, that's serendipity for you.'

Wendy relaxed further into the seat. Now that the adrenaline had gone down she realised how fortunate she'd been to be picked up by Didi. She'd done everything she always warned Rosie against.

'You were lucky, but then again, maybe it isn't luck. Maybe we only think we have control over our destiny because it makes us feel better to think we do. I often wonder about these things. I mean, what are the odds of anyone even stopping for you? At this time at night. Anyway I am just as lucky as you. You could have been a freak for all I knew.'

'So why did you decide to stop then? What if I'd meant to rob you? Or worse? Surely you are as vulnerable as I was?'

'Being on the road is a lonely life; I take more chances than I should maybe, but the company keeps me grounded. I find co-riders mostly at gas stations, where I talk to them to suss them out, before offering a ride. But something about you, tonight, made me slow down and trust my gut. Glad I did.'

'Me too. I feel so ashamed about my stupidity.'

'Don't be. It happens to the best. You need to keep trusting. If you lose that sense of the good around you, the world becomes a very cynical place. You got caught in his net, but don't forget these types of men are very good at what they do. They too work on instinct. They have a nose for a chink in the armour and know exactly how to play you.'

'You speak as if you know.'

Didi nodded grimly. 'I was in a relationship with a sociopath for 14 years. Got involved with her when I was 17. At first, she made me feel like I was a Disney princess. She adored me. Said all the things a young girl likes to hear. It wasn't until I realised she had alienated me from all my friends, and then my family, that I began to see it was all about her need. I lost a ton of weight, was always on edge. She accused me of not loving her when I'd object to staying in yet again. She'd threatened to kill herself if I ever left. I mean, I adored her. She was funny, and easy to talk too. Beautiful too. But I now know how unhealthy it all was. Your man, well, let's say I recognise the pattern. He moved in much quicker, but still. Let me guess, the sex was mind-blowing?'

Wendy looked at her hands. Yes, the sex had been the best she was likely to have for the rest of her life. Even thinking about it made her ache for more. But sex and love. Different things altogether. 'Yes,' she whispered, 'if it hadn't gone too far, if he hadn't drunk too much tonight, I guess I would still be there.'

Didi looked at Wendy. 'Again, don't beat yourself up over it. If they were easy to spot, nobody would be a victim. You got out in time. You didn't get hurt too bad. Thank the Lord and move on.'

'So shouldn't I phone the police? Don't I declare the rape?' She thought about the girl who had been in the room next to them. Nobody bothered to report what was going on there either.

'Rape? Girlfriend, no police officer is going to touch your case. It isn't the way they do things here, and certainly not in Atlantic City. The room was in your name? You paid in advance? You invited him into your bed? For more than one night? You like it rough? Don't go complaining afterwards.'

'But I said I didn't want to.'

'Your word against his. You think he won't be able to manipulate the truth? You fell for him. What makes you think he won't talk his way out of any allegation against him? No sister, whatever you call it, it is yours to get over. And to move on. Count yourself lucky he didn't rob you of all your money as well.'

Wendy flinched. That too was something to get over. All those hours she had slaved away behind the bar. And now she had hardly anything left to get through the rest of her time. Should she go back to New York so soon? Maybe she should find some work in Baltimore, or Pittsburgh before traveling on to Graceland. Maybe she should just go home. It was a huge mess anyways. She had hoped to find herself, but she barely recognised the person who was sitting next to Didi. Sure, that person was free, driving her own fortunes, but it was not what she had hoped she'd be.

Didi switched on the radio. Some country dude whined about picking up his life again, smiling his best smile. She gestured to the bed behind us. 'You can curl up for a few hours, catch some sleep. No need for both of us to be up. You must be exhausted.'

Wendy nodded and slipped through the seats. The mattress was firm, the pillow thick. The soft piano and Didi's humming along were the comfortable blanket she needed right now.

'Are you all right over here? Would you like another fill-up?' The teenager dangled a pot of see-through coffee above Wendy's half-filled cup. When it came to food, the USA certainly was the land of plenty.

She considered the three eggs still sitting on her plate. How big were the stomachs of these truck drivers?

'No thank you, I'm still on my first one.' Wendy saw Didi come in from the car park. She had a big grin on her face.

'I found you a lift to Pittsburgh. It means spending most of the day in Baltimore, but this friend of mine out there radioed a guy coming through Baltimore around six; he can take you to Pittsburgh Airport. You can fly out to Memphis, that's the closest to Graceland you'll get. Two miles or so.'

'Didi, really, there is no need for you to make all this effort. Getting me here is more than I could have asked for already.' Didi leaned back on the plastic chair and lifted the massive glass full of cola and ice. Took a large swig and burped.

'Whose money did you gamble with?' And when Wendy didn't answer she continued, 'Thought as much. This breakfast is on me. I'll take you to the place he'll pick you up. At least I don't have to worry about you that way. And you won't have to say much. He'll do all the talking. He is generous with smiles, full of tall tales and laughter, and definitely a good guy.' Didi paused and leaned over. 'Look Wendy, I might act nonchalantly, but trust me. I know how filthy you feel. How small, dirty, stupid. You'll go back over it all for a long time yet. When I say to move on, I don't mean for you to forget, or to make little of it. But being on your way will help. It will take your mind off it long enough to stem the panic. It's a bit like after a bad car crash. If you don't get into the car straight away, you might not dare to later on. Take your time to give all that shit from yesterday a place, but move on, move away first.'

Wendy nodded. She took another bite of her syrup-saturated pancakes. Her night had been a clammy affair and right now, the thought of getting into another guy's truck filled her with dread. But if Didi trusted him, she should be able to relax a little. 'Thanks Didi, I do really appreciate this.'

'I'll take you to the next truckers' rest; there's a shower there, you can clean yourself. Here, take my battered copy of Jack Kerouac. It'll be six before you know it.'

Didi had been right of course. Wendy had turned the shower up hot, and scrubbed away at her skin, unable in the end to say whether it was the water or the rough cloth that made her skin glow. They had burned the clothes she'd been wearing, sprinkling them with white sage. *It is cleansing!* Didi had whooped. *I didn't tell you I am really a witch and this truck driving is only a rouse, did I?* She had given Wendy, a pair of sneakers a size or two too large, but it beat going barefoot again. Then she'd blown her horn in a long farewell, and left Wendy with a large coffee and infinite refills until six. Wendy was grabbed by the book almost immediately. Strange to think that a classic that old, would echo some of her restlessness. The need to find IT; wasn't she doing a similar thing? After a few hours though, she spent some of her time writing a blog entry in her notebook. At some point she'd find an internet cafe where she could type it up. The writing was also her cleansing. And just maybe, sharing her embarrassment of what had happened to her, could be a small gesture of support to another woman needing to find their way out. Thinking someone might, helped.

Big Dave had not asked many questions. Instead he'd talked about the glory of John Denver, and vented his frustrations about handbag dogs. *How do you even call it a dog? A rat, at most! With those pop-out eyes. A real dog has teeth, strong legs. What's the point of a dog if it can't protect you? You won't see me with my Rottweiler in a bag any day soon.* The image of Big Dave dragging a huge duffel bag behind him with a great black dog in it made her laugh despite the sickening stone she still felt in her belly. Dave had insisted on treating her to dinner in Baltimore. *You gotta crack a crab when you're down here.* He said he would leave for Pittsburgh straight after, in time for her to camp out at the airport. And be first in line to buy a flight to Memphis in the morning. When she had retorted that she did not eat meat, Big Dave nearly parked his truck in the crash barrier.

'No meat? No wonder you are so skinny. I bet ya I could snap those bones of yours with two fingers only. My mother, may she rest in peace, got it into her head that eating meat was cruel. Went cold turkey on it, excuse the pun, but after eight years changed from a tall upright woman into this crooked hunchback. No strength in any of her bones. Her spine couldn't even hold up her head no more. At one time, she had a silly fall, broke her hip and didn't recover after. A crooked, lopsided waddle-ma, my mother was a sight for sore eyes. Girl, you gotta eat meat.'

Wendy had replied she ate supplements, which was a lie, but if these past few weeks had taught her anything, is that Americans seemed to trust the supplement more than real nutrients.

Big Dave had grumbled, 'Like what?' Ready to start his lecture all over, but when she identified Zinc, Iron, Vitamins D and B12 as her essentials, he gave in a little.

'Just make sure you have extra fats too. A shot of Omega 3 a day…'

Wendy had promised on her mother's grave that she would add Omega 3 to her diet of supplements. When they had stopped at an Exxon gas station just off Interstate 70, Big Dave had loaded his plate with meatloaf AND chicken wings along with mashed potatoes and gravy, stating real men were mean machines running on meat.

'Hagerstown was the scene of the bloodiest day in battle during the Civil War. I don't think General Robert E Lee fed his soldiers on carrot sticks and cauliflower florets. History was made right here, and meat is what they ate.'

'Maybe it wouldn't have been so bloody if the battle had been fought by real women. Nothing like a scone and tea to settle an argument,' Wendy had quipped. To that Big Dave had just shrugged and dug into his meatloaf. Wendy didn't want to upset him; he was taking her to Pittsburgh after all. She added, 'But listen, I appreciate being taken to Pittsburgh by a kind man. So enjoy your protein slaughterhouse my friend.' She had then started on her baked potato with beans and cheese, a bittersweet reminder of home. Although, she could not realistically call the fatty, stringy, yellow mess cheese. Still, it was hearty and tasty enough. It would see her through the endless hours at Pittsburgh airport until the morning.

They pulled into Pittsburgh airport around eleven that night. None of the desks were open, so Wendy walked around the concourse for a bit. She found some curved benches near the main security check point. She pulled on an extra hoodie, wearing it backwards, so she could eventually pull the hood over her eyes, tied her rucksack to her wrist with a luggage strap, and drifted off to sleep.

She was woken up around 5:00 am by a security guard cleaning up the area for the red-eye flights that day. She found a Starbucks and ordered a Grande Americano to kickstart her day and open her veins. She wandered over to the Delta Airlines desk and found herself waiting behind the broad backs of five Springsteen fans. They were talking excitedly about how brilliant the show had been.

'Excuse me,' Wendy interjected in one of the rare pauses between exclamations of superlatives and incredulity, 'Springsteen was in Pittsburgh? Did I miss it?'

The man with a bald head turned round. He was wearing a denim jacket without sleeves, and a red bandana around his gleaming globe. Nothing like a cliché. The rest of the group looked at her with pity. 'Sorry, but under which rock have you been these last few months? Springsteen in Pittsburgh, it is the show of the tour!'

'Apart maybe from the Philadelphia and Jersey shows,' a woman with a wrinkle-free smile and smooth forehead added. The man was about to argue back when the woman wagged her finger at him. The move shut him up. 'Are you a fan also?' she asked Wendy.

Wendy nodded. 'I went to see him in New Jersey, but the ticket I bought was a fake. By the time I got in with a cheap ticket, he had just started *My Love Won't Let You Down*, and the people around me were already on their fourth beer and second nachos and sausage.' Wendy could cry. She had lost all sense of time and urgency when Dwayne took her to Atlantic City. She could have tried to get to another show, and maybe get up closer this time. See his actual face instead of a small pixelated image on a huge screen and warped sound echoing off the stadium seating.

The bald man noticed the quiver in Wendy's voice and softened up. 'Sorry darling, that stinks. Yeah Springsteen was here last night. He opened with *Jackson Cage*, and just revved it up. *Streets of Fire* just killed me, you know?'

The woman hushed him with an impatient tap on the wrist. 'You don't sound like you're from here?'

'I'm from Scotland. Came to America to reconnect with myself, and to see Springsteen's homeland. See where it all started. I had not realised about the show yesterday. I ended up in Atlantic City and well, let's just say time has a way of slowing down as the roulette tables turn.'

'Ah, yes, that happens. But he's still doing a few more places around here. Philadelphia is sometime next week. Maybe you can still catch him. Look it up. Where are you off to now?'

'Memphis, I hope. See the wall that Bruce jumped. Find out where the King died and the Boss got put back in his place.' She smiled. 'And, like you say, maybe there is still time to see Bruce one more time, who knows. And if not, I saw him in his backyard, even if he was a million miles away.'

The man behind the Delta Airlines service counter beckoned the group of Springsteen fans forward. As they tried to upgrade their flights to Chicago, Wendy decided not to look back. One day it would all seem funny, Bruce would say. The main thing was to get to Memphis today. No plans, just going where the winds took her. That's how she had gone into this journey, that's how she would continue.

As she sat waiting for an airplane to fly her to Memphis, she found her chest unclenching for the first time since the night in Atlantic City. Her limbs were heavy, as was her heart, but she was still here. The group of Springsteen fans had invited her for breakfast as a consolation. They had recorded some of the show on an MP3 player and Wendy had spent some blissful moments listening to the tinny sound of *Blinded by the Light* and *No Surrender*. When one of them had pulled out an Apple MacBook and connected to the free Wi-Fi at the airport, Wendy had asked her if she could maybe use it for a few minutes to write her blog. After she had explained the purpose of her online diary, the woman had offered her laptop without reservation. And now, for the first time, she considered the possibility of going home, her restlessness battered down enough to perhaps consider a reinvented path into the familiar.

Dreaming of ways to make her glow

It took two phone calls and one sob story to find out Wendy's return flight. Rosie chewed on her pencil. Danny had come home a tad less morose than on other days, and he had left in lighter spirits this morning. When Rosie came down to the kitchen she found a note with a promise to cook, signed off with a squiggly heart. Rosie hoped nobody at his work was into reading blogs. She would be mortified if her dad found out the way she had.

She had tossed and turned last night trying to figure out a way to protect her dad from the reality. He was still hoping Mum would come back to him. Why else did he keep her side of the bed tidy? Leave her favourite book and a small candle on her night stand? She had heard him cry too. Not that he would share that with her. But the thing that really gave it away was his new repertoire. He played the songs off *The Rising* almost every other night. She loved Bruce's voice but to hear her dad sing *You're Missing* floored her every single time. Not that she'd let on to him. Rosie cringed at the thought though, that despite her mum intending to fly back, her blog did not seem to suggest she'd be moving back in any time soon.

The other thing that kept her up was Lea. She still felt the back of Lea's hand on her cheek, hot and burning as if she had just been touched. Why had Lea come 'round' last night? To say something about the cutting? To make her feel better about her mum? Or because she was interested in her? She had seen Lea before; aloof and a bit uppity, Maria and her had decided. But uniquely herself too, Rosie had always secretly added in her mind. She appreciated people who did not feign interest, who clearly couldn't give a hoot about the current fashion. Without thinking, Rosie touched her bottom lip. Up to this point, sex of any kind had been one big disappointment. Today she felt fuzzy with anticipation, like waking up from a long hibernation. The light cut the trees more sharply against the sky, the baker's smelled sweeter. She was hyper aware of the noise of the cats outside, the children's voices. Were they always out on the street? And this loud?

The bell rang impatiently. Maria! She was the only one who applied Morse-code-techniques to the bell. Long dot dot – dot dot long long dot dot – dot. Rosie laughed. Dude! Maria was clearly excited about something. Rosie jumped down the stairs and flung open the door. 'Dude!' she called and readied herself for the convoluted High and Low fives.

Both Maria and Lea stood on her front porch. Maria barged past her, ignoring the high-five set-up, but Lea hung back.

'Hey,' Lea said quietly.

Rosie felt her cheeks get warm. How childish she must have looked. Lea touched Rosie's arm and then followed Maria into the house.

'Right, first things first. I should've let you bash her head in. She is such a tyke. You'll never guess what she did. Oh Rose, I could smack her one in that miserably horsy gob of hers.' Maria was pacing around the kitchen, opening the cupboards until she found what she was looking for. She snapped open the can of coke and ripped at the bag of McCoy's. Rosie looked at Lea, and shook her head sheepishly.

'Sharon printed out your mum's blogs and glued them on all of the toilet doors. On the insides, so the teachers didn't know until well after lunch break.'

'And also on the boys' toilets! Don't forget the boys' toilets!'

Lea nodded. 'Also on the boys' toilets.'

Rosie began to giggle. She couldn't help it. 'God I must be the first teenager in the world who needs to sit down their mother. I am supposed to be the bane of my parents' life, not the other way around!'

Maria stopped sloshing her coke and let out a huge burp. 'Quine, are you not worried? Your reputation is shot, kaput, you are a pariah. Because whatever your mother does, obviously reflects on you and is a predictor of you. Duh!'

Lea took the cup of tea and smiled at Rosie. 'Maria, I reckon Rosie is more concerned with her status as artistic nerd than her fuckability.'

Rosie walked over to Maria and gave her a big hug. 'Sista I love you. I could not wish for a better ally. Did I read all the blogs or is there more? Was there more on the doors?'

'Your mother hasn't written anything new, clootie dumplings be praised. We can only hope she is too busy shagging men to write about it.' She stuffed another hand of McCoy's in her mouth.

'Thing is Maria, it is obviously gross to us. Who wants to read what their parents get up to? I mean, nightmare. But you know what, I actually read the comments. Did you know people are reading this? And they are commenting too.' Lea nibbled at a crisp.

Rosie groaned. Her mother was such a computer nitwit. No common sense. The world wide web was called that for a reason. Yet here is her mum, who treats this writing as a personal diary that she can hide in the attic.

'Rosie, the women reading this are loving it. They are very supportive of your mum's experience. Many women wish they were as brave as her.'

'Seriously?'

'Aye, seriously! Wanting to throw off the yoke they made for themselves. Talking about being brave …'

Rosie looked at Maria. She clearly did not know that Lea had come by last night.

'Lea was here yesterday, she was worried. I decided to look up if my mum had planned to come back at all. Well she has. I'm thinking about going to see her before she comes back.'

'Rad!' Maria smacked her Coke on the bar. 'That's my bestie Rosie, right here. Rosie is the most amazing, funny, and brave confidante I have ever had Lea!'

'I know,' smiled Lea, 'I have been watching.'

'Creepy,' mocked Maria, 'but fair. I'd be watching the two coolest chicks from 5C too.'

Rosie gave Maria a hug. 'Nutter! Glad you're still here Maria. Glad to have you on the team Lea.' Rosie said the last bit a little softer. Maria raised an eyebrow. Rosie hastened past any awkwardness, snatching the crisps packet, dumping the rest of the crisps into a small bowl and folding the packet into a small triangle.

'So, what's next? Raiding the old-folks credit card? You may think Rosie's cool Lea, but the best tricks she learned all from master imposter herself.' She winked.

Rosie explained her plans whilst Lea and Maria looked at the atlas. One phone call later, a questionable credit card transaction in her father's name, and Rosie was set to go. She'd miss the actual start of school, but summer school had been a dumb enough idea in the first place, and she didn't expect the start of the new year to get any more interesting. She'd catch up no problem. Adventure was beckoning, and who knows, she might convince her mother to come back home after all. Her dad walked in with two heavy shopping bags as the girls went out. He knocked Lea in the ribs accidentally.

'Oh sorry, erhm …'

'Lea.'

'Lea. These new Wimpey-sized houses, eh? They don't build hallways the way they used to. This feels mean, you girls are welcome any time normally, but tonight I have a date with my daughter.'

All three of them laughed and left Rosie's dad to it.

Rosie had to admit she was genuinely impressed. Not only had her dad cooked as he had promised, but the food was also delicious. Okay, it was the obligatory lasagne, but he had really gone to town on the spices and creaminess. She put her fork down. Now that she had booked her ticket she had to tell her dad without kicking him further down.

'This is really yummy Dad. I didn't know you had it in you.'

'Well, I did live on my own before I met your mum.' Rosie was about to comment when her dad stopped her, and added, 'And after I met your mum, for a bit. But, I confess, I did look up a recipe. I learned how to make a proper roux to thicken the cheese sauce.' He smiled. Rosie grinned back.

This was as good an opening as any. 'I don't think Mum really enjoyed cooking. But right now, I even miss her bland potatoes.' Her dad nodded. Rosie stared into the flames of the two tea lights on the counter. Her dad had made the effort; she sighed. The tea lights fluttered. This line of questioning felt like premeditated character murder. She had to make it clear though, that she had no option but to seek out her mother. 'Dad, do you know what the last book was that Mum read? Or the last film she cried at?'

Her dad shrugged. Rosie continued, 'How come you don't know? Did you guys not talk, like ever?'

Again her dad didn't respond. He reached over and took Rosie's plate, stacked it up on his own, and put them in the sink. He unscrewed the red wine and filled a clean glass to the rim. He came back to the table, offering her some. She put her hand over her glass. She needed her wits about her.

'So, if you had to mention three things you loved about Mum, what would they be?'

'She is a great mother.' Danny took no time to answer that question.

Rosie looked at the man across from her. Really? 'Dad, you think, really think, that's what Mum wants you to say? Of all the things she could be, you think being a good mother would be highest on her list? Not that she's intelligent, brave, creative, I dunno – funny?' She let out a deep sigh, 'Anyhow, I don't see a lot of mothering right now.'

'Just because she is not here, doesn't mean she has stopped being your mother. And I reckon she did a fine job with you.'

And now for the jugular. The bit where she'd theoretically self-harmed a little, but also was about to shake the foundations of her mum's husband's life of the past 16 years.

'Dad, have you ever considered maybe Mum never wanted to be a mum, not really. I know you weren't keen on the dad bit, but do you honestly think she wanted to keep me? I reckon with gran dying ... she just wanted her mum to know she'd be a grandmother, even if a belated dead one. All I am was an unlucky accident. Dad, I know this sounds horrible, but did you ever contemplate Mum might not have had me out of love for you, but love for her own mother?'

Danny cleared the plates noisily. 'Coffee?' On Rosie's affirmative he put on the kettle and started to load the dishwasher. He had this particular system that apparently nobody understood, so Rosie didn't bother to help out. He would simply sneak back in when she was in the shed to redo all the stacking.

Rosie was relentless. 'When you two first met, what did you love about her?'

'Easy, she was wild, not scared of anything. She had this energy, it was impossible to deny her anything. But then she went so dark a few years into having you. And life … well … all marriages get into this stale rut. It's inevitable.'

'Poppycock!' Her mum's archaic but favourite expression broke the ice enough to tread lightly but deeper into the murky waters. 'What did you do, in those dark periods? Did you talk to her? Hold her? Ask her what the demons looked like? Did you check under the bed for the crocodile?'

Danny turned on the tap and scrubbed the lasagne dish with a raging fervour. She could see he was close to tears. 'Dad where WERE you all those years?'

Rosie felt bad. She heard herself rant and knew she sounded like her mother. After the nice meal it felt unfair to her dad. But if she was going to drag her mother back home, her dad had better change his ways. 'Dad where did she go? Where is that wild life-loving girl you embraced? All I saw for as long as I remember is a control freak scared shitless of anything that's out of place. Never seen anything as un-wild as Mum to be honest.' She paused for a moment, time for the kill. 'Dad, what do you think Mum's doing?'

'Well, chasing Springsteen?'

That casual remark stopped Rosie in her tracks. She had not expected her dad to be this close to the truth. But her dad needed to know there was more to it.

'You think that's what she's doing? Dad, really? She is not chasing some old rock and roll guy, she is chasing herself. She is looking for her lost self. Maybe she too wondered where she went, that girl you fell in love with.' Rosie paused to let the words sink in. And to find the courage to tell him what she'd done. 'Dad, I have loved being with you these past few weeks. It's been good hanging out together, hasn't it? I am not sure Mum planned for that to happen. But it did. And now you start cooking me lovely meals. But I need to find Mum and I want to be there when she finds that sixteen-year-old her. So, I have booked a flight to the USA, the day after tomorrow. I'm going to find her.'

'Rosie,' her dad shook his head. 'Your mum could be anywhere. This is lunacy.' Rosie was quiet. She wouldn't let him in on her detective work and deductions. Elementary, Dad, elementary, she thought.

Then the statement sank in, 'But hang on, how did you pay for the ticket?'

'Never mind Dad, I'll pay it back to you. I have a good feeling about bumping into her somehow. And if I don't, at least I will have seen some of the landmark sights.'

'School?'

'Can wait. You, maybe you could do something apart from waiting. What if you became less predictable? And actually write her some poetry or do other soppy things. Go nuts on the romantics? Maybe you'll feel better too.'

Her dad ignored her remarks. ‘I guess you want me to write you a note now, saying you have my parental permission to travel on your own?’

‘Dad, you are a class act. And while you are at it, put Mum’s name at the bottom too. I can fake her signature.’ When her dad frowned, she laughed, ‘Come on Dad, don’t tell me you never used the ‘loophole” of falsification to get out of things at school. Please don’t tell me you were that square.’

‘Maybe I should come with you,’ Danny suggested. ‘I mean, I am not exactly at my best at work anyway.’

‘Nope, Dad, definitely nope!’ Rosie’s heart jumped. If she was going to convince her mum to come back at all, the last thing she needed was her dad there. Who knows what new version of her mother she might actually meet, and how much damage control needed to be done. Anyhow, she had things she wanted to discuss with her mum first. ‘No Dad, let me do this on my own. Trust me on that one.’

Start all over again

Wendy stood in front of the white gates with the Elvis silhouette and the music notes leading up to the very unromantic sky-blue pavilion that would allow her entry to the inner sanctum. People milled around her, cameras on their chests, sunglasses on the top of their heads. It was hot. She had missed the morning session in the memorial gardens. By the time she had walked to Graceland from the airport, the Rock & Roll circus had already been open for a solid hour. It meant now she was faced with buying an extortionately overpriced ticket to walk through a dead man's house. It felt odd, although she couldn't understand why. She'd been to houses of historical figures before. Why should this be any different? She looked at the droves of tourists. There were loud welcomes, and big-bosomed hugs from family members that had agreed to meet up here. Japanese tourists did everything to fit the cliché, including group choreography like a flock of starlings, and the matching Elvis Lives bucket hats. She twirled the credit card in her fingers.

She imagined this is how Elvis had felt. Surrounded by people, the glitz of celebrity at the centre of it all, but somehow completely detached from it. Noises started to swirl over and past her like a hazy veil, a muted murmur in which her own thoughts started an uncoordinated tap dance routine. The thought of shuffling in a line of tourists past Elvis's troubled life suddenly filled her with incredible sadness. She would be gawking at all the bygone glory that had been the man's wealth, but ultimately had been no more than a trap. Rhinestones instead of diamonds. Maybe she should just walk along the wall, peek over it from the street and catch some of the exterior. She tried to imagine how Bruce must have felt that evening in 1977. Pumped with adrenaline and admiration. Still, he must have been feeling cocksure youth too, how else would you simply decide to jump a superstar's wall?

Did it count as a milestone, if she was very close to but didn't actually see the Pink Cadillac? Wendy decided it did; it was her who was making the rules this trip. She retraced her steps out of the wide pavement. She walked to a small parking space off the Boulevard and took a closer look at the wall. Fans from all over the world had left their hearts and names on the bricks. Bruce hadn't taken a sharpie but song lyrics that day – at least he had been original. She glanced at the white mansion. A prison manifested itself in many different guises.

'Hey, are you all right there?'

Wendy slid down the wall and turn around apprehensively. The last thing she could use now was a fine for trespassing. She turned to see a middle-aged woman wearing a long panther-print gypsy skirt over combat boots. She jingled as she moved, her body bent under the weight of six strings of glass beads around her neck.

The woman waved a left arm full of bangles, and repeated, 'You all right?'

'I wasn't trying to get over, honestly.'

'Ha, you wouldn't get far girl. There's cameras everywhere. Ticket too expensive eh?' She grinned knowingly. Wendy noticed a gaping hole where the woman's front teeth used to be, but not a hint of sarcasm. She felt the urge to turn her head, but the woman looked at her with kind eyes. Wendy relaxed and approached the colourful woman on the curb side.

'It was more the sadness that stopped me, if I'm honest.'

'Come, come, sit with me.' The woman took Wendy by the arm coaxing her to a beat-up Buick. She opened the tailgate to reveal a hidden home. She sat down and patted the cushion next to her.

'It's what travelling does to you, sometimes.' She took a pipe from a deep pocket in her skirt; from the other she fished a paper bag of tobacco. She gingerly filled her pipe, looking at Wendy sideways. She compressed the tobacco with a tamper, and took a test draw. Wendy expected her to talk, but the woman simply hummed and mumbled to herself. Wendy relaxed. And remained quiet too. The woman trickled in some more tobacco and stamped it until it was level with the top of the bowl. She struck a match and circled it a few times over the pipe, taking short puffs. Then she continued. 'Memphis is a town full of souls, many searching. I wouldn't call them demons but they do bring with them a coldness that can creep into your bones.'

Wendy touched the felted blanket that was spread out over the bottom of the boot. It was pasted on the inside walls too. A simple pattern: spirals and suns that reminded her of tribal tattoos.

'My name is Teata, Bearer of Dawn. Are you fleeing from or fleeing to?'

The question flummoxed Wendy. So far, she had been fleeing from her old life, fleeing from routines that suffocated her, hollowness that filled her so completely and quite literally, the past few days, a man who assumed control over her. So yes, she was fleeing from – all the time. Could she also be fleeing to? She looked sideways. Teata's flat forehead emphasised the woody wisdom of her face. All she answered was, 'I'm Wendy.'

Teata talked right over the answer. 'I go away often, but always return to the intoxicating lure of after-hour Beale Street. And of course, the Chickasaw festival that takes place in a few weeks' time.' She puffed on her pipe in short bursts. 'Everything I own is right here, this van is my home.' Teata fell on her back and looked up. Wendy did the same. The sky's constellation was painted on the roof of the van in bright pinks and golds and greens. 'Still, no matter how far I take my van and no matter how hard I claim it to be my home, my true home is here. In the soil that holds the memories of my tribe. So, no matter where the roads take me, each year I flee back to my roots. From these roots I flee to other experiences and adventures that enrich my tapestry of life.'

Teata shifted her skirts. 'On the banks of the Father of Waters, the spirits of my past are coaxing and seeking out the lost souls: the white jazz singer who plays for her meal and bed, the greasy-haired, unwashed backpackers that obscure a path of expectation and ambition with booze or drugs and keep the weight of decisions at bay for a while. The penniless, the fat cats, the dealers, the jokers, the dreamers – all fleeing from the void and loneliness that comes when the beating of your heart is out of sync with the drum of life. They congregate in Memphis, seeking out Elvis, the notes seeping from small stages on Beale, to find their melody. Many never find it here. And that's where the chill comes from. They are looking in the wrong place.'

'Elvis was arguably the biggest singer of his time. He only strayed 80 miles from where he was born. You would think he was "home" here. So how come he died utterly alone if he was right at his roots?' Wendy glanced sideways at Teata who had sat up to pull deeply on her pipe.

'Elvis's roots were not his birthplace, or even his family. It was the music that went through him. With all the fame and fortune came a distancing from that music. His performances were just tricks of the trade in the end, he was clawing at fake connections with fans who were in love with their image of him. His addictions muted his true voice. The root of Elvis was music, not place or family, he got distracted.'

Wendy sat up. She got distracted with Dwayne. But she knew that if she were to return to Aberdeen she'd still not find roots enough to keep her, no matter how much she had grown to love the place. Something was missing.

'When you get distracted is when things tend to go south. It is about tuning into your own individual truth. Most likely, it isn't the place, or music, that is your anchor. Have you ever considered your roots might be something more intangible?'

Wendy sucked in some air. 'Are you some sort of soothsayer, or tarot card reader, Teata? I mean, what do you know about my roots?' Wendy was aware she was biting her nails. Maybe she had spoken aloud without realising it.

'Come on, let me take you somewhere. You don't need to tell me – I want to try something.'

They got out of the back of the van. Teata shook out her pipe, stuffed it in her pocket, and closed the tailgate. Wendy followed, closely observing this strange woman. They walked to the front of the car.

'Get in. Door's open!'

Wendy had her hand on the door handle but hesitated. This woman did not come highly recommended, like Big Dave. Then again, she must be at least twice her age; nothing Wendy couldn't handle. She got in and squeezed her rucksack under the dash, between her legs. She stared out of the window, whilst Teata searched her bag for the keys.

'How long are you staying in Memphis?'

'Just passing through. I have a flight back to Scotland in a few days.'

'Scotland, eh? So that's the accent. You do know it is always possible to postpone, don't you?' Teata started the engine and turned up Elvis Presley Boulevard.

'I came to America to find out about Springsteen's roots. At least, that's how it started.'

'Springsteen? The *Born in the USA* guy?'

'Yes, you sound surprised.'

'I had you down as a Mitchell girl, or something spiritually akin. Your spirit seems flightier than the four by four of rock and roll.'

'Ah but when I first saw him, he was like a preacher, you know. He spoke to us like we were his flock somehow. I can't explain, but something shifted. It went beyond the catchy tunes, it was a spiritual awakening. You ever listened to Springsteen?'

'Can't say I have, really. Just know he calls the women in his songs little girls, and that bothers me. And I know he's got this thing with cars.'

Wendy didn't feel like defending Bruce, and stayed quiet after this. Teata put her hand on Wendy's knee and squeezed it briefly.

'I didn't mean to offend. I just feel you have a mystical river inside you that goes beyond your musical taste. It is not a judgment of any kind. You said it started that way, what has changed?'

'Instead of experiencing Springsteen's reality, I keep having to face my own demons and shortcomings. I find I can't run away from them.'

'Memphis is the birthplace of soul music. Do you know we've got two museums dedicated to it? Not one, but two! If that's not telling you something! You ever considered why it is called soul music?'

'Because it touches your soul?'

'Because it comes from the soul. What is the soul anyway, Wendy? Is it the same as the heart? How does the soul speak? Springsteen might have touched your heart, but does his music speak to your soul?' Teata indicated right, whilst nodding ahead. 'That's the Stax museum up there. Inside is the church where gospel song educated the soul before soul educated the white man. If we were to drive even further up to Beale we'd be right by the Rock and Soul Museum, telling the same story, differently. I'm not taking you to either.'

'So where are we going now then?'

'A cemetery.'

'A cemetery?'

Teata chuckled and added, 'Not just any old ring-fenced grounds with dead people in it. The Crystal Shrine cemetery is the alternative to Graceland I believe you were meant to see here, not the grave of the man who inspired Springsteen. It is the place I think you'll be closer to your roots.'

At no point did Wendy feel she was walking through a cemetery. Green open spaces and tranquillity. This felt like a park, not a place where people found their final resting place. Teata pointed at the flowers that were standing in neat rows to the left of them.

'Those are the graves. Horizontal plaques because in death everyone is equal.'

They crossed over a wooden bridge that Teata pointed out was actually made of concrete. Wendy stopped and retraced her steps. On second feel, what had looked like wood was indeed not wood at all. They walked through Abraham's Oak and came upon a stump of a huge tree.

‘Not real, of course, but another of Rodriguez’s concrete structures. And the door to God’s Garden.’

‘I’m not really into God, to be honest. I mean, if you think that is where my roots are.’ She felt suddenly very creeped out. Had she found the one wandering zealot in Memphis? She began to seriously doubt her judgment of character these days.

Teata laughed out loud. ‘Listen, I am not trying to convert you. Don’t worry. It’s called that because inside you’ll see depictions from the life of Christ. But that is not why we came here. I want you to keep in mind, as you step through the door, that this is not a natural phenomenon. This is all man-made.’

Wendy couldn’t believe her eyes. From the Memphis heat she had stepped into a grotto dripping with crystal stalactites lit up in many different colours. She saw lots of different scenes from the Bible even she recognised. It looked properly tacky.

‘Just like Graceland, an overkill of kitsch. But be quiet. Sit yourself down somewhere and close your eyes briefly.’

Wendy found a space next to the Good Samaritan and squatted down. She closed her eyes. She focused her mind on nothing in particular and heard harp music from somewhere. Her breathing slowed down. Underneath the melody she heard faint noises from outside the grotto, and let them float past her. A calm came over her. The knot in her stomach, that she had felt ever since she walked out of that motel in Atlantic City, began to loosen. She started to sob, first quietly but soon found she couldn’t hold back the tears. She let them flow, rocking back and forth like she used to do when she was a child. It wasn’t pain she felt though, but openness and clarity of mind. Here in this moment she felt rooted. Belonging not to the space, not to art. Someone had spent six years giving attention to every detail. He had placed crystals exactly where it felt right. He had had a vision and seen it through. What was it that Teata had said: keep in mind this is all man-made. Life then, as a malleable and makeable thing? Life had mostly happened to her, from the moment she decided to keep Rosie. This trip, for the first time, she felt like she was making her own life; her confidence was growing. The idea bounced off the sparkling walls. She felt rooted to an unseen energy she guessed was akin to the inspiration that had driven Rodriguez 65 years ago. His desire to make beauty, not wait for it to be accidental in his life, but to claim it. He'd kept the techniques a secret, taken with him to his grave how exactly he created tinted concrete to resemble wood. He'd assembled the crystals and devised their placement, driven by nothing more than the desire to be a creator of beauty. His energy and inspiration somehow still breathed inside this space, filling her with lightness and warmth. She could be like that too. Writing the blog had given her a taste again for her old passion. She would make her own life, by writing other lives. Deep inside a voiced sighed: *you can let go now.*

When she opened her eyes, she expected to see Teata smiling at her with a smug look on her face, a twinkle in her eye, or smoking a pipe whilst chanting softly. But when she looked up, she was completely alone in the grotto. She walked outside. Maybe Teata had not wanted to interfere, but no matter where Wendy looked, she couldn't find her. Wendy's heart skipped a beat. For fuck sake! All her stuff was in that van. Wendy looked about frantically. She had to get back to the van. She cursed her lack of orientation. She recognised the oak and passed through it, but couldn't for the life of her remember how they had gotten here. She cursed out loud this time.

'A little respect would be nice.'

Wendy turn and saw a lanky man inside the oak, legs stretched out now, cowboy hat deep over his eyes. He had to stoop to get out. His skin was weathered through years or the sun, she couldn't tell which.

'Did you see a woman go by? Long gypsy skirt, beads, bangles, combat boots?'

'I did.'

'You did? Oh, please, where did she go? I need to find her. Where's the exit?' She walked up to the man. He didn't flinch, not even when she grabbed him by the arm.

'Relax,' he said, smiling a dopey grin, 'one question at a time. Which one do you want me to answer first?'

'Relax? you don't understand! My bag. God I am such a gullible fool!'

'What bag?'

'My bag with all my stuff. For f …' she stopped herself, 'why did I trust that woman?'

The man strolled back to the oak. He leant in and looked over his shoulder. 'Because at some point in your life, you have to trust. Without reservation.' He dragged something from the side and when he turned around she could see it was her backpack 'My name is Randy, I believe you would be Wendy.'

She'd do almost anything to get you back

Rosie checked the small piles on her bed one last time. Three T-shirts, five socks and four pants, spare jeans and shorts, swimsuit and towel – you never go anywhere without a bikini her mum admonished her in her mind. All black of course. She patted the sweater she had found in the back of her mother's closet. Her mother might be sex-crazy, off her rocker, and frankly, troubled, but she was frugal too. And these days, nothing said punk more than vintage.

Danny had fussed about like an old biddy, dragging out his old rucksack for her, making a list and checking it twice, made her promise on her life that she'd be responsible with his credit card. She had just let him play overbearing parent for once. She picked up the book he had just given her for on the plane. Over 650 pages on the Sex Pistols. It was more thoughtful than anything he'd ever bought her in the past 15 years. She might have been upset with her mum at first, then worried as time passed and she found out what her mum had been getting herself in to, but the shock of her disappearance had definitely jumpstarted her dad's empathetic side it seemed.

She sat down and felt the cover with her fingers. She lifted the book to her nose to smell the pages. Musty from long years in the charity shop in Bieldside it had come from, which was only open a few days a week, so her dad had really made an effort. It smelt fantastic. She had to give it to him, his choice was bang on. She sounded out the words: England's Dreaming, Anarchy, Sex Pistols Punk and Beyond. Definitely more interesting than summer school.

If you are taking your music seriously, you have to study it. Commit to knowing how the minds of the stalwarts of punk worked, understand the political climate, and act accordingly, he had said. *Nothing's as horrible as a lazy derivative version of the real thing.* She couldn't agree more. She shoved the book in the front pocket of the bag, zipped up the toggle, then lifted each small pile from her bed into the main compartment. She walked over to her beanie drawer and rummaged until she'd found the red oversized cabled one that Maria had made her last December.

Speak of the devil, she grinned when she heard the familiar Morse code ring. She threw the beanie on the bed, and jumped down the stairs two steps at the time. 'Got it Dad! It's only Maria.' She ripped open the door. The wind tore at the scarf Maria had wound tightly around her chin and nose. A tiny tornado of leaves rustled at her feet. Autumn was definitely on its way. Maria smiled liked the Cheshire cat though, waving a set of clippers in front of her face.

'Here we go, your PhD has arrived. Your Personal Hairdresser,' she added with an exasperated sigh when Rosie didn't catch on. 'I went past Hair by Dare today to ask for advice, so you have nothing to worry about. I know exactly what to do.' She stepped past Rosie, nipping by the living room. 'Hey Rosie's dad, A-okay?' Before he had time to answer she had dashed up the stairs. Rosie closed the door, then followed her friend to her room.

Maria flopped on the bed. She kicked off her shoes without undoing the laces. 'You ready Rose? You can still chicken out, stick with the henna.'

Rosie connected her mp3 player to the speakers. 'Letter between A to Z.'

'C'

'The Cure it is.' She turned up the volume. 'This way my dad won't hear us. He's definitely not going to approve, but what's done cannot be undone. Let's go Maria.' She plonked herself on the second-hand baroque chair she had restored last winter. She had ripped off the worn-out green velvet fabric, and replaced it with a tote bag with the Velvet

Underground album cover. The yellow of the banana contrasted sharply with the neon green nails she had used to hammer the fabric taut. 'Do your best!' She held up an image she had torn out of a magazine she'd found in one of her mother's loft boxes.

Maria giggled nervously. She plugged in the clippers, stood behind Rosie and looked in the mirror. Rosie stuck up her thumb. Maria slowly moved the clippers over Rosie's temple towards herself. The red hair fell on the floor in large chunks. The buzz reminded Rosie of a tattoo gun; this was painless though, a symbolic mutilation as a first step on a new path. Maria buzzed on with deadly determination once the first strands of hair had hit the laminate.

'Hand me the scissors, Rose.' Maria took the long hair that was left on the middle part of Rosie's skull. 'About an inch?' Rosie nodded.

A few minutes later Maria squatted next to Maria and together they looked at their reflections. Rosie gelled the bristles into a Mohican and smiled. 'Next step!'

'No, Rose, I can't. Just thinking about it makes me sick. I mean, you saw what happened with Olive.'

'Oh Maria, Grease was just a film. She might have looked awesome in those black leathers, but that scene, come on, it's no more than a pinprick. I've got ice in that cup over there.'

'Rosie, why not tell me about Lea first.'

'What do you want to hear?'

Maria shrugged. 'I don't know, is it serious? How long have you known? You never said anything about this to me.'

Rosie tasted a reluctant bitterness. Was Maria jealous? They'd been as thick as two peas in a pod for such a long time they considered themselves sisters. Maybe she would feel a little threatened too if Maria suddenly introduced a third player into the mix. But it had never been a problem when it was boys. Maybe Maria instinctively felt that this went deeper than the misguided teenage fumbles earlier. She was right, of course, the boys had meant nothing whereas Lea's breath set her skin on fire, one look from her shifting her heartbeat into overdrive. It was a glorious yet terrifying experience. 'Honestly Maria, I don't know. I didn't realise what was so out of kilter with me, really, until Lea came out to me. I hadn't even considered it an option. But there's nothing solid. It is no more than reconnaissance right now. I think.'

Maria nodded. She scooped up some of Rosie's locks of hair and held it against her cheek. 'So soft. Your face is sharper without the mane of hair. You look like a boy.'

'Would it bother you I might be into girls? And before you ask, no not into you. Not that way.'

'Nah not really, I just didn't see it coming. Lea, is she kind? Will she look after you?' Maria lowered her eyes as she asked the question.

'Maria, you sound like my mother! I don't know, she seems to be kind. I have to trust my guts I guess. There's no alarm bells with this one. And she makes me feel good. She's sickly optimistic, like you. But she is not you. Love and love are two very different things!'

'It's just that I know that Lea was off school for a wee while, and there were all these rumours.'

Rosie raised an eyebrow. 'Rumours? Like what?'

Maria slapped her knees and got up. Her dodgy right knee buckled. 'Goddamnit, and on top of all of that shite at school I've turned into an old cripple overnight.' Both of them snorted at the joke. 'They said she was seeing a shrink at some point because she tried to, well ... you know.'

'I do know, but that's in the past. She is still seeing a shrink, but that's a good thing. She told me the first time she came round.'

Maria stood behind the chair, bent over and hugged Rosie from behind. 'Just be careful. I know what you've been doing to yourself. It worries me you two might get into a downward spiral together.'

'Definitely my mother. Don't worry Maria, I got this.'

'I'm gonna miss you Rosie, just promise you'll come back. Snatch that mother of yours from the claws of sexual predators and her own stupidity, shove her on a plane back, and be done with it.'

'Promise. Now let's get down to business: Blokus, Scrabble or Trivial?' Rosie pointed at the concave bookshelf loaded with games and jigsaw puzzles.

Maria placed the brown pie piece in the wheel with a satisfied grin. 'Let's take a break, I'm dying for a coffee and a fag.'

'You are such a junkie, you are.'

They sneaked down the stairs as quietly as possible to avoid a premature reveal of the hairdo. In the living room Danny was having a heated debate with Lineker on the TV. 'He can't hear you Dad,' Rosie shouted.

'Oh you girls in the kitchen? Give us a beer would ya?'

Maria rapped on Rosie's forehead with her knuckles. 'You should have been quiet; I'm not bringing it to him.'

Rosie steeled herself when she walked into the lounge but all her dad said was, 'Ah didn't realise you were going to take the book this seriously.' Then turned back to the screen, pulled the ring, and took a swig.

'He didn't even flinch.'

Maria leant against the backdoor and offered Rosie a drag of her cigarette. 'Rosie, am I a good friend?'

'Of course you are. You came over to cut my hair, didn't you?'

Maria shrugged, and scuffed her boots against the harling of the back wall. 'But I knew what you were doing, and I didn't try to stop you. Or ask you why. Do best friends not protect each other?'

'What do you mean, what I was doing?'

'Rose, I suspected your scars, but I didn't tell anyone. Is that bad?

There was only a sliver of moon in the sky. A sickly yellow mist slid in front of it, obscuring but not killing its light. The wind had picked up. The willow at the back was sweeping about its flexible branches. It reminded her of Kate Bush's dancing. She was surprised Maria had known before, as she had been careful to keep her skin covered at all times. Then again, it had taken Lea only one touch to realise. She felt a pang of shame. She wasn't even clever enough to keep something this simple hidden. 'No of course not. I didn't want anyone to know. So you did good.'

'Ah, but being a best friend is more than dancing to the other person's tune. It is about confronting them whilst standing right next to them when doing so. Goddamnit, I feel shite. Rosie what made you do it?'

'Oh Maria, it's complicated, can we leave it just now?'

'I have been so worried. Been covering it up with my frantic optimism, but I don't want to lose you Rosie. You can talk to me. Always, even if you did snog my waste of a brother when I asked you not to.'

'Now there's a mistake you were right about, 100 percent.' Rosie walked in to make the coffee. She came out with two steaming mugs. 'Here, you can have Sponge Bob.' She warmed her hands on her mug before she continued, 'I just didn't know what there was to say. I kept reaching for things that would cut through the numbness I guess. But it started out just a niggle. You were such a bright star of your own right. I couldn't share. So I kept it quiet. If anyone's at fault here, it is me.'

Maria didn't say anything. Two minutes passed, three. 'But friends are not just there for the good times. Best friends only truly matter in the bad times. I have been with you in all our fun moments. It's been a blast, but then in your darkest pit of shit, I chose to cover the lid. Pretend it would blow over. Just a phase, nothing serious.'

'You stayed. You didn't judge. That matters. Maria, I couldn't have wished for a better friend. This thing with Lea has brought me a strange peace of mind. I thought I was a freak. Imagine me being the lake and life is skimming stones. Everything bounced off the surface, stress, nasty things but also the good times; the only thing that penetrated into the depth that is me is when the stone finally sinks, when I slice through that surface. I know it sounds freaky, but it is the best I can explain it. Does it make sense?'

Maria nodded. She emptied her mug. 'So what next? Are you going to stop? Can you? Can I do anything to help?'

Rosie swallowed hard. The urge was still so strong at times, but despite the turbulent last few weeks she had managed to control it more or less. Feeling confused and thrilled at Lea's kiss was the first time she had felt anything that strong without the cutting. It felt real, and she hadn't had the urge to use the blade to seal the event. Things had landed. Hope. It tasted sweet. She found she liked this new sensation. Now that she had opened up to Maria, maybe she could ignore the urge by continuing to confide in her best friend. But first things first, her mother. 'I'm not sure Maria. It feels different now. At least I am taking control now. Finding mum.'

'Are you scared? Going on your own?'

'A little. But more that I am going to miss her, not find her. I'm all right with going. Americans are just like people.' She let out a nervous giggle.

'Bump fist, girlfriend! If anyone can find your mum it's you. Speaking of your mum … maybe there's another blog. Let's go up, find out. Also, I've only got the orange slice to go. I feel good about my chances.' She hooked her arm in Rosie's and dragged her up the stairs.

POET DOWN HERE

making an honest stand

WEDNESDAY, 06 AUGUST 2003

Still hoping for the dope

I disappeared off the radar, I know. Sorry Brendan: I am safe now. The emphasis is on *now*. How deceptive good looks can be. Dwayne's pecs might have been the hottest north of Havana, his tongue smoother than silk in many ways, his hip thrusts capable of ecstasy that left me screaming for more and mercy at the same time, but I had not seen the truth beneath the smooth. And God was I scared when I did.

I am not proud of the mess I got myself into. That is not why I am writing this entry today. I write it to support anyone, who finds themselves caught in a situation where you think you're going mad. That you are imagining things, because your lover tells you, you got it wrong. Trust your gut. You are most likely absolutely right.

I write this, because I have seen that some of you are actually reading these entries. And if some of you are struggling to escape a similar position. Please read on.

Here's the quick and low of it all.

At first this Dwayne dude and I fell over each other. We were both hungry for sex. It was good, more than good. I don't think we slept any the first night. I am still amazed at how easy this whole sex-thing is. Dwayne was a pro at the tables, so I let him take the lead. I lent him $50 to get going; he promised to get money later. As Dwayne had the bigger pockets he kept our winnings safe. We were doing well. When we got to the blackjack tables, he denied having the money. I was surprised, and challenged him. He started to shout at me that I didn't trust him. Right there in the casino. That he had driven me here as a kind gesture and why would he lie about something stupid like that. He didn't need the money. When I started to cry – remember, I had slept very little – he took my hand and softly led me to the toilet area. He started to kiss me, saying he didn't mean to upset me.

Previous Posts

POET DOWN HERE

making an honest stand

WEDNESDAY, 6 AUGUST 2003

Still hoping for the dope

That I was gorgeous, and hot. We went into a cubicle. Afterwards he whispered, we'd forget about the screaming and just win some more. He stroked my hair, and squeezed my hand. I figured I had got him wrong.

The pattern was the same for the next few days. Him accusing me of lying, me crying, him making up. Sex. Very little sleep. Lots of alcohol.

Obviously, no casino is there to make the punter money; Brendan was correct about that. We lost heavily. Dwayne was all blasé about it, saying he had plenty in the bank and this was all just a bit of fun. I should relax. It never occurred to me to check my own wallet, that I left in the room for safety. The night I left Dwayne, things got really ugly; I'll spare you the details. This time I didn't fall for the apologies afterwards, his honeydew lies of love, and his presents declaring his love. I managed to sneak out after I discovered he had taken my cash out of my purse and that all along we had been gambling away my money.

I am mortified writing this down. All the red flags were there, but I simply ignored them. It is so clear now that I have stepped away. All I wanted to say is, trust the first signs. If the first argument is unreasonable, get out, straight away.

I sit here in Pittsburgh airport, waiting for a cheap flight to Graceland. I don't even like Elvis that much, but Bruce did. Elvis cracked open his world, like Bruce tore down all the walls around mine. Let's see what my hero's hero has got to offer. And of course, I need to see that pink Cadillac with my own eyes.
I meant to get away, I still mean to get away. I got on the wrong train for a bit but I am stronger for it. Clarity comes over time and by accepting the road you follow, bumps and all.

posted by poetdownhere@ August 06, 2003 comments

'Holy shit!' Rosie and Maria stared at the screen. Rosie bit her bottom lip, scrolling up and down the screen to take in what her mum had written.

'Enough already!' Maria slapped her palm on the desk. 'Your mother, what on earth? Is she losing the plot completely?'

An annoying tremor had crept in Rosie's voice when she responded, 'What if that had gone wrong Maria? I mean she always tells me off about these kinda things! And that is Aberdeen, not the United States where all the nutters own a gun.

Maria took out the atlas and looked up Graceland. She showed it to Rosie.

'Well this is where she is at.' She pointed at the map. 'This is not what you had figured, is it? This is much further south.'

'No, you are right.' She scanned the map, Arkansas – that made sense. She let her eye go even further west, then pointed at Amarillo. 'That's where Cadillac Ranch is. Not a million miles from Memphis.' When Rosie had first heard it on *The River*, she had been surprised by the party atmosphere. It had taken a few spins for the words to land properly. The lyrics were so much darker than the music belied. At first she had struggled to do much with that incongruence. Now, reading Wendy's last paragraph it dawned on her that perhaps there's not much more to do in the face of death than to enjoy every single moment you are given. Cadillac Ranch made perfect sense.

'Did you notice the date of the blog?' Maria held the piece of paper with the tour dates scribbled down on it. Day after the Pittsburgh show. She must have missed it, because she would have talked about it otherwise, right?'

Rosie took the sheet from Maria, 'Uh huh, you are right Watson; I taught you well.' She gave Maria's left flank a friendly dig with her elbow. 'So it doesn't look like mum is chasing concerts at this moment. Interesting. I still think that she'll go back up the east corridor before travelling home.' Rosie turned the paper over to scan the map she had drawn. 'She's done New Jersey, New York, but not yet much of

Pennsylvania I reckon. I thought she would be there right now to be honest, but maybe she needed to put some miles between her and that Dwayne dude. I reckon she'll go back there though. It's too close to the airport not to.' With that she switched off the computer. 'I'll grant you the victory Maria, let's just go to bed and listen to some Springsteen to get me in the mood. Early start tomorrow.'

The secret garden of her heart

Randy's RV was not a thing of beauty. He had explained that in the USA there is no such thing as a MOT, and it showed. It was an eyesore amidst the gleaming Hondas and Subarus waiting for their owners to return to their daily commute. Rusty patches had been sanded down, filled up with body filler and primed but most patches were still waiting for the base coat. The floor mats inside were threadbare. Randy had partially covered these with old Faux-Persian carpets, cheap and nasty but warm on the feet. But looks are deceiving, so Randy had claimed, like in the Grotto. It wasn't the sparkle of the fake stalactites that drew in the drones of folk. It was the experience of being in it. Consider my wagon in the same way, he had advised when he first placed her bag against the filthy wheel hub on the driver's side.

It all sounded a bit happy clappy to her, but something in the way he had lingered over the words, and his slow and deliberate delivery had caught her off-guard. Was Randy another smooth talker with only one thing in mind? When she had looked inside the RV she saw the same tribal images she had spotted in Teata's van. It gave her confidence. She pointed at them.

'So, you want to explain how it is you and I are here?'

'To be wise is to know when your role has ended, and when to pass on the torch.' Randy sat on his haunches and swayed to a silent tune. 'You are on the land of the Chickasaw. You were passed along to me so you can follow your path. Teata has given you all she could, the first step over the threshold. I'm here to guide you deeper into the search you are ready to open up to. I too, shall walk out on you at some point. But first, coffee!'

Randy walked into his RV and waved Wendy in. 'Take your bag, dump it on my bed.' The heat pressed down on Wendy the minute she put her head around the door. She saw a neatly arranged kitchen area, a bed, and cupboards tied shut with brightly woven leather ribbons. A small bookshelf offered sanctuary to a guide on indigenous plants, a volume of all Shakespeare's plays, and numerous *Folk Art Messenger* magazines. The rest of the shelves were stacked full of yoghurt pots with oak seedlings. Gingerly, she took a step inside, grabbing the baseball bat that was next to the door. At least she would be able to defend herself. Randy clanged about and soon stumbled past Wendy again with an armful of cups, blackened kettle, wood and matches. Wendy breathed in the smell of white sage. The potent smell clung to the curtains which would separate the bedroom from the kitchen when drawn. She took the fabric and pressed it to her nose. It calmed her nerves. She scanned the interior once again. There was no hint of violence. If anything, this man was hippie stuck in the Peace-Love-and-Understanding groove of the 60s. She took her time to regulate her breathing and push down the anxiety that was brewing in her chest before she followed Randy outside.

'I'm glad you decided to leave that bat inside.'

'Well, you have to admit it is a little weird. How come you were around at the right moment to have me passed on to you?'

'To seek for an explanation limits growth, to accept frees the path.' Randy blew on the small flames that hesitantly licked the starter sticks he'd stacked.

Wendy smiled inwardly at the sloth-speed with which this man moved, and at his distinct lack of interest in her other than sharing words of wisdom. Could her sixth sense for danger be on the mend after the episode with Dwayne?

Randy put an iron barbecue grid over the fledgling fire and placed the kettle on top. After wiping his hands on his jeans, Randy extended them to Wendy and drew her down gently. 'Relax doll, you are quite safe with me. You can ask me anything you want. I won't ask anything of you.'

Wendy stared into the flames. Why would she trust this stranger? She might have been passed on to him by a woman, but that woman knew nothing about her travels. Icy pricks crawled up her spine as she remembered Dwayne's hand around her neck. What would make Randy any different? After all, had Myra Hindley not been the expert to lure young prey into Brady's trap? Perhaps Teata had simply recognised easy pickings.

'You have no proof to trust me, but whatever happened in the past, if you replace trust by suspicion it makes a person weaker, not stronger. I see you are wondering what to do with me.' Randy poured instant coffee into the boiling water. 'I have no proof of who I am. I have no passport, and my driver's licence could easily be a fake. I have no home, no employer. The only reference I have is my desire to be your guide.'

Wendy drew in a quick breath. Were Teata and this man really mind readers? Was that even possible? 'It's just that the last man I trusted, was quite different from the man I took him to be. Seems I am not such a good judge of character.'

'Trust, without reservation, makes anyone vulnerable. But ultimately if you don't, you lead a poorer life for it. Do you want to tell me what happened?'

'No, I'd prefer not to.' Wendy looked at the long fingers that held the cup out to her. The coffee smelled dark and strong. It tasted sweeter than she expected.

'Star anise, honey and one vanilla pod.'

Wendy chuckled, 'That's it, you are a mind reader.'

'I am good at making informed guesses. I might be a native of this land, but I am also a fifty-two-year-old wanderer; I'm streetwise, I read people's body language. I like to keep it real. It dramatically increases my own safety.'

'Well, I can safely say that this is the best coffee I have had in the US so far. So if the coffee is a reflection of your character, I'd not worry a bit.' Wendy inhaled the dark sweet roast again. Her stomach grumbled.

'Oh, I beg your pardon, how rude of me.' Randy slunk back into his RV and after a few moments returned with a loaf of bread and butter. 'Here, have some rye bread,' he broke off a piece and smeared a thick layer of butter on it. 'I was not expecting guests so this will have to do. We will get some extra food if you do decide to journey on with me.'

The two of them were quiet then. Wendy pretended to look across the river to the other half of Memphis. She had never realised that the city was like a heart with two chambers, each part beating to the tune of a different state. She observed Randy's deliberate movements, never in a hurry but always sure. He shifted to keep the fire going. He seemed quite unperturbed that he was tending an open fire in a public car park. She would be looking over her shoulder all the time, ready to douse it should police officers be about. He didn't look at her much, had taken out some tobacco and rolled a cigarette. He inhaled deeply, spitting out the loose bit of tobacco after the first drag. He too stared out over the water.

When the sun started to dip into the Mississippi river, Wendy made up her mind to trust. The M-bridge stood out starkly against the orange sky. She loved how the golden hour created the strong black outlines. Ever since Kyle, her aim had been to savour this moment each day. She was glad to get back to the routine. She and Randy sat without speaking for an hour or so. It felt completely natural. She recalled the inner voice she had heard in the Grotto. Let go now. So she had made a foolish error a few days back, but so far her time in the US had given more than it had taken. Maybe she had been reckless before, or maybe people on the whole were indeed a relatively safe bet. Back home, she had moved around amongst a tight circle of good friends. They had become her second family. Everyone in the village had known her, and she had known everyone. Small-town life had been comfortable; going into the local Spar for a natter, nodding her head at neighbours in the post office. At the same time, she hadn't realised how shallow her breathing had become. How limited her aspirations. But that had changed now. If she was not going to settle for the stale rut of past glory, she'd have to keep her faith in the goodness of people. A second chance at life was still beckoning, it was only to be expected that she'd stumble at times.

'Can I see your gun?' she asked.

Randy looked genuinely surprised. 'My gun?'

'Yes, your gun.'

Randy composed himself within a nanosecond. 'Come,' he motioned. He shook his limbs standing up, as if to waken them. She followed him into the truck. He dove onto the bed and picked up his pillow. Below it was a small hatch that he lifted. He took out a small hand gun and showed Wendy. 'It's on the safety catch, but it is loaded. I have not had to use it yet. But I do know how.'

'Teach me.'

'I'm not sure what you think American law is like doll, but let me tell you, it is nothing like in Hollywood films. If I start giving you shooting lessons in this parking lot, I'll be thrown in a cell in no time.' He coughed a wheezy cough. 'Would you feel safer if we locked it up and I gave you the key?'

Wendy considered the offer. It was probably better protection than her attempting to hold a gun, let alone use it. 'Can that hatch be locked?'

'No, but I have a safe where I keep the few valuables I own. We can put it in there.' He dug into his shirt and took out a long leather necklace. It had a key on it. He showed her the safe welded onto the floor of the vehicle, behind the heavy chest with his spare shirts and jeans underneath the bed. Randy opened and closed the safe.

'Keep the key around your neck until you leave me.' Randy smiled. 'And no, I haven't got a second key here. The second key is in a safety deposit box in a Memphis bank. That bit is like Hollywood I guess.' He grinned.

'Okay, I'd like to travel on with you for a bit. Where are you going?'

'Where you want to take me. I have no specific place to be.'

'Do you know if Cadillac Ranch is close by?'

'I know where it is, and wouldn't call it close. We can go there though. Why?'

'It's a place Springsteen sings about, and I wanted to see it with my own eyes. I saw a picture of it on the inside of one of his LPs and it looked like a cool place. Quintessential U S of A, to me.'

Randy moved closer. He sat himself behind her and wrapped his legs around her waist. Wendy stiffened. 'Relax, doll. Here, let me.' He started to circle his hands on her shoulders slowly, occasionally stopping to apply pressure when he came across a knot. He then worked his way from the nape of her neck down, vertebra by vertebra.

'When Teata passed you on to me she briefly mentioned your quest and the Springsteen thing. Close your eyes and think about where you are headed. Is Cadillac Ranch still where you need to go?'

Wendy softened under his touch. Randy was reading her skin and muscles as if they had been long-term siblings and touch was a natural part of their communication. He took liberty without ever crossing the thin line into sexuality. Her muscles spasmed, sparking a cold shiver along her spine. She gazed into the dying fire. 'I understand what you are saying. That's part of Springsteen's path, is it truly mine to walk? Randy, I don't know if I need to, but I want to find what's waiting for me there.'

Randy burst out laughing. 'Slam dunk! Here is me saying I am a practical guy, and on my first attempt to be more spiritual you put me right back in my place. You want to see it, I will take you there. Dead right. Let's clear up and get some food.'

Wendy stood up and grabbed Randy by the arm. 'Listen Randy, whatever happens, we travel together until we part, right? There is no promise in the hours I spend with you. You see, there's one other thing I came here to find. I travelled from Scotland to reclaim my own reflection in the mirror: an uncluttered image of the woman I left behind somewhere along the way. The woman before I met Danny, before I had Rosie, before I lost my mother.'

'What would possibly happen? I drive you to the Cadillac Ranch and beyond if you want. When you tell me to leave you, I will head away into the desert and find substance in my own company. It is how I have lived for over 30 years. You are a beauty doll, but I'm not changing the ways of my days. Fate might have thrown us together but my destiny is the familiar solitude on the horizon.'

It was dark when they pulled into Clarksville. Randy had been content to concentrate on the road, humming along to KSSN radio, tapping his thumbs on the steering wheel. The two lane highway was mostly straight, and it hadn't been long until Wendy had slumped against the window, occasionally twitching awake with her heart pounding. Disoriented, she had cleaned away the drool from the corner of her mouth, a clear sign she'd actually slipped into REM sleep. She had missed Little Rock completely, and although they were still in a river delta, the surroundings now boasted trees and the promise of mountainous nature nearby.

Not long after Wendy woke up, Randy had pulled over to a rest stop and prepped some food for them both. Spaghetti with a Bolognese sauce. The pasta was fresh, but the sauce came from a tin which he heated up in the microwave after he had transferred it to their separate bowls of spaghetti before she could stop him. Wendy didn't have the heart to tell him she was vegetarian, but at the same time the idea of actually swallowing meat made her gag. In the end she ate the spaghetti with as little of the sauce as possible, leaving the meatballs untouched. How she'd kill for a leaf of lettuce and a piece of cucumber. Randy glanced at her a couple of times but didn't mention it, until they were both done.

'So is it an eating disorder, or are you a very polite vegetarian?'

Wendy looked at her bowl and poked about it with her fork. 'I'm so sorry Randy. Here you are taking me with you as a grand gesture and the first things I do is bore you out by sleeping most of the way and insulting you by nibbling away at your food like some hyper-critical chipmunk. I am vegetarian, sorry.' Wendy shrugged her shoulders. 'I really do appreciate your efforts and kindness.'

Randy took her bowl and started on her leftovers. 'No offense taken doll, more for me. Do you eat eggs though? I was gonna make us omelettes in the morning. It's dry bread or grits for you otherwise.'

'Grits?'

'Wait, I picked you up in Memphis and you don't know what grits are? Doll, you are in for a treat. I happen to make the best breakfast grits west of Nashville.' He cleared away their bowls and rolled a cigarette. He kicked off his boots and moved over to the bed. He opened a map and patted it flat. Then he motioned, 'Come Wendy, I'll show you where we are.'

Wendy lay down on her belly and looked at the map. Randy tapped on it and explained. 'The I40 runs all the way from the east to the west coast. At some point near Oklahoma the old route 66 joins it. We are doing this section. We are pulled over here because tomorrow, I will teach you how to use a gun.'

Wendy looked sideways but saw no inkling of irony on Randy's face. 'I know what I said, but I don't need to learn. I would never be able to shoot anything alive.'

Randy pulled himself into a seated position and held out his hand. Wendy took it and let herself be dragged next to him. He wiped away some strands of her hair that had come untangled from the loose bun she had hastily scraped together. 'Wendy, doll, you are a woman on your own in America. You take rides with folks you do not know. You must have an angel on your shoulder to have come this far without getting really hurt. Do yourself a favour; learn how to shoot.'

'What's the point? I'm a tourist, I can't walk into a store and buy a gun just like that.'

'You'd be surprised doll. You'd be surprised. The law and reality are two very different things. You don't need a licence to buy a gun here, and we can walk into a store tomorrow and get you one right there and then.'

Wendy turned in towards Randy and thumped him on the chest. 'Be that as it may, I have absolutely no wish to carry a weapon.'

'Controlling a gun is a great feeling. Controlling it well makes you feel magnificent. You say you want to explore where the unabashed you has gone. The one from before. You asked me to teach you. Your words.'

'Your interpretation is that I am scared. Wendy paused. 'Well, maybe I was a little when I started out, hesitant more like. Cautious now, more than anything, after … well, whatever.' Wendy fell quiet. She hugged herself. Randy put his arm around her shoulder.

'Cautious, after what, Wendy?'

'Forget it. It happened. I was a fool. Ignored my instincts.'

Randy squeezed her shoulder slightly. 'You can tell, you know. Maybe it will help. Was it something Danny did?'

'Danny?' Wendy sat up. 'Danny, no, what makes you say that?'

'You said something about a Danny before, so I was thinking maybe he mistreated you and you needed to get away.'

'Oh no, not Danny. Danny's my husband.'

'I might not have had much of an education, but I figured he was. If not Danny, who or what else? Trust me, I won't judge. I won't think you stupid. Or weak.'

'I'm not weak, or scared, just lost. I am still in here somewhere.' Wendy outlined her figure with both hands. 'This was never really about some macho thing. About being strong. It is not about the strength to shoot a gun. It is about being true to my own path.'

'But the path is blocked if you let things fester. To see yourself, don't you first have to look the ghost that is haunting you in the eye? Take away the hurt, before you try to heal.'

'Not really a ghost,' Wendy sighed. 'I told you about a guy whom I mistook for a friend. Not Danny, a guy here, in fact. Only a few days ago.' Randy massaged her neck. Wendy let out a sigh. 'I took a ride with this guy. We had a fun time, he made me feel like a goddess. Until he didn't.' She didn't want to cry. She'd promised herself to take Didi's advice to store the memory away and move on. She thought she'd shed her last tears in the Grotto. But in the soft glow of the oil lamp, sat on the bed with this kind man, the tears came out all over again.

Randy said nothing. He took her in both arms and rocked her. She smelled the sweat in his shirt, and the campfire from earlier. Her howls came thick and fast. She felt stupid. He wiped away the snot with his sleeve. Still not saying anything. He followed her breath and then took over the rhythm slowly, but surely easing her into a less frantic pattern.

'About eight years ago, I met this gorgeous woman. Chrissy her name was. She was like a model. Legs up to here, strong shoulders, stomach like a washboard, long auburn hair, eyes to match. She walked up to me one day, when I was having breakfast in a service station along the I80 near Lincoln, Nebraska. I couldn't believe my luck. I might be a lone ranger, but I am still a man. We got chatting, and she said she'd walked out on her lowlife husband. She left her dog and all her belongings. Wanted a lift, and was I going anywhere. I had been pretty solitary for five months or so, and I offered a ride thinking, well hoping, maybe. Still, we made no plans, no promise. We had the best time for a week or two. We talked, we grew close. She opened up, I told her about my scars.'

'This one?' Wendy traced the scar on Randy's neck.

'Yes, amongst others,' he stopped her hand. 'Then one morning, I wake up with a gun against my head. She is sitting across of me, looking at me with this deadpan stare.' He paused. 'The gun was cocked. She cuffed me to the wheel, took all my savings, walked away. I watched her get into another truck only a few hundred yards further up the road. I managed to radio my location and the cops cut me free. Next day I went out and bought myself a gun. I swore never again after 'Nam, but she changed my mind. I never heard from her. I never used the gun. For years I felt stupid. Weak. I met Teata and she took me to the place I met you today. After I had confessed to her, she took me to the gun range, and I fired my gun for the first and the last time with Chrissy in my mind's eye. That was four years ago. Until today, I never gave that girl a second thought.'

Wendy took Randy's hand. 'Holy Moly! After that, you offer a lift to another woman with a sob story and even give her the key to your gun?'

Randy smiled then and said, 'You gotta trust completely if you want to move on. Yes, I choose vulnerability because in the end it makes me stronger. Like you said, most people are decent. Acting out your revenge and "shooting" the bastard on the firing range might give you the closure you need to move on. Strip off the you-now and get to the you-true.'

'He choked me, and took me from behind. I said no. But I had let myself be tied to the bed.'

'Well, well doll, I didn't see that one coming.'

Wendy continued more shyly than she cared for, 'I've been exploring my own sexual appetite. I figured it was one of the layers that kinda muffled the real me. I mean, I have never done anything like it.'

'Did you get off on it?'

'Nah, I did it because it excited him.' She fell quiet. Goddamnit. She heard herself say it. Her self-pity changed to loathing. In New York she had felt liberated with a new vigour because she chose what and where, and she was emboldened by it. Dwayne had blindsided her. Worse than him taking what he shouldn't have, was the fact she let herself be swayed to betray herself. Because it excited him.

'Don't blame yourself. I made a mistake. You made a mistake. Tomorrow at the shooting range, I'll teach you how to use a gun. Trust me. You'll feel like a million dollars. And you'll love the place. It's in the middle of the woods.'

He got off the bed and dragged out one of the plastic containers from underneath it. He took out a blanket, and a head torch, pushed it back and took out a bucket. 'Make yourself comfortable. I'll sleep in the front seat. If you need to go tonight, use this bucket. We'll empty it in the morning. I'll lock the doors. Despite of what I said, it is safer to stay inside at night.'

With that he turned his back to her, stepped out of his jeans and stripped off his shirt revealing a threadbare vest. Wendy noticed a long scar on the back of his left calf. When Randy had moved to the cabin and closed the curtain, she took off her jeans and top, and slid underneath the quilted blanket.

The shooting range was deserted when they got there. Like Randy had predicted, Wendy loved the setting. She hadn't realised how much she had missed being away from traffic and slow company that had nowhere to go. The leaves shimmered in the low morning sun that spread a diffused light over the low-floating fog. She saw some pheasants scatter away, crowing their rusty two-note crack. Randy pinned up some old tins as targets, then walked back to the shooting bench, and took Wendy through the basics of his gun. When he handed it to her, she found it heavier than she had anticipated. Randy put some ear protectors on her head.

'Finger on the frame, gun horizontal pointing at the target.' Randy handed the magazine to her left hand. She clicked it in.

'Good, now squeeze, pull back, and let go.' Wendy struggled to draw back the slide without moving the gun, so Randy steadied her right hand briefly.

'Hold your arms extended. Square up your feet, feel the ground beneath them and lean forward. Wrap that left hand over your right. Keep both eyes open, breathe and with a slow, steady squeeze, pull the trigger.' He quickly covered his ears with his hands and stepped back.

Wendy felt her head snap back at the recoil of the gun. The power of the release sent jolts from her hands and wrists right up to her shoulder. The gun buckled, but Wendy managed to hold on to it. She smelt gunpowder, and saw a speck of dust as her bullet hit the dirt berm that acted as a backstop.

‘You shot down and to the left. Beginner’s thing. Often people subconsciously anticipate the recoil and move the gun while pressing the trigger. Not to worry.’

Wendy’s hands were shaking. It was truly terrifying, but exhilarating at the same time. She turned to Randy full of what she had just experienced.

‘Whoa, hold the gun towards the target. Steady now, take out the magazine, and put the gun down.’

Wendy laughed sheepishly. ‘Sorry, of course. Sorry, damn, man that was ... wow!’

Randy laughed. ‘I told you! You want to try again?’

Wendy considered it. She would like to hit the target. And unlike gambling this was not a matter of luck but of control. ‘Yeah, but maybe can you hold my arms straight?’

‘I need to protect my ears. I’m kinda attached to my hearing. Wait. Don’t touch that gun!’ He reached underneath his shirt and started tugging at something. Wendy heard the ripping of fabric. Randy held a strip of cotton and started to tear off small strips. ‘It’s an old vest. Time for a new one.’ He rolled the cotton tightly into small plugs and pushed them into his ears. Then he made her go through the whole sequence again. As she squared up, he stood close behind her and stretched his arms alongside hers, his hands over hers. His mouth was in the nape of her neck and he breathed slowly and steadily. ‘Over there is the bastard who took what wasn’t his. Twice over. Show him who is boss.’

They breathed out together, she squeezed whilst he held her arms steady and straight. There was no dust at the far end. Wendy’s ears were ringing, even with the protectors. She worried about Randy’s ear drums. He guided her finger off the trigger, helped her unloading the magazine, then made her put the gun down.

‘I think you might have hit the target doll.’ He secured the gun, after which they walked to the tin together. The hole was unmistakable. The adrenaline was still pumping through Wendy’s veins. Randy untied the tin and handed it to Wendy. ‘Here, we’ll tie it to your rucksack so you can remember. This is how powerful you are. It is also part of who you are. All that power didn't blow you away, you can handle it. You planted your feet firmly in the ground and you breathed. And nothing else matters.' He slung his arm around Wendy's shoulder. She let him. It was a comfortable gesture. Their hips bumped against each other awkwardly. She hopped so their steps matched. They swaggered back to the road like drunk Buccaneers lavishing on the rich spoils hidden in the fo'c'sle, after having just hoisted the Jolly Roger on a ship they'd been chasing for months.

'We'll make a quick coffee, I need a cigarette after this, but then we'll move on. We've got a long way to go still if we wanna get to those Cadillacs by tonight.'

A Second's Glance

Lyrics and Music by Will o' the Whisperer

A Second's Glance

Lyrics and Music by Will o' the Whisperer

to listen / download
scan – open link – click on image – enjoy!

Cadillac Ranch

The shy sun lit her way to the front of the cab. Carefully, she pulled on the lace sliver of red. Lace! Really? Beauty before itch. And yes, she did feel beautiful today. Like a new woman; no, that wasn't right. Like the girl of old before she chose Spandex over Versace and with that, practicality over lush, setting the tone of her own sexual desert.

Randy's leathery torso was splayed across the mattress. The wiry muscles shimmered under the timid rays that seeped through the window of the trailer. She bundled up the rest of her clothes and opened the door. The cool of retreating night licked her thighs. She shook her hair loose and sat down on the step. In front of her, the Cadillacs still buried their heads in sandy Texas, behind her the interstate yawned, the occasional Kenworth truck pulled out of the layby and continued its long-distance trip. Randy had pointed out the sleeker, newer designs with the sloped hood lines, the rectangular headlines and massive air horns between the two exhaust pipes. The train-whistle blasts. Whilst there was something very powerful and independent about these giants of the highway, she failed to see the aesthetics that so excited Randy.

'Hey doll, sleep well?'

She turned to see Randy scratching his bollocks. He was himself if anything.

'Enjoying the sunrise,' she muttered, making a grand sweep with her arms. The sand was amber in the morning sun, the tufts of grass summer pale, even though the air was still cold and grey.

'Oh boy, avoiding the question?!' Randy chuckled.

She got up, and eyed him up: soul patch, moustache, one long grey lock that fell half over his eye. His skin showed his past: scars, and pot holes of teenage acne. He gazed straight back. His wanna-come-in-for-coffee eyes were calm. 'Yes, I slept like a baby,' she touched his cheek and smiled.

She shuddered when she thought back on the last time she found herself in her pants and vest, at early-o'clock. She kissed Randy on the cheek; obviously princes do exist. They arrive not on white horses but in beaten-down RVs and jeans that could do with a wash, smelling of garlic and engine grease.

'It is some sight eh? Those Cadillacs. The sun came up behind them just then. For a moment I could imagine them like dinosaurs. Like they were bones sticking out from the ground, waiting to be dug up further. Got me thinking about my own skeletons – if you know what I mean.'

Randy shrugged. 'I don't really do metaphor shit. All I see is a set of wheels, lost to the idiocy of art. But hey, at least we get to be part of it.' He read her confusion and continued, 'I've got some spray cans in the back. We'll add a bit of our story to it later. First, I am starving. And, I'm thirsty. I'll fry us up some eggs – you want a beer?' His hand lingered on her shoulder, then he disappeared through the plastic beads before she could answer.

Only seconds later his head appeared again. 'Can you light the fire? It's a nice day for some outdoor cooking.' He held out a few logs; she took them. Like she knew what to do next.

'Really, what is a pretty gal like you doing on her own, if she can't fire a gun, and now can't even make a decent fire?'

'I never dug scouts, I guess'.

'Scouts? No doll, that is far too hardcore. Take one of my vests, sprinkle some gasoline from the jerrycan on it. Then construct a tepee from wood over it. Chuck in a burning match … On second thought, hang on.' Seconds later he tossed a tub of Vaseline at her.

‘There could be so much more use for that,’ he winked. Then he held up his hands and continued, ‘I know, you told me, it is fine. Before soaking my vest in petrol, put some of that on it. It will burn much longer.’

‘That sounds like scout wisdom to me.’

Randy roared. ‘Too true doll, too true.’

As she heard him clanging his way through his kitchen, she prepared the fire stack as instructed. She cleared the area of loose-lying trash. She found some rocks to make a fire pit, and followed Randy’s instructions. She struck the match and threw it into her “Pyramid of Amarillo”. The fire took hold immediately, and ferociously. She smiled: can’t start a fire …

Randy reappeared with a metal grid, a kettle, and a frying pan. She passed him going inside to fetch the eggs, coffee, and some mugs. She glanced at herself in the shaving mirror: tangled hair, roots too obvious to be mistaken for a fashion statement, smudged eyes. She liked what she saw.

Randy pulled a rock near the fire and sat with his legs wide open. He invited her into his leg-embrace and smelled her hair. She let him hold her.

‘You are quite something else when you take your foot off the brakes, doll. That waterfall of hurt was a raging mess, so much wilder than I had imagined.’ He paused and stroked the nape of her neck. He nuzzled into her hair and whispered, ‘What’s the hurt? How long back since you opened up like this?’

She bent forward and kissed him on his arms. ‘Is it enough to say that you came at the right time? I let my guard down temporarily. You gave me a missing piece, that’s all. And I’ll treasure it. Build on it.’ She stopped to move the logs around in the fire. There was a loud hiss of oxygen fuelling the blackened wood. ‘One day I’ll have enough pieces to make a better version of me. One I can wholly believe in again. You lit the fire. That’s all, stirred the dying embers.’

The water started boiling, and she poured the hot water into the mugs. She always got that wild-west, cowboy-explorer feeling when she drank from enamel. Must be all those terrible spaghetti westerns she used to watch as a kid, blue-eyed Hill and stubble-bearded Spencer eating beans from a tin. Drinking from bashed mugs.

Randy clipped open his can of beer. He started on the eggs, but kept his body pressed against her. It was comfortable, this moment of lingering.

'Take the label off, and open that can of beans. We'll cook it in the tin.' He slid a pocket knife over her shoulder. She sure was getting the full western treatment. Behind them, the highway shuddered to life as trucks that had spent the night parked near them revved up and slowly pulled out. She wondered where she'd go after this. Her return journey was beckoning. She sank back into Randy's chest and decided to worry later.

He heaved as he caught up with her. 'Maybe I should go easy on those cigs after all. That was some sprint.'

Ha! She smiled and laid back on the hood of the nearest up-arsed car. The sun was hot on her skin. She bathed in the light, the hot cool steel in her back. She closed her eyes and spread her arms. Randy whistled through his teeth.

'That's some car mechanic's dream picture right there doll. I got an idea. Trust me.' He dumped the spray cans from his shirt, and shook them. 'Take off your top, and them jeans. Keep your panties on if you want. There's not that much fabric in them anyway.'

She considered the idea. Was she ready to once again go along with some sort of male fantasy? Or did she owe it to herself not to? 'What's your idea?'

'It's a rites of passage to leave your marks on these cars. That's what all that mess is; empty spray cans of visitors. We will do a bit more. Not just leave our signature. I'll make you disappear into the car. You and the car, blending together.'

'Don't need to be naked for that, do I?'

'Clothes will be too prudish. Not exciting. Like your old life. Throw them off! Live. Be naked. Be free.'

'Ah, like a metaphor?'

He grinned.

'I don't want some dude wanking off over me though. It's gross and demeaning.'

'Your limbs are so beautiful, the curves, I promise you it is going to be art.'

'So, I can do you too?'

Randy didn't flinch and stepped out of his jeans in a breath. 'Why don't you start on me?'

He pulled himself up on the angled tail fin and morphed onto the car. One leg squeezed into the seats, he leant into the car. He held his T-shirt over his eyes, nose and mouth. 'Make me roar!'

'Will it come off?' she hesitated.

'Eventually, sure. I got some white spirit too, somewhere in the back of the truck. Another reason to take off our clothes, eh?' The bile of a slight panic rose up, but she swallowed it back down. He was volunteering. It didn't mean she had to go through with it. She shook the yellow and sprayed her first line. Randy looked at her as she concentrated on his torso. She marvelled at his ease in his own skin, wondering whether he'd always been like that. She could see his ribs, the leather of working shirtless on menial jobs. She picked up the green.

When she stepped back to admire her work, the sun was out, adding a golden hue to her twenty-first century "Van Gogh". When Randy flexed his muscles, the leaves moved as if a gentle breeze touched them. She laid her hands on his chest and felt his breath. He grabbed her ass and pulled her in and held her there. When she pulled away there was a line of paint on her shirt.

'It's your turn.' Randy smiled. She hesitated. He took off her shirt, 'Trust me. Anyhow, we'll use your camera, so you get to control who sees it. You're quite safe.'

She felt the heat on her skin. She laid on the vertical hood and looked over her shoulder as Randy took out the red. 'A field of poppies, intoxicating like you. Fleeting too.' He looked her square in the eye. 'I know what we said. But you lit up my night. Don't underestimate the power of a woman opening up. Like you did, not holding back. I haven't had that, in a long while. That sort of trust is intoxicating.'

She never considered that her being vulnerable, could be someone else's liberation. And suddenly she understood what "George" had meant when he warned that the iron fence of protection would impoverish her, rather than protect her. She closed her eyes and felt her new skin inked on her.

She closed the buckles of her rucksack and stared out of the window. After she had gathered her trash off the cab floor she looked sideways. Randy wasn't looking her way.

'Wanna grab a coffee before the Greyhound gets here?' She touched his arm lightly. She wasn't prepared for the sense of loss, so quickly after she had felt found. Randy's white knuckles told a similar story. He rummaged through his shirt. 'Here,' she helped him find his packet of tobacco and handed it over. He hesitated.

'Nah, I'll wait until you're gone. How long till the coach leaves then?'

She shrugged. She had no idea really. 'I'll ask the office.' With that she opened the door and climbed out. The station was empty. Not a promising sign. The streets were wide open and empty.

'The Greyhound doesn't leave until one. We've got a few hours to spare.' She smiled apologetically at Randy. 'This is not my normal self; I would have planned this to the T normally.'

'Ah, okay.' Randy fell quiet. He twiddled his cigarette in his bony hands. The silence started to thicken between them; the awkward what-happens-next moment they had tried to avoid by being clear from the onset. Then an idea struck her.

'You know what you said about the graffiti fading and all? Seems like a waste of a good moment.' She pointed at the one roughly-drawn poppy she didn't scrape off. 'Do you know if there's a tattoo place here at all?' She cast her eyes over the long empty street that ran along the deserted bus station.

'You mad, doll? A tattoo on that beautiful white skin of yours? You have too much class.'

She considered the compliment. What exactly is class? Money? Privilege? Luck? 'Class is about character. Character doesn't sit on my skin. It is underneath. My skin is just a canvas of life. It shows the journey I made; the journey I am making.'

Randy touched her brow. He whispered tenderly, 'Like this scar?'

She laughed. 'Oh, that's nothing. It is one of the many battle scars.' Randy looked disturbed. 'No,' she added hastily, 'not what you think. I didn't get hurt that way. I trained with some boxers for a while. Needless to say, my defences weren't always up to scratch.'

Randy grinned. 'That's where those strong thigh muscles come from then? But doll, tattoos, they're for lowlifes like me. For the lost and deserted. For men who wanna etch out some of their pain and make it visible because they haven't got the words.'

'Even classy types like me sometimes fall silent. I could write poetry, or a book about what you gave me. It will sound soppy. Maybe some will say it is romantic. I reckon, it just is. I don't want to lose it. A tattoo will remind me. When I die, nobody will know you, but your moment will be with me. When I was 100% at home within me.' She had no idea where the words were coming from. She had not planned this. But as the words tumbled out, she knew with absolute certainty that she needed to get that tattoo done.

'It's trashy. On a girl.'

'Well mister, you better get used to the fact you offered your place up to real trash these last few nights. Hit the gas.'

A muscled beardy guy sat on a stool outside the Music Box Art Studio. His arms and neck were a brightly coloured canvas of dragons and roses. He wore an immaculate vest and tie. Randy glanced at her, raising an eyebrow. She smirked and shrugged, 'Class is more than the outside. Let's wait and see what he says.'

Randy stopped the RV alongside the wall of intricate graffiti design. In true American fashion there was no unnecessary detail in the architecture. The building was a box. But the box was purple! The straight violet pattern on the façade had an Art Nouveau quality to it. It gave the building an artificial sense of depth. In the round window with a stained-glass tree of life, flashed a bright neon sign stating the shop was indeed 'open'. Sunbeams radiated around the window. The massive dragon on the edge of the rooftop seemed out of place, or at least inappropriate in this mix of quasi-intellectual iconography.

She got out of the cab as Randy drove the RV round the back to park. Mr beardy got up lazily and addressed her with a drawl, 'Howdy.' All her childhood cartoons flashed in front of her eyes at once, but she realised he wasn't taking the piss. She saw his eye wander all over her. He spat on the ground. 'Are you looking for a tattoo?'

She was sure he thought she was some stuck-up prissy who was here for a fashion statement. A rich, bored housewife with too much money and time on her hands. Randy came around the corner, and Mr Beardy made a quick one-two. His attitude softened. He opened the door and invited them in.

Now it was her time to reassess her prejudices. She walked into a squeaky-clean room. Jewellery was displayed in organized glass cases, and the black leather sofa was simple, but elegant. The place didn't resemble a cosy living room, lulling the customer into a false sense of homeliness; nor was it a dingy backroom in a sailor's bar, smoke-filled and separated by a heavy burgundy velvet curtain. The whole place was brightly lit with simple strip lights. On the far right she saw a young girl of about thirty, covered from head to toe in tattoos. Surgical mask on, hair tied back in a bun. On the massage table, covered in plastic foil, a customer seemed to be asleep. The tattoo artist looked up, and did a quick once-over. She rolled her plastic-covered stool a little to the left and concentrated on her art again. The whirr of the pen-like contraption was quite hypnotic. Randy touched Wendy's arm.

'You sure about this?'

'Yes! It is only skin.'

Still, the humming of the tattoo gun did not drown her mother's words: tattoos are for sailors and criminals. You'll never find a job if you have a tattoo. In fact, you'll probably get cancer. After that, she had never considered one. And yet, here she was, at thirty-four, in what looked like a surgical operating room. Appearance was only skin deep, she had discovered with Randy. Not in her wildest dreams had she ever considered a man like this in her life. And now she was willing to get a permanent reminder of him on her body. She knew the tingling of his touch on her skin would become a vague film over time. She knew she would not be able to draw an accurate depiction of him in a police enquiry in a few years. But this tattoo would remind her of essence and kindness; of a man that allowed her to be free by giving her all of his attention, and cutting deep into her protective layers. True, she probably would not forget that memory, or even how it felt, without the tattoo. But she might forget to search for it in darker times. This tattoo would be her visible Control-Alt-Delete button. The reset button. The start-over-from-scratch-with-hope-and-faith button.

Beardy guy pointed towards an empty table next to the young girl. She moved across, and scuffed off her shoes before laying down. Beardy grinned. She blushed at her own betrayal of her 'proper' upbringing: never sit on anyone's furniture, sofa or bed with your shoes on.

'So, any ideas of what you'd want? Want to have a look at the catalogue? Maybe a nice butterfly? A hummingbird? Or a small ladybug?' She looked. He wasn't teasing her.

'No,' she rolled up her sleeve, 'I want you to outline this. And then some colour?'

'My name is Barry, by the way. What's yours?'

'Wendy.'

'Well Wendy, don't want to offend ya'll, but that is a red splodge. You sure about this design?'

Now it was her turn to grin. 'I can see why you are saying that. So how about this. It represents a small detail of a larger canvas – a field of red poppies ... Can you make it look like a poppy, maybe done in the style of a spray can? The original artist may not have been a Monet, but the meaning is real. You are an artist – go for it. Just don't make it so perfect I won't recognize the original hand.'

Barry considered her arm. He turned it up and down. 'Okay, hang on. Darlene, love, can you pause for a moment and have a look at this?'

The girl put her ink-gun down and scooted over on her stool. Surprise passed her brow for only the briefest moments. It was obvious to Wendy that Darlene had clearly thought Randy was the customer, and she only the trophy woman tagging along. Darlene took out a thin marker pen and, following most of the outline, drew an arty poppy.

'I'd use some watercolour effects to keep the idea of movement, of flow. And to avoid this looking like a child's attempt at colouring-by-numbers.'

She rolled back to her own customer, and continued working. Wendy looked at her arm. Yes, that would do fine, thank you. She nodded at Barry.

'That's why I employ her. She has a quick eye, and first-rate awareness of her canvases. Let me get some mineral spirits to erase this paint and get the inks set up.'

The needle didn't hurt half as much as she had expected. Barry reassured her it was the fine outlines. But, he did warn her about the colouring in. And he was right. She took a deep inhale and remembered the exercises from sixteen years ago, when she gave birth to her only child. Randy caressed her cheek, and she relaxed her jaw. As she let go of her unintentional fists she could feel the endorphins being released. Her body was taking charge and she settled back in the moment.

She had not been able to stop Randy paying for the tattoo. As the original artist, he had insisted on at least acting like the patron to the art. Now, as she loaded her things onto the coach, they stuttered one last wistful goodbye. Randy held her tight as she caressed his hair.

'I got ya, doll.'

'Under my skin,' she murmured. She let go, took off the necklace with his key, handed it back, turned around and disappeared into the coach.

Forty-two hours to New York City. With a whistle-stop in Philadelphia. Her swollen forearm had stopped throbbing. She took out her iPod and turned the wheel. It sounded like a Geiger teller. She scrolled through to S and went back and forth: Springsteen, Southside, Springsteen, Southside, Springsteen. She was going to Philadelphia, but decided she really didn't want to go home. So she might as well fill the last leg of her journey with the glorious sounds of the horns and the most under-appreciated bar-band in the land. *I know we had to try …*

Right to run after all was said and done

'ID? Here you go.' Rosie held out the fake ID boy-genius Finn had doctored for her a year or so ago. It had gotten her into any club in Aberdeen without a hitch. She smiled inwardly. Good thing she had brought it after all. Maria had woken up at 3:00 am that last night before she left, and grabbed her by the arm because she had suddenly remembered about the strict drinking laws in the USA. So she had added the fake ID to her travel documents. It transpired now that Maria was a friend with excellent premonition.

'I'm afraid this won't quite do. We need an official document to verify your age. Have you got a passport of driver's licence?' The woman folded her arms and leant against the doorpost with the confidence of someone who's got all night.

Rosie's heart sank. Shit, she was only half a day into her quest and already she had to climb hurdles. 'No,' she improvised, 'I left my passport in the hostel for safekeeping. It's my first time in New York, and heard so many horror stories about muggings that I thought it safer.'

'No passport, no beer.' The woman rummaged in her pocket and found a stub and some matches. She lit the cigarette. 'Maybe go back to the hostel and get it.'

Rosie dismissed the idea right off. Maybe she should just take a punt. In the end she wasn't interested in the beer. She had wanted to keep her questions low key, but really all she needed was the owner. She might as well put her cards on the table.

'Okay, okay, you know as well as I that my passport won't do the trick. Can I ask you a question? See, I'm really looking for my mother. I think that she worked somewhere around here for a while. I'm just trying to find out where she stayed. Meet people who knew her. Have a wee chat with them. Her name is Wendy.'

The woman straightened up. She dropped the stub, swirled her toe on it and took a step inside the door. 'Come in. Please.'

She walked into the bar gesturing Rosie to follow her into a small backroom. Rosie saw a desk stacked full of paperwork, a flickering computer, plastic flamingos, parasols, various tangles of coloured fairy lights. The woman shifted three boxes of crisps, pulled the one chair into the middle of the makeshift office and said, 'Here, sit down. I know Wendy. My name is Aimee. I worked with your mom.'

Rosie sat down, folding her hands into her lap. God, she felt like a little schoolgirl at the headmaster's desk. She waited.

'So, you are Wendy's daughter? My, I would never have thought. I didn't expect such a …' she twirled a ballpoint in her left hand, '… such an … unusual … uhm … you, I suppose.'

Rosie patted her Mohican. 'You mean this? You didn't think my thoroughly bland mouse of a mother could have sprouted a punk daughter?'

Aimee looked at Rosie. 'I wouldn't say your mother is a bland mouse, exactly. When was the last time you spoke to her?'

'About five or six weeks ago I guess. Not long before she left for New York.'

Aimee rummaged in her pocket again. 'Do you mind …?'

Rosie shook her head, then said, 'In fact, I'll have one.'

Aimee paused, shrugged and held a crumpled pack out to Rosie. Rosie took a cigarette and found her own lighter. She took a deep drag. Waited for Aimee to continue.

'Your mum worked here every night for a solid three weeks. Always on time, got paid in cash. Got on well with the customers. Good chat on her. Her leaving was a blow, and quite unexpected. Customers miss her. They opened up to her, you know.'

'I know how it is, a customer who is relaxed, opens up, drinks more. I explained that to my mum once, when she shouted at me for taking some free pills at a night club. Any-old-how, how did she seem to you?'

Aimee seemed to consider her words. 'Well, initially she was like these two people. She didn't say much about herself, was even withdrawn at times. I suppose that is what you mean with bland mouse. But it was like the bar was some sort of stage for her. She would slink in for her shift, take off her jacket, hang it up in here, together with any personal issues and then become this bright beacon lighting up the bar the minute she walked out of this door. She turned heads, an easy talker and friend of all.'

'Did she speak about home?'

'No, not really.' She looked at Rosie and added, 'Sorry. But just before she left she was smiling much more, even when there were no customers. She did seem more confident. Somehow more herself. As if each day she had to leave a little less of her personal stuff in this back room in order to make it through the day.'

Rosie thought back to Lea's parting message to her: *Go with an open heart. Accept the woman you'll find.* Her mum had blossomed here. That much was clear from the blog. Maybe it had been more than only that embarrassing sexual revolution. 'I read her blog.'

'Oh, well, yes ...'

'So you read it too. God, I am mortified.' Rosie hid her face in her hands. Other people would think her mother such a fool. Could she not have used her brain? This would haunt both of them forever. 'It came as rather a shock. No daughter wants to read about these things. I mean, your mother! In the end it got me a little worried though. Like my mother has definitely lost the plot. And then, well …' Rosie stopped. She wasn't going to let this stranger into her personal problems.

'She's gone a bit wild, right? I did warn her about that guy who took her to Atlantic City. Not sure if it helps but she seemed strong and happy when she set off.' Aimee patted Rosie on the knee. 'Don't be ashamed. So many of us would want to grab this kind of freedom. Instead we hide behind what is respectable, expected, safe. She's trying to live her life despite conventions she herself signed up for, for so long; that takes courage.' And when Rosie looked at her in disbelief she added, 'Serious.'

Rosie was not going to accept such wisdom easily. It wasn't Aimee's mother who was flaunting their sexual adventures for all to see. No matter what other women might think, or say, she had to live with the fall out. 'Do you know where she stayed? This hostel with Brendan, do you know where it is?'

'Sure, I walked her home sometimes.' She scribbled something on a beer mat. 'Here. But she isn't in NYC anymore.'

'I am up to date with the blog; I just need to see some of what she saw. I'm trying to figure out what to say to her when I find her. Thanks for this.' She pocketed the beer mat and got up to go.

'Where will you go?'

'Maybe my mother is not the modest mouse I had her down for, but she's left enough clues for me to have an informed guess at her route. Thanks for this.' Rosie stood up, took a last drag and stubbed out her fag. Aimee let her out of the back door after giving her a long hug without a hint of pity or judgment.

Rosie sat down next to the two bronze women on the bench in Christopher Park. So this is where it had all gone wrong that fateful day in 1969. It was humbling to think that the people involved in those riots had paved the way for the likes of Lea, and, she had now shyly started to admit, herself. Hate turned into a movement that advocated acceptance. She was surprised at how inconspicuous the four statues were. If you hadn't read up about anything and simply happened on this small park you'd only guess if you took time to observe the statues closely, and even then, it could just be two pairs chatting. The whiteness took her aback a bit. She had read the riots had involved many people of colour. Maybe 1979 simply was too early to also include race in liberation art.

She sipped her milkshake. She had found the hostel no problem and spoken to Brendan. He was indeed as friendly and generous as her mum had reported. He showed her where Wendy had slept, after which he had offered her a blueberry muffin and a cup of tea that tasted like weak coffee. They'd talked for about an hour in the kitchen. Rosie had ignored the stove. She didn't want to think about it. Brendan had obviously read the blog also, and again he too had nothing but praise for Wendy. But, just like Rosie, he was also worried. Still he had argued, Wendy had gotten herself out. Fit for living.

Fit for living, what did that even mean? Was living some sort of activity that you could train for? She thought about marathon runners who went out every day, a constant pounding of feet on concrete. After a while that in itself became common place. They were fit for running, but not necessarily fit for racing. It was the bits where the unexpected happened that made them race-fit; how they turned around the obstacles, the gale force winds, a change in the route, a tummy bug on the morning of the race; all these variables determined their success. Life happening, day by day, hour by hour was far from being fit for living if you never meet the obstacles head on.

A pigeon landed at her feet, seemingly unconcerned with her presence. She people watched. An old woman scuttled by, bright eyes scanning the street, tortoise pace, dragging a battered shopping bag on wheels behind her. The day was way too warm for her scarf, hat and fingerless gloves. A group of three girls swooped through the park, leaving a trail of bergamot, rose and lily of the valley mixed with sandalwood and vetiver. They were each clutching books Rosie noticed had come from the bookstore on the corner of the block. Two of them were busy arguing about the state of the world, seemingly having forgotten the third member of their party. That one was closely considering her own footsteps, only glancing up occasionally, living in her own world. She met Rosie's gaze briefly; Rosie felt a warm invitation to un-see the world. She nodded and raised her hand ever so slightly, mouthed, have a nice day. The girl nodded back hesitantly, but Rosie thought she saw the girl pick up her step. And all the while the businessmen and women in their slick shoes and high heels and iron-smart suits strutted past without ever veering from their trajectory. The boy in the shiny parachute trousers and immaculately white trainers, rapping and swaying along to whatever was blasting into his ears from those big black over-the-ear headphones stepped off the pavement to avoid bumping into the business people. The tourists huffing and puffing with unnecessarily heavy day packs, jumpers bound round the waist, passed the little park a number of times, their eyes buried into the guidebook rather than looking at the objects they were reading about. All of them had their own stories. How many were fit for living? How many were simply living?

Sitting in the noise and chaos of New York on her own, she began to reconsider her mother's story. The buzz of possibility these strangers embodied, the excitement of not knowing what's around the corner, the everchanging landscape of emotions, hopes and desires were catching. Some of the heavy mists that had clouded her thoughts for so long lifted. Feeling free was easier now that she was an insignificant face in the crowd. She inhaled deeply through her nose, filling her lungs, diaphragm, and belly.

Rosie stroked the scars on her wrists, which immediately reminded her of Lea's kiss. It had been an invitation to see herself without judgment or comparison. Is that the beauty and curse of the doubled-headed monster of love? If loving someone was liberation as well as suffocation, being fit for life was no more than a balancing act between those two, and you are the one controlling the scales. It was time for her to be in charge. She need not careen out of control like her mother had done, overstepping all boundaries of promises made, motherhood and decency. Still, for the first time in a long while, the urge to cut was gone. The critical eye kept its gaze down, the condescending voice was quiet.

She started humming a tune, tapping her feet. She grabbed her notebook and a pen from her rucksack. When she looked she saw it was one from the bar she had visited earlier. She started scribbling away as words and phrases flooded her mind.

Bruised and battered but recognising herself

'Excuse me, could I sit next to you?'

Wendy opened her eyes. Her head was heavy on her cricked neck; she must have been out for the count because she could feel a sliver of spit slither on her chin from the corner of her mouth. Not a pretty sight she knew from pictures taken during school trips when she was young. Momentarily she panicked; she had probably snored. And probably farted too. Then she shrugged her shoulders. Heck, it was the stage coach life after all. She looked up to see an attractive young black woman. She wore her hair in one of those loose, hastily scrunched pineapple knots that looked so hip and fashionable on everyone else. Wendy never managed to make it anything less than an uncoordinated mess on herself. One eyelid of the young woman was slightly droopy, but the grey-blue eyes smiled with a hint of a spring brook in early dawn. Wendy scooted up straighter. 'Of course,' she stammered, 'erhm, let me rearrange myself a little.' She had taken the advantage of the double seat as she boarded the bus. Quickly, she gathered up the wrappers of the salad, sandwich, and empty cartons of juice and looked about for a bin. In the vague shimmer of the sparse overhead lights, she saw nothing, so opted for her own small rucksack, taking out the sweater and her notebook. The woman waited patiently, even as the bus lunged into action again.

'My name is Fay, by the way,' the young woman said as she slid effortlessly into the seat. She held out her hand.

'Wendy, pleased to meet you. Are you a poet then?'

'Why would you say that?'

'I'm Fay, by the way.' She knew the joke was lame, but couldn't resist.

Fay appeared to appreciate the comment, and chuckled, 'I am actually. Besides teaching thirty-two eight-year-olds their times-tables and spelling. Poetry still doesn't pay the mortgage. Unfortunately.'

Wendy laughed. 'Okay, you got me there! So what's the poet doing on a greyhound bus at ten-forty, in … ehh …'

'Tulsa,' Fay volunteered. 'I was down there for a conference about poverty and language acquisition. I teach poor kids in the Knoxville neighbourhood of Pittsburgh. You been to Pittsburgh?'

Wendy nodded. 'I slept at the airport. Took an early morning flight to Graceland.' She had contemplated stopping at the steel city on the way back, instead of Philadelphia, but Liberty Bell and the desire to run the Rambo steps had flipped the coin – besides it was another Bruce landmark. It seemed almost sacrilegious not to walk the streets of Philadelphia.

'Knoxville is a particularly poor neighbourhood. Even with a lot of developments going on right now, we are noticing the income gap is only getting bigger. Studies have shown links between high poverty and school results. Many of my kids won't graduate from high school. I want to help close the gap; seems it is a long-term struggle.' Fay fidgeted with the frayed edge of her denim jacket. 'But enough of the boring professional bullshit already. To lift my professional gloom, I stayed on a bit for the open mic at the Gypsy Café House.'

'Ah, I see. Grabbed some late-night glory. So you are on your way to Pittsburgh?'

'Yes, you?'

'Newark ultimately, I'm supposed to catch a plane. Back home.' Wendy felt the nausea rise as she imagined going back. These past five weeks had flown by, and she had started to feel her young blood rush again. Her skin felt youthful, not just where she could feel the sting of her tattoo. But all over. She had started to notice small things around her, and found joy in them. Cracks in the pavement were a source of artistic potential rather than an ankle-breaking nuisance. The way the light changes throughout the day, and cuts out the silhouettes of buildings in the glamour of the golden hour, amazed her each day; she loved watching the sunset. The shifts in tints brought a calm that didn't sedate but invigorated. She felt like a blinkered horse that had sniffed the open prairies but was now coaxed back to the stables and the oval racetrack. She'd stretched her legs, and felt great. Would she be able to keep that sense of free-roaming after she returned to Aberdeen?

'You don't seem all too sure about it.'

'I know – I don't, do I?' Wendy shivered involuntarily. These Americans with their obsession with the AC. She put on her thin sweater, but knew that she was facing a cold night without her fleecy top. The fleecy top that was rolled up in her backpack in the hold. Randy had tried to warn her, but she figured, in the dazzling Amarillo heat as she left, that a jumper would be enough.

'You cold? Here, I brought a blanket. You're not the first Greyhound tourist that gets caught out without a blanket. I should start selling blankets at major stops – I'd make a killing.'

Wendy hesitated. The offer was kind, but she barely knew this person. Still, the night was long, and a bit of warmth would probably help her to sleep. She heard Randy's warm voice admonishing her about trust without reservation. 'Thanks, that would be lovely.'

Fay spread the blanket out over the both of them, pushed the back of the seat as low as it would go and said, 'Lovely,' then winked. 'Seeing as I am just over twenty-four hours from home, you've got plenty of time to tell me all about what's not to like about going back to your home, and what you've been up to here. For now, let's catch some sleep.'

They had a two-and-a-half-hour layover in St Louis, so plenty time to get some movement back in her legs. Danny could sleep anywhere; it was one of the things she was secretly jealous of. Hard sweaty seats at an odd angle with little-to-no headrests would not have done to his body what it did to hers. Fay took her by the arm.

'Come on then, let's get to the Arch and down to the river.'

Wendy couldn't help but immediately sing that line in her head, and it seemed so fitting for how she felt. 'Do you have dreams, Fay?'

'Dreams? So many I need three lives to make 'm all come true.'

'I used to be like that. And then, I don't know, I slipped into a version of me that stopped dreaming them. Funny how you don't really notice until it is way too late.'

'Whoa… woke up feeling down, did we? Hang on, let's get some coffee and something to eat. You'll feel better with some sugar in you.'

They found a Starbucks along the way. Wendy liked Starbucks. So far it was the only place she'd been able to buy a decent cup of coffee. Asking for a double shot solved the problem of watery mud other places put in front of her. She was glad too with the healthier food option; the bus station's supply of crisps, chocolate bars, and various meat products had looked far from enticing, and definitely heart attack-inducing.

'So, those dreams then, when, or why did you lose them?' The arch rose majestically over Fay. The grass around them was filled with young people, whose carefree laughter added to the good vibes around them. Wendy spotted a small group in a heated debate over what seemed a game of chess. The two players were stoically peering at the board, but their friends around them clearly had their own opinions on the next moves. The player with the white pieces was an older woman, a headscarf in rainbow colours wrapped loosely around her head. Wendy registered a gut response and wondered whether there was any hair underneath. Her face looked healthy enough, and not puffy. The woman moved her knight into position, hovering at first, then letting out a small snigger, and gently putting the piece down. The others exploded in hoops of agreement and high fives. The young male peered over his sunshades, a smile appearing on his face. Slowly, he put his index finger on his king and with a nod, pushed it onto its side. The two players shook hands amicably and a scuffle ensued for another game with different players.

As they watched the scuffle for the next chess game, Wendy thought about Fay's earlier question; when exactly did she let the dreams fade away? Fay seemed comfortable in the silence. Good teacher practice to wait for answers. 'I don't even know if there was any specific time. It is just that I woke up one day and my world didn't make sense any longer. Days started to feel like ill-fitting boots that give you blisters, but that you won't chuck because you've worked so hard to buy them in the first place.' She considered the many years of relative comfort she had lived. They weren't rich but Danny's job made them comfortable enough not to have to worry about where the next washing machine would come from, should it break down. 'Sometimes I wonder if I am just spoiled, and this restlessness is nothing more than a sign of a good life. And that all I have to do is get my act together.'

'True, getting your act together is important, but that is easier said than done sometimes. And being comfortable is okay. No need to beat yourself up about that. You are here, in St Louis, right now. Is this part of your dream?'

'Sort of, I guess.'

'Tell me about it. Why are you on a Greyhound to Philadelphia? But more so, is it important? Why?'

'Okay, one answer at a time,' Wendy sipped her coffee, glad she'd asked for *extra hot*. 'When I was fourteen I bought my first record. It was *Born to Run*. It was playing in my local record shop and the minute I heard it, I couldn't move on to the punk section I would normally head for, or concentrate on anything else for that matter. I still remember the shriek of desperation in the saxophone and the howl that ended the song.'

'*Jungleland?*'

Wendy looked at Fay. 'Ehrm, yes. You know Springsteen?'

It was Fay's turn to take a long sip of her Latte and look across the water quietly. 'Yes, my mother's a fan. When I was nine she sat me down in front of the record player. Gave me a cup of warm barley milk and a piece of banana bread and hushed me. She told me that she wanted me to sit quiet, close my eyes, and just listen. This, she swore, is the most important song you'll ever need to know. And then she played Thunder Road. So yeah, I know Springsteen.'

'I like your mother. You know a spooky thing? Before I left Scotland, I highlighted the Thunder Road lyrics on the album and wrote a note for my girl. It said: *This song will change your life*. Imagine that.' Wendy smiled at Fay. 'So anyway, that afternoon, in the shop, I didn't even listen to any of the other songs. I went up to the counter and asked for the record. When the girl flashed the cover at me, and I saw Bruce and Clarence I fell in love. Not with the music – I hadn't heard more than a sax solo and a howl – just with everything that cover promised. I raced home and played the album. And promised myself that one day I would go to New Jersey and ride my car with the windows rolled down and the wind in my hair. It took me twenty years.'

'So that dream did come true?'

'I guess that bit did, now you say it like that. I found so much more once I got here. The search for real love crashed at sixteen, motherhood came at seventeen, curtailing the grand plans of adventure and exploration. And that was all fine, because I really love my little girl, and the boy that got me pregnant stayed, and is a good guy. God, that sounds so much like middle-class white privilege.'

'You make the privilege sound like a prison sentence. Something to be ashamed of. Don't be ashamed! Be grateful for it. It's not your fault that you were lucky in life. Others might not be so lucky, but that doesn't mean you can't have issues. Come!'

Wendy looked up at Fay, who had started collecting their stuff in the bag. Not following her didn't seem to be an option.

'Come, we'll talk as we go up the arch. Sometimes being above things clears the mind. We should just have enough time before we set off again.'

Fay, Wendy, and three full-fat Americans were squeezed into the rickety orb. As it hiccupped its way up the steep legs, Wendy closed her eyes to the nausea of the movement and was glad there was no way to look outside whilst they were travelling. The sliding exit came as a relief and with a rush of fresher and welcome oxygen.

Fay started up the stairs at a pace of someone who knew the climb to come was something to be accepted, and best gotten over with. 'Too often people cut you down for daring to have issues if you are not also at least rolling in the gutter somewhere with an abusive father and crack addict as a mother. Nonsense. The feelings you have are genuine. So you meet a guy at sixteen, pretty soon start eating for two, he sticks around, and without warning life has passed you by?'

Wendy decided to ignore that Springsteen bait, and answered, "Yes. I slipped into a pattern of menial household tasks and of practical wishes. I stopped asking for poetry, and went for Tupperware boxes instead. And I was not unhappy. But I felt something was missing. Then, I went to see Bruce last year. I queued up, got front row, and all at once I felt it. This black hole, this innumerable sense of loss, loss of … I don't know… spark …'

'Wildness? Unlimitedness?'

'I guess. Everything I had done up to that point was measured, responsible, grown-up. But when I looked in the mirror, I saw nothing.'

'You didn't recognise yourself?'

'I had become something I swore I would never be. Where had the wild me gone, the one that defied her parents, the teachers, the status quo? So, a wee while after the concert, I asked people back home what they felt I had achieved.'

Let me guess: '*You're a great mum! Look at your child*?! They used to tell my mom that, whenever she had one of her dark weeks.'

Wendy nodded. 'I asked my husband. I asked him why he loved me. He literally said that I was the greatest mother a child could wish for.' Wendy thought back at the skinny ghost that Rosie had become in the last year. She could feel the trouble brewing, but Rosie had closed off the door into her heart's wishes. Wendy was no longer privy to her daughter's private world, fears, and thoughts she had tried to foster and guard back in the days when Rosie looked at the wonder of life with open surprise and curiosity. She could no longer be the shield. 'Not so sure my girl agrees, anyway.'

'Cause that is what women should aim for, in the end? We should be grateful to be seen as good housekeepers, good mothers, excellent planners, superb lunch makers, dinner ladies.' Fay dragged Wendy over to a tiny window. 'There's the courthouse. Looks quite European to me; all our old buildings do.' Wendy considered the green dome, and the neo-Greek pillars. Funny how Americans considered any faux-classicism architecture as European. Technically they were right of course, but so much more distinct European architecture had come from it since. Fay went on, 'It is known for two landmark cases, both of which were lost. Firstly, a black slave's right to buy freedom. And secondly, a woman's attempt to register to vote. Both issues have since been redressed, but sometimes you do wonder how much further we are these days.'

'Thing is, I have definitely tasted it, that unlimitedness, here – these last five weeks. I have loved every minute of it. But I am not so sure I can hold on to it when I go back. I am afraid to lose the old me that has begun to resurface.' Wendy moved to another window and saw the Mississippi meander its way past St. Louis. A bulking ribbon of murky water stretching out as far as the eye could see. It looked languid and lazy like a line of slow-moving orangutans swinging from branch to branch. From up here, it was hard to imagine the swell and noise caused by paddleboats down below. 'How do you make lasting changes to your life without moving away from that which constituted it for so long? I know the native Americans have this saying that you can't step in a river twice. Because of the flowing waters, where you are at is in constant motion. Married life seems to be more of a lake though. You can throw a pebble in it, but the effects last only a few ripples. Then it falls quiet. And it is itself again.'

Fay had joined Wendy at the slit overlooking the river. 'Don't consider life as an outside force that brings liberation, fulfilment, only if it flows. That's the Nomad way. Constant changes of what's around you is not living.'

Wendy was intrigued where this would go. 'So I should just stay put and take life as it comes?'

Fay shook her head. 'Absorbing and changing with the surroundings without making shifts inside, you mean? That would be the chameleon way, like basking in the sun and changing only skin deep. No, you are doing the right thing. See the world, change perspective, and figure out how to find new life on the well-trodden paths. Travel beyond what is comfortable to change something deep within. That's the pilgrim way.'

Wendy looked at Fay. How did someone so young come up with all this?

Fay continued. 'Don't get me wrong. I'm not telling you to be on the road for the rest of your life. The journey can be in the mind also. Just be a pilgrim. That is when you'll continue to find bewilderment.' Fay took Wendy's hand and squeezed it. The river rolled on below. Fay checked her watch. 'Shit, we gotta run!'

Wendy looked at her watch too. They had seven minutes to get back. They would never make it. All her belongings were on that bus. She couldn't miss it. As she sprinted after Fay, Wendy cursed herself. By now she should know better than ever leaving her stuff anywhere but on her back. Fay and Wendy rushed past the people and jumped the queue for the first pod down. The four-minute ride seemed to last forever. Fay and Wendy sprinted out of the building. 'I know a quicker route!' Fay sprinted off. Wendy followed blindly. Soon they saw the junction to the bus station. Slowly the nose of a coach became visible.

'Noooo!' Wendy heard the shrill panic in her own voice. A long line of funeral cars arrived at the junction from the other side. The coach held back and waited.

'We can make it!' Fay sprinted on. Just as the last funeral car had passed, she slammed the door of the coach. Wendy joined her only seconds after. For a moment nothing happened, then the coach let out a hiss. The driver had decided to open the door for them.

'Ladies, you are dicing with the devil. I'd have left without you but for paying respect to the dead.'

'We are so, so sorry,' Wendy panted, 'next coffee is on me.'

'You're all right. I could see you sprinting. You've got some legs on you. Like two greyhounds in a chase.' He chuckled at his own joke. 'Just find your seats and buckle up.'

The coach had gotten busier, but they found their seats still unclaimed. Nobody had dared to move their blanket and jackets. After they had made themselves comfortable, Fay picked a book from her bag and was about to open it. Wendy squeezed her arm. 'Thanks, that was … well, thanks.'

Fay shrugged and blushed a little.

'What happened to your mother, Fay. Is she still a fan?'

Fay took a deep breath. 'She took an overdose when I was fourteen. Too many *burned-out Chevrolets, too many wedding dresses in rags at her feet.* She really did try but, I guess, my mum was a chameleon that could never find her true colours. She never learned to become a pilgrim.'

When they got out at Indianapolis, Wendy and Fay decided not to stray too far from the bus. The driver winked at them when he saw them sitting inside the bus station. 'You girls have time to get lunch along the canal you know.' Wendy shook her head and showed the driver the Starbucks carry out.

'But we can move into the sun,' Fay urged. They sat outside on some steps nearby and were comfortably silent for a while. Some teenagers were throwing a football about.

'Fay, if you were fourteen when your mother passed away, who looked after you?' Wendy had been thinking about the grey-stained hurt she had heard in Fay's voice five hours earlier. She had meant to ask at the time, but Fay had been engrossed in her book, and it had felt like the conversation was over for a bit. 'I mean, if you don't want to talk about it ...'

Fay gazed at the boys chucking a football about. The skinny, straggly-limbed one with the blue basketball shirt threw a fifteen-yarder that went straight over the others' heads. Fay jumped up, ran towards the ball and caught it. She tossed it nonchalantly to the boy on her left. 'I learned how to play.' She walked back. 'I learned to play the system, so I could keep the apartment in my mom's name; got a job by pretending I was sixteen, and got on with it. I worked eight-hour shifts at McDonald's after school and ran some postal rounds in the early mornings. I managed to hold on to the apartment and pay rent each week. I then followed night classes and graduated from school.'

'No father about?'

'I'm an African American woman from a poor background ... what do you think? I realise I'm a stereotype, but that's that. Got on with it. It was hard work but I like learning. Also, I was not going to end up like my mom. In a soulless cashier job that couldn't really sustain the both of us.'

Wendy felt her own shame burn. That was a tough life. She'd have to stop navel-gazing and feeling sorry for herself. 'I hear you, and I feel ashamed – you have every reason to feel angry or resentful, and hard done-by. Yet, you are full of sympathy for my problems.'

Fay touched Wendy's shoulder. 'You remind me of my mom. I don't hate her. I don't even blame her for what she did. She saw no other way. It is not my place to judge what's going on in someone else's head or heart. Like I said before, your experience is real to you.'

Wendy was silent. If Fay could pick herself up at fourteen, surely she could at thirty-four. She had come this far; the next steps were only a matter of being truthful to herself. Facing up to the inevitable.

Fay continued, 'That doesn't mean I won't tell you to buckle up and just go out and fix it. Become the pilgrim, use the time you took wisely.' She coughed. Then she was quiet.

Wendy looked at the youngsters play. At their age she had been a mother. Learning about life had been quick and relentless. She wondered about their lives. Would they be as stuck as her in twenty years time?

Fay stirred next to her. 'I've been thinking about this for a bit.' She hesitated, and then opened her bag. She rummaged about, and produced a diary. She opened it and handed Wendy an envelope. 'Here, but you must promise this is the start of the pilgrimage. Don't be my mom. Go back and reconcile. If not for you, for your child's sake.'

Wendy opened the envelope and took out a ticket. Her heart stopped when she saw what Fay had just given her. 'I cannot take this. Were you on your way here? This is yours to experience, to enjoy. I mean, we have only just met – Fay, I can't …'

'Listen, I went to the show in Pittsburgh before I came down to St Louis. And cried my way through it. It was phenomenal. He opened that show with Jackson Cage.'

Wendy nodded. 'I know, when I slept at Pittsburgh to catch the plane to Graceland, I met a few fans who told me all about it. I felt so stupid I missed it but they told me to trust that another opportunity was going to present itself. I can't believe … it is too much.'

Fay looked surprised. 'There you go! It is fate Wendy. As Bruce played the first chords from Jackson Cage I realised what my purpose is at this point in my life. It's Rochelle, Kadeem, Razi, Tyrell, Velinda and all the others. I am going to do everything I can to give them a chance to never get caught in the rut of life. To rise above their stations, and to believe they can. I don't need to go to multiple shows to know what path is right for me. I did travel, got on that train – alone, my first concert, without my mom to share it with me. I can't even describe how every riff tore at the ragged stitches of loss. My students have many wounds like that. Being at the concert on my own, feeling my mother's presence all around me, reminded me of where I am needed. And I don't need another concert within a week to wallow in that epiphany. You do. You're still not free from that Jackson Cage.'

Wendy stared at the piece of paper. Bruce Springsteen, Lincoln Financial Field, 11 August. $77 – a pit ticket! The last day in the US before she had to fly back, and make her choices. 'Fay …'

'Just take it. Nobody wins until everybody wins.'

'1984, Born in the USA tour – wee speech before he started Born to Run …'

'Well, I'll have to take your word for that one …' Fay chuckled and nudged Wendy. 'Find out if love is real, Wendy! Find out if it's wild still. Find out what's back home for you.'

'You don't, I can't, at least let me …' Wendy began.

'You'd insult me for life! No way. I know that if you ever meet someone who is lost and trying to navigate the alleyways of confusion and despair, you will pay it forward. That's enough for me. Anyhow, I'm dog-tired from this last week. I'm starting to feel my age!'

Wendy burst out laughing. 'Wait until you get to past thirty!' She sighed. 'Fay, wow. When I started this trip, I wanted to visit Springsteen Mecca. I thought the road and everything on it was going to change everything. I was ready to start something. Now it seems to me that the real pilgrimage is right at the end of it.'

'Isn't it always?'

Fay hugged Wendy, and started to pick up her bag. 'See those kids,' she pointed at the boys who had stopped throwing their football about. They were sitting on the steps not too far away, laughing and play-wrestling over a can of something. 'They are the lucky ones. I suspect they might own very little, but they have each other to hang out with. Without the kindness of people, this world is a tough place. Be kind, I know you will be. You will make a difference, and that will be the difference of you.' Then she got up, held her hand out to Wendy. Together they walked back to the bus for the last stretch of their journey together.

Small things become big one day

Saying goodbye to Fay in the deep of the night had been warm and wistful at the same time. Fay had written her address in Wendy's notebook, and Wendy had vowed to write and stay in touch. Fay also promised to read up on the blog; another reader. She was amazed to find out that Brendan had been right. People had been reading her blogs, even commented on her posts. She was shocked to learn that the personal demons and adventures of a lone individual could be of any interest to anyone else. She was sure such diary keeping wouldn't take off, ultimately. Still, it had been fun keeping track of some of her more memorable moments.

Wendy had held Fay a little longer maybe than what could be considered decent, and had inhaled the ginger-orange of her hair. She'd not forget it easily. Wendy had offered to pay for a taxi, but Fay had reassured her that Pittsburgh was quite safe that late at night, and that she had not that far to walk. When the coach pulled into Philadelphia, Wendy's legs ached, her heart was heavy, but her spirits were raised.

Fay had told her about a few must-go-to spots. Wendy knew about the Rocky Steps, of course. She was a child of the 80s after all. Although Liberty Bell had been on the list, she hadn't realised why it was such a thing. Another symbol of independence, right at the end of her trip this time. Fay had also mentioned an area around South and Alder street. Apparently, it was some sort of street art project. Wendy decided that those three things were what she'd do before heading out to the stadium, and join the queue for the pit. The only thing she had to do before all of that was to see if she could somehow change her coach ticket so she could arrive at the airport a day later. And find a place to sleep. She got her bag from the hold, took a deep breath and started out to the ticket desk.

'Yes, how can I help you miss?' The old man looked over his square reading glasses, and did a once-over. The briefest of smiles flitted across his face when his eyes rested on her small fanny pack that she'd plunked in front of her. The station was cold and deserted. Despite the metallic tone of his voice, he sounded friendly and warm.

'Well, Jackson, I was on my way to Newark, to fly home in time for my daughter's 16th birthday, and I met this person.' The old man looked at her in surprise. She pointed at the name tag on his shirt.

'Is that so? You met someone, eh. And now you're gonna follow this fella wherever he goes? Exactly, where do I feature in this blossoming tale of romance?'

Wendy decided to ignore the old man's romantic fantasies. 'This person, Fay, well she wanted me …'

'A woman? Interesting,' Jackson smirked.

'No, well yes, a woman. But we're not, you know. She left the bus in Pittsburgh. Anyhow, thing is, she gave me a ticket to see Springsteen tonight. Here! In Philadelphia.'

Jackson whistled through his teeth. 'You sure you and her are not …? That's an expensive gift. Where are you seated?'

'Pit.'

The man grinned and then he slapped his hands on the desk. 'I knew it the minute you walked in! I saw that fanny pack of yours with those buttons and patches, and I wondered whether you were here for the concert. A pit ticket. My, that was mighty kind of this woman. Are you a lucky woman, or what!'

Wendy realised that she had once again given away much more than she intended, just by a little thing she was unaware of. That bum bag; she hadn't considered those patches as anything but decoration. No longer a statement, like it had been when she was fifteen. 'Yes, I know.' She was keen to get past the polite American chit-chat and down to business. 'Now the thing is, my flight home is from Newark tomorrow, but if I catch an early coach I reckon I can just about make it. So I was wondering if it is possible to swap this last bit of the journey.'

Jackson inspected the bus ticket she had slipped under the glass. He looked at it, turned the page, and looked up. 'Officially, you have to pay a fee for that. But seeing as you are here to see the Boss himself, I might be able to bypass some of the rules.' He winked at her. 'Which side are you going to choose, once you get in?'

Wendy was taken aback by the secret code of concert going this old man seemed to know. Her interest was now piqued. 'Why, are you going too?'

'Not me, but my granddaughter is. She'll be on Clarence's side.'

Wendy smiled. Every fan worth their salt would choose The Big Man's side, if the middle wasn't open. The energy between him and the Boss oozing down from the stage straight into the public, had been one of the most precious things she had treasured from the previous times she had been close. Also, when she and Sofia had been discussing US plans after Wembley, Sofia had said Bruce tended to notice people on his right more too. She laughed at herself. At thirty-four she was still such a fan-girl. 'I will be too, if I can't get somewhere close to Bruce, in the middle.' Jackson chuckled. His grey eyes seemed even softer now. Wendy continued, 'Is there a bus leaving around 6:00 am?'

Jackson ruffled his grey hair, and started typing away on the computer. 'There's one at seven am. Or straight after the concert. But they arrive only an hour apart in the end. I'd get myself a rest tonight.' Wendy nodded. As she handed over her bank card, Jackson shook his head and went on, 'You got a place to sleep then?'

This time Wendy was the one shaking her head.

'Didn't think so. Want me to help you with that too?' When Wendy looked at him in surprise, he chuckled again. 'I've lived in this here city all my life. I have connections. Here, let me make a few phone calls. A fan of Bruce is a friend for life.'

Wendy was embarrassed by the generous kindness of this man. Truth be told, she was very grateful. This meant she wouldn't have to go back to the station to find a bench to sleep on. After two days on a bus, a bed sounded like heaven.

Behind her an unhealthy-looking young man shuffled his shoes impatiently. 'Are you going to be much longer? Stop flirting with that man already. This is a ticket desk – not some speed-dating venue.'

Wendy caught a whiff of stale deodorant. Or maybe it was his unwashed hair. He was wearing a long grey overcoat that had seen better days.

'Okay,' Jackson scribbled down an address. 'This is Larry. His place is only a few minutes from the station. You can catch up on your sleep tomorrow. He'll have you for twenty bucks. He might even throw in a protein bar in the morning.'

Wendy could not believe it. How did she land on her feet like this? All these years she had imagined herself invisible. But here in America, not only did people see her, they also saw her needs. And then went out of their way to help. 'Thank you so much Jackson!' She slid her hand under the glass separating them.

Jackson took her fingers. 'Now, listen here young lady. If, tonight, you meet this gorgeous looking kid on Clarence's side called Billy, tell her granddad loves her very much. And to have fun and enjoy every minute.'

Wendy folded the piece of paper and put it in her bag. It was an easy promise to make. After all, what were the chances. 'Sure, I will Jackson. It has been a real privilege to meet you.'

'Don't get soppy on me, now. Off you go. Go wander the *Streets of Philadelphia*. I was born and raised here and I love my city. Being hospitable seems only right. The Boss loves this city too, so I reckon you're in for a great night.'

When Wendy got out of the station, she was hit by the warm breath of a hot day to come. She blinked her eyes against the blinding light, and decided to get rid of her bag first, before looking where the fun was. Larry's place was indeed only a few streets away, and he was kind and generous, just like George had been. When he found out she was on her way to the Museum of Arts only for the famous steps, he'd tut-tutted her a little, the grey eyebrows above his green eyes in a mock frown. But when she explained there was a Springsteen concert to attend, and just under 24 hours in this town before catching a plane, he had relented and accepted her limited, hotspot-only itinerary. In fact, when she told him about the streets with the art she wanted to go see, he was visibly surprised, and pleased. After a brief rummage he had produced a battered map of the centre of town. It was held together by Sellotape. The many creases of excessive use obscured some of the street names. It would do just fine. Larry circled her points of interest and drew out the route that would be most enjoyable for a mere tourist such as her. She had to promise him she would come back one day, to do the city justice. She asked him if she could take a shower to which he had replied, *thought you would never ask! That Greyhound sweat is clinging to you.*

The water on her skin washed off the tiredness of two days in cramped seats. She could feel her neck muscles relax, and the faint headache subside. She knew she needed more than water to feel clean though, but realised she'd forgotten to take her travel bottle of shampoo with her into the bathroom. She looked about the door and saw Larry pottering around in the kitchen. It was only a few steps to her bedroom, so she wrapped herself in a towel and dashed across. She dripped all over the threadbare carpet and searched her bag. In the end, she simply threw out all the contents onto the bed and found the wee travel bottle in the plastic bag that served as her toiletries pouch. It was empty. She had been too skimpy to buy a big bottle she'd have to throw out when she left; hand luggage only was a curse for the non-wasteful at times, certainly stingy ones like her. She had counted on shampoo left in the shared showers of what would have been her last hostel. But Larry was no hostel. She cursed and, after another quick glance into the kitchen to check the coast was clear, returned to the bathroom. It was the bathroom of a man. She hated the cliché, but it really was practicality before design all the way. A plastic medicine cabinet, and only a small shaving mirror. Toothpaste, toothbrush and razor teetering on the small ledge next to the tap of the sink. Soap in a small plastic take away tub on a rusty holder hung off the shower. No shower curtain, so no matter how she tried, it was impossible to keep the closet-sized bathroom dry. But it was all clean. And Larry obviously washed his hair. She took up the bottle of Head and Shoulders. Clean is clean.

She put on her souvenir Jersey Girl T-shirt. A little bit of a cheat – traipsing around America in search of all-things-Springsteen didn't really give her the claim to being a Jersey girl at all, but she was in the mood for the sparkles on the T-shirt. She applied some eyeliner that would have to last the day and night, and lay on the mattress to close her tight jeans. She stuffed her ticket, credit card – she wasn't going to make that rookie error again – a sharpie for the unlikely chance she'd get the opportunity to ask for an autograph, and a $50 bill in her bum bag. That should see her through the gates quickly. A coffee, some water, and a quick bite before entering the stadium was all she needed later on. At the last minute she remembered the key to the front door, and with the map in her hands and a see you later Larry, pulled the front door closed behind her.

The area around the park entrance was what she had come to expect of how American cities were built. Wide avenues for cars and high-rise buildings bearing down on the pedestrians. It still struck her as so odd, this mixture of clean-lined high-rise architecture in combination with the low, detailed, historical stone buildings that felt stranded like out-of-place furniture. The park was a roomy, green oasis in the concrete around her. She passed a class of school children and their teacher. For a moment she figured she could just plonk herself down, pretending to read, and listen in to this free history lesson, but the Bell was little more than a tourist point to tick off and she wanted to get to the Rocky steps. The queue wasn't too bad, and she was glad she joined it now, early in the morning, as already the sun was beating down. She settled for half an hour of patience and appreciated the sound vacuum that took out most of what she hated about big cities.

She had not counted on the impact of the Bell. The massive crack seemed such a fitting metaphor for how she had felt when she'd left Scotland. Like the Bell, she had rung out once, but the years of ignoring tiny hairline cracks in her life had silenced her bit by bit, almost imperceptibly; or rather, she had simply ignored those tiny fissures. The first chords on the guitar at Wembley had torn open the cracks – and she found herself unable to pretending any longer. She looked across the bell and saw a young mother with a baby in a sling. They locked eyes over the ancient yoke that held up the near 1000 kilograms of copper and lead. For a moment she and the young mother just stood there, staring at one another, but then the young woman pushed a strand of hair behind her ears, let her eyes glaze over, sighed and turned away.

Maybe she was just tired. Maybe she was just sad. Wendy suddenly could not hold back her tears. She didn't feel sad though, just relieved, and proud. Yes, this whole trip was perhaps a ridiculous excuse; she was spending money she didn't really have, and she had left no trace of her whereabouts to the people closest to her. She had not thought it through, but deep down she had known the only way to move on was to move way back first, and fulfil the promise to her fifteen-year-old self. The bell was tolling for her now, telling her to let go of self-pity. It wasn't the things she had done these past five weeks – living like a single woman, ignoring the ties forged for all those years – that had given her freedom. It was exactly those binds back home that gave her the freedom to be her true self, and to fulfil her life. The restrictions she had felt were of her own making, in her own head. She had always been free – she just hadn't believed it because her ideas of freedom had been like a skipping record, playing the same bit over and over again. Her life was not one scratched record; it was a whole collection of fine vinyl. A rich, varied, and precious collection, there for the playing if only she cared to keep the needle dust-free, and the sleeves at hand.

The revelation hit her with such force that Wendy decided she needed to write it down. It would be the last blog she'd post. She had time on her hands, an empty and protesting belly, and fire in her soul. Not too far from Declaration House she found a small internet café where she set to work. She ordered the usual watery coffee and a wholegrain muffin. She was the only customer at that time of day. Way too early for youngsters. And the place was too bare and pragmatic for holiday makers who came in organised coach trips. She set to work; her Rocky run could wait an hour or so.

Wendy cursed herself for not bringing her iPod. She had the Rocky Theme tune on her playlist but now that she stood at the bottom of the steps she would have to simply imagine the song. She looked up the 72 steps. Nothing she couldn't handle. Just as she was about to make the sprint up, a young girl with a skateboard turned on a boom box. *Gonna Fly Now* rang out. She smiled at the teenager. For some reason this last stretch of her trip was one long stretch of serendipity. Wendy took a deep inhalation and started her steady run. The music faded into the background as she neared the top steps. Five, four, three, she jumped the last two. She faced the city below her and raised her arms in victory. Benjamin Franklin Parkway and the Philadelphia City Hall stretched out before her like a sure thing, the sun beat down and all was perfect. All around her, excited tourists were panting and reliving the epic run amongst groups of friends. She saw what looked like a seventy-year-old Vietnamese man head for the top. She didn't remember passing him, and she admired his slow but very steady and determined pace. She held up her hand for a high-five to welcome another member of the underdogs who had felt compelled, for whatever reason, to rise to the challenge. He grinned and slapped her palm, then turned around and like she had done only seconds before, he raised his hands in triumph.

'Mum? … Mum! What the … Mum? Wendy!'

Wendy felt the shove at her shoulder before she had time to register the voice. She turned. And there she was. Her daughter! The asymmetrical bob had made way for an even shorter number-one job with a Mohawk cut at the top – green. Rosie's eyes were rimmed darker than she remembered them, and the nose piercing was new too. But this was definitely her child, in Philadelphia, at the top of Rocky's steps.

As they weaved their way to South Street, Wendy couldn't keep her eyes off her daughter. She seemed changed somehow. The outside was the obvious difference, but there was more. But the only thing she could think to ask was, 'How did you find me?'

'Read your blog. Every single entry. And so did my classmates. Brilliant move to dump your inner demons and weird sexual preferences in the open wasteland of the internet, for all to see! I mean, TMI Mum, really TMI. Mortifying. Deadly.' Rosie was gesticulating emphatically as she spoke into the winding streets they were following.

'But how, I mean, how would anyone in Aberdeen find those few pages I scribbled down? It's the world wide web, isn't it? Isn't that way too big to find any of my words?'

'Why did you even post them, if you didn't think anyone would read them?' Rosie stopped in her tracks and threw up her hands. 'God Mum, why is everything with you always so melodramatic?'

It wasn't quite the reunion that Wendy had imagined during lonely mornings where she'd allowed her mind to wander back home. No open arms, just exasperation and disbelief. She tried to take her daughter's hand, but Rosie shrugged it loose, and took a sideways step to keep the gap between them. 'You are not an island, Mum! The world doesn't centre around you!'

Something broke inside. Wendy didn't want to fight, on the streets of Philadelphia, with the one person she surely loved more than herself. But she had not come this far to retreat. 'Neither does it revolve around you! For sixteen years, all my hopes, all my aspirations shrugged back into the grey wings of the stage, for the spotlight was on you, always from the moment you let out that first wail.' She swallowed hard. 'You think you know it all, don't you? Tell me, what have you lived, actually? What roads not taken? What tears swallowed? What fucking rivers driven to, only to stand on the bank unable to move on?'

Rosie made an attempt to butt in but Wendy was not finished. 'Don't even try to belittle me with your barricade-brawling. You want to really know why I up and left? Here's a very brief low-down. I didn't mean to seek attention; but all of a sudden my head wouldn't stop talking. Every minute of the day, and night, it was just talk, talk, talk, in my head. And the only way to break through seemed to be to run. Then I met a guy here, and he told me to write down my feelings; it might help me get some things straight, he said.'

'Yes, that is why you have a diary. With a lock! So that if your thoughts taste sour, not the whole world has to bear witness to the bitterness.'

Wendy went in for another defensive reply, and then remembered Randy again, to communicate is to say less. She took a breath and took out the map. Just one more corner and they should arrive at South Street. She swallowed hard and asked Rosie, 'So talk about you then. Why are you here?'

'To stop you making an immortal fool of yourself. To get you to come home before you ruin it all for me, for Dad.' Rosie slowed her step. She looked about her and stared at the bright graffiti on the wall. It wasn't the run-of-the-mill tagging that defiled the back alleys of Aberdeen. These were tiles. A tapestry of thousands and thousands of tiles. Swirling mosaics of blue and orange broken tiles. She put her hand out and felt the smooth tiles, the rough grouting. The wall was topped with blue bottles and bicycle wheels. Faces in a naïve style, reminiscent of Picasso. Wild, almost crazed patterns that hinted at Van Gogh's Starry Night. The turmoil of a worried mind brought alive in colour, pattern, motion. She looked at her mother. Wendy had moved to the gate and was quietly tracing the rusted bicycle spokes. A twig-thin man shuffled out. He wore gym shorts and an orange cap. He stroked his beard and moved over to Wendy. He rummaged in his pocket, and held out a piece of cloth. Wendy took it, and Rosie saw her frantically wiping away at her face. She moved closer.

'Mum, are you okay?' Rosie looked at the man. He had deep blue eyes. But it wasn't the beauty of azure that was remarkable. It was the endless depth of them, a twisting pool of a dark past for which there were no words. He was still, simply holding Wendy's shoulder. As Rosie drew closer, she saw her mother sob.

'Ma'am, would you like to come in and have glass of water?' The old man didn't wait for an answer but motioned Wendy into the gate.

They stepped through the gate, and walked through a maze of walls erected of rubbish, broken plates, teapots, garden ornaments. Grotesques made from bathtub ducks. Wendy perked up somewhat and the first thing she said to Rosie was, 'Alice in Wonderland on speed'. She smiled through her tears. They sat down at a garden table. The old man moved away and pottered about with cups and a jerrycan of water.

'Mum, are you all right? I didn't want to be mean. I'm sorry Mum. But, well, things are shit at home, and then with you gone. It's kinda all falling apart Mum.'

Wendy looked at her child. She knew there was so much to talk about. Still, the change she had suspected – some of the 'shit-at-home' – could wait a little longer. She needed the last pieces of her own journey to fall into place before she'd pick up her role as mother. The path Fay had sent her on, found its fountainhead right here, as if from where, like a spring, all her soul searching had sprung. Wendy had not been aware there was a spring to be found. But she knew this place had shown her the gate to her future.

The old man put down the china cup. It was chinked, and even though Wendy saw a hairline crack, the cup didn't seem to leak. She noticed with a smile that it had a faded picture of the Queen on it. The Americans and their hunger for a bite of the Royal Family. Rosie's water came in a red plastic tumbler. The old man pulled out a can of beer. The fizz of the tab was his cue to speak.

'My name is Isaiah Zagar. I created these gardens and streets. Thank you for crying.'

Wendy smiled weakly. 'I feel a little silly.'

'No need. I know what happened.'

Wendy looked closer at this man. His eyes were kind, and his face remarkably young despite the white beard. When he smiled, his rosy cheeks and button nose gave off a garden gnome vibe, including the feel of pleasure and optimism. But his hands betrayed a colourful past. His calloused finger tips were the result of many years of working with broken pieces and cement. The man continued, 'I had the same experience way back, when I stumbled across an art installation that lies deep at the foundation of this. I get many people who come and admire my work here. It strokes my ego, I guess. Many more shout abuse at me. This is filth, not art!'

'Art is the gap, the missing link.'

Isaiah looked at Rosie. 'Duchamp. I'm impressed young man.'

'This here is Rosie, my daughter.' Wendy put her hands on the old man's arm as she corrected him. She could feel the bones through his fleece. 'She took art at school. I thought all they did was brutalist architecture, but I guess they teach them more thoroughly after all.'

'Question is, what is it linking? I think I know, but it is probably best if you figure that out for yourself.'

Wendy nodded. She looked at Rosie. 'There is so much we have to talk about Rosie, we'll have time later today. You asked me why I would spill my guts for the world to read. These past weeks, writing became a way of searching. I knew I was hurt. I thought it was because I had missed out. So I went away and decided to make a grab at it. Whatever ‘it’ is. I thought I had fixed the leak yesterday. But as I stood in front of this gate, it suddenly became so crystal clear. The root of the rot.’

Rosie looked at her mum. Mother and daughter had not spoken about personal turmoil in the past year or two, unless it was to call each other names, slamming doors. This dizzying, colourful place only added to the irony of misunderstanding. ’What is the rot then Mum?’

‘I thought I had wasted my life away, that I hadn’t made any difference. I felt useless. I had dreamt of being more than just a mother, Rosie. But outside, when I touched this mosaic tapestry of lost and found, I knew it wasn’t the lack of something, it was the overwhelming weight of it. I have been surrounded by many, many people I love; I love you Rosie, but I have been so goddamn lonely for so long.’

Isaiah nodded. ‘I started the first mosaic as therapy. Like Duchamp I try to be indifferent and from that absence of judgment I hope to create. It is the moment I become one with the process, and I’m one hundred percent in the now. The presence is present when I work. And that’s because I see each single tile, broken plate, garden gnome, broken bicycle for what it is each time I move to fix it in place. And I am no longer empty, or lonely. In noticing the pieces of trash I am seen too.’ He sipped on his beer. He checked his beard for any remaining foam after a few sips.

Wendy picked up the thread of Isaiah’s conversation like married couples do after a lifetime together.

‘Just there, I felt the presence of the deep seed of loneliness. I can’t believe I didn’t get it earlier. It was so obvious. No matter the people around you, if you are not seen for who you are, warts and all, loneliness just consumes you. I am not simply a mother. I’m not only a wife. I am a barrel full of contrasting things, that tug, shout, barter and plead. That smile and laugh. That are out-of-line, fiercely protective. That are older than the past and younger than the future. For too long I have allowed all of these things to be buried.’

Isaiah mused, 'Communication is all we've got. Eye contact, touch, what we do on a daily basis with these small gifts we're given, is what counts.'

Wendy cupped her drink. Rosie stayed quiet. They sat in contemplation for a while, sipping water, inhaling the quiet of the crazy chaos of the patterns around them. She could faintly hear the voices of passers-by. Then she asked, 'What was the art that moved you Isaiah?'

Isaiah squeezed his eyes into small slits as he peered closer at her. 'The House of Mirrors in Woodstock, New York.' He gently twitched his right leg, as if sitting still this long was uncomfortable. 'It has long burned down but through those windows, it was like I peered right into myself. I didn't find my path straightaway, but it was the missing link for me. Mind, that was thirty-five years ago.' He chuckled.

After all three of them had finished their drinks, Isaiah took them on a guided tour of his place. He told them about his wife and children, his life, his successes. But also about his failed projects, the hardships and his mistakes. He explained about the many community volunteers that were now helping him create the newer pieces. After two hours of marvelling over his works, they thanked him and said goodbye.

When they stood outside on the pavement, Rosie hugged Wendy. 'Sorry Mum, I shouldn't have shouted. But jeez, please promise you won't spill your worries online like that again. I am right here. I will pay closer attention, and see you. Just, don't make me defend you again like that.'

Wendy looked at her daughter in surprise. Rosie waved away her mother's quizzical looks. 'Leave it for now, Mum, I'll tell you later.'

Wendy drew in her daughter. 'Well, who knows, maybe I'll write a book. Or take up painting, or mosaicking.'

Rosie laughed. The tension of the first half hour had dwindled in the Magic Garden. Rosie's anger had softened, seeing her mother cry openly for the first time in years. The last time, Rosie had stood like a thief in the night, outside the kitchen where she had heard her mother softly whimpering. She had peered around the door carefully, and seen her mother with a fist in her mouth, pacing back and forth, back and forth between the sink and the fridge, the fridge and the sink. In the kitchen sink she had noticed two bottles of white wine. And assumed them empty. Wendy never did handle her alcohol well. Rosie had fled upstairs, terrified to see the "sane one" losing it. These tears now, were different. No more the angst-ridden hysteria. They were embracing her rather than pushing her out. 'You can join me at art college – just kidding!! Where to now? What's the plan?'

Wendy grinned and hooked her arm into her daughter's. 'Well darling daughter, roll down your window, we're pulling out of here to win!' She unzipped her bum bag and held up her ticket for the Springsteen show. 'This … is a ticket to heaven, to celebrate your 16th birthday. This is where the band is! This is where it is all happening tonight. I have one for you. We just have to find me one! So let's go down to Lincoln Financial Field!'

The metro to Pattison Station was clunky and loud, like any underground Wendy had taken in New York. It made speaking cumbersome, so she just held Rosie's hand and looked into the dark, as the train rattled its way down to the stadium. They weren't the only ones. Fan shirts filled the platforms and the seats. The nearer they got to the venue, the more she could feel that nervous anticipation tie a knot in her stomach. No matter how cool she tried to act, being near to her hero made her feel fifteen again, when the earth shook and all changed. It was a miraculous thing, this fandom. Last year at the arena she had felt she was continuing the conversation she had begun all those years ago. She truly believed he had seen her then, and that she somehow had helped him to perform even better, by opening her heart in the moment, allowing her own energy, her fears and hopes and dreams to reach out to the man on stage, where he had prowled across it like an unleashed Jersey Devil, with his battered guitar and working man's boots. Ridiculous of course, to think that he'd ever noticed her, and even more fan-girl-silly to think he cared. When she had tried to explain the conversation thing to her colleagues they had all laughed. Tonight, her Rosie would not need any explanation. She would experience the conversation. She was sure of it.

The parking lot was buzzing with fans too. Beers were shared generously, and the chat was all about the previous shows. They were strolling about the parking lot and Rosie clearly could not believe her eyes. Wendy knew the gigs she went to at the Tunnels were small, grungy affairs. Most of the nights, youths would turn up after the gig had started and walk straight in with their Vodka breath from pre-drinks. Here there were people out with their barbeques, the back of vans open to showcase a veritable bar. Waiting, waiting patiently, to be let in.

Unfuckingbelievable! What a way to open the stadium; the only guy to do that justice!

Man, Tougher? I have been chasing that for so long. He doesn't seem to like ToL – and then on Saturday, boom! Where did that come from?

What can I say man, it's a great night for it. Clear skies man, nice and warm – gonna be epic.
Bruce sure does like Philly.

Where you sitting? I've got pit tonight. Yeah baby!

Wendy's ears pricked up at this last bit of conversation. She turned to the woman who proudly raised her beer. She had flaming red curls in a ponytail. She wore a Giants' shirt, so was clearly a repeat offender. Better to ask than forever hold her tongue. Do or die.

'Excuse me, I heard you saying you had a pit ticket for tonight's show. So do I. But my girl here flew over unexpectedly, so I am looking for another. You don't happen to know anyone with a spare?'

'After Saturday's show? That's gonna be a tough one. Anywhere else, sure, ask about. But no can do here, I can't help you.'

Wendy thanked the woman and was about to turn when a big man with a Born-in-the-USA shirt asked, 'Hey, where is home for you? Where's that frolicking accent from?'

'Aberdeen, Scotland.'

'Did I not see you at the Giants' show a few weeks back?'

Wendy was stunned. She looked at the guy. Black curly mullet, definitely stuck in the 70s. Jeans that only just held in the bulge of his beer belly. She did not remember seeing him before, or even talking to him. How could he remember her? The guy laughed as he saw her stunned face.

'I'm not a stalker or anything. My pop's from there-abouts. So when I heard the lilt back on the Jersey boardwalk at Giants, I couldn't help but notice. My name's BigBalls, by the way. That there is Red-headed Woman. MaryJaney'sPlace and Magic Rat have just gone to seek out the merch table.'

'Pleased to meet you Bigballs. I'mma ...' Wendy paused. She was acutely aware of how corny Wendy would sound. 'I'mma ... Poet-down-here.' Rosie rolled her eyes, but when Wendy made a start at introducing her, she interceded quickly.

'I'm Rosie. Yes, after the song.'

Red-headed Woman laughed out loud. 'Hey kiddo, it's a tough life being the child of a fan of Bruuuuce.' She elongated the uuuu on purpose, and the response was immediate. From all around them came the echo of the name with the same long and lazy vowel. 'Why don't you guys hang out here a bit. It's some time yet before gates open.'

BigBalls added, 'We got beer and meatballs, and some cardboard and pens.'

Wendy looked at BigBalls, bemused by the pen and paper comment.

'You wanna buy, you can't be shy! Make a sign, walk around with it. You never know. Rosie, you look like an artistic person – go nuts!' BigBalls threw some sharpies Rosie's way as Red-Headed Woman reached into the car booth for a pizza box.

'If you get in, there's plenty space on here for a request too.' She smiled. 'Your first concert?'

Rosie nodded.

'Well you've come to the right place for it. Maybe your mom took her fandom a little far with the name, but she sure knows where to come for epic shows'. With that she turned to Wendy and threw her a beer.

BigBalls winked at Wendy. 'You done sowing your wild oats yet?'

Wendy didn't know how to answer this insinuation. What did BigBalls know about her? She started to think he was a stalker after all. She glanced at Rosie, who pretended to be oblivious but the way she was gripping her sharpie betrayed her.

BigBalls grinned, and continued, 'Poet-down-here, the name rang a bell. It just clicked. While tailgating in New Jersey I heard you talking to some woman about an online diary, so I looked it up. I'm interested in the web, and hadn't heard of this diary thing. Figured if I searched for diaries to do with Springsteen, it might pop up. A bit of imagination did the trick. But woman, wow, if you put a cover on them words and some cute bunny on the front, it will sell like hot cakes, I tell ya. Us fellas like that kinda sheet action.' Rosie cringed visibly now. Wendy took in a deep breath. So things on the internet did travel far further than she had imagined. Rosie was right, she had really not thought it through.

She raised her beer trying to make light of it all, 'Finding out if love is wild BigBalls, just finding out.'

Redheaded Woman raised her beer as well. 'Absolutely right you are! Why, if Springsteen can sing about it? And go after it, why wouldn't a young woman like yourself do the same as he? Power to the pussy!'

Wendy couldn't resist, despite the embarrassment, and retorted, 'It takes a redheaded woman to get the dirty job done.'

'Haha, touché! But seriously BigBalls, can we just dig deeper into this male chauvinist thing you got going on here?'

BigBalls leaned forward on his foldable garden chair. 'I'm not saying it is a bad thing, just saying it was detailed. Ya know. Not many women talk dirty like that. It is a compliment. Just saying, it's a turn-on.'

Wendy looked him up and down. 'I wasn't talking dirty. I just talked about having sex. Like one of the boys. The biggest revelation so far has been how easy men take down their trousers. Far, far quicker than any of the women I met, including myself, despite what you assume from my blog.'

Redheaded woman whooped at this. BigBalls was about to make a defensive move, when a middle-aged woman in sneakers, wearing a denim jacket and red bandana – and yes a white T-shirt – accompanied by a slender man who was chewing tobacco and wearing a cowboy hat, walked into the conversation. Redheaded Woman introduced Wendy and Rosie, and warned the newcomers they had walked into a women's lib encampment, just in time for bra burning. Then she asked if they had seen anyone trying to sell tickets for the pit.

'No, but the keen ones are starting to line up for the pit, so maybe it is worth your while walking to the gates. Just don't be too obvious, because it is illegal, technically.

BigBalls touched Wendy's arm. 'Didn't mean to make you feel bad. I am a traditionalist. I like it the old-fashioned way. Man woos woman kinda-way. But good on you for losing the sociopath!'

Wendy smiled at him. 'It wasn't really about wooing. It was about sex. They are not the same thing, are they? That's the thing. With the sociopath I still confused the two. I know better now.'

MaryJane'sPlace chirped in, 'Sex is about power. So if we want real equality, we need to update our dating rules. Women get to call the shots when they feel like it. Right, Magic?'

Magic Rat shrugged, 'Listen, I see four women here and two men. I know when to shut up and change the subject. Any guesses on the setlist tonight?'

Redheaded Woman called over to Rosie, 'You should make a sign for *Rosalita* you know, with a Scottish Flag!'

Magic Rat nudged Wendy, 'I guess you guys really should try your luck nearer the gates for the pit entry. Scotland is a mighty long way to come and listen to a concert in a car park.'

Wendy walked over to Rosie. 'He's right, let's get on this train.'

They returned the sharpies to Redheaded Woman who bump-fisted Rosie, and high-fived Wendy. Wendy took the sign Rosie had made and rested it on her bum bag. Then they slowly walked to the gates. Rosie shuffled a few paces behind her mum, looking straight at her feet. There was a long line of people patiently waiting to be let into the pit. The buzz of anticipation made Wendy nauseous – New Jersey had been such a let-down. This time it needed to be perfect, like her own first time. She wanted Rosie to experience the baptism from close up, so she would be drenched in the energy that lifts you so high in the stratosphere you really believe you can take on the whole world. She held the sign out so it was more visible, and tried to catch people's eyes. 'Tell you what Rosie, you should probably get in line, for when we do find that ticket. Hold a place for us.'

'If we find a ticket.'

'Show a little faith child! Things fall in their place, if the universe demands it. I believe this is such a moment.' She wandered off, leaving Rosie in line.

'Hey lady! I might be able to help.'

After half an hour of aimless wandering through the carparks, past the many vans tailgating, and even a trip past the closed box office, Wendy had begun to consider letting Rosie go in by herself, as all she got was apologetic shakes of the head. She thought about what Fay had made her promise when she handed over the ticket. After the Magic Garden, Wendy knew her path forward lay ahead unobstructed. Sure, she wasn't naïve enough to think that it would be one straight road, with rows of gleaming billboards plastered full of promises of penthouse glory, and diamond-necklace-sparkle for the remainder of the journey; a white line to the stars and untold treasures of the universe. She wasn't expecting the dry suffocation of the Badlands to leave her for good, sure to encounter again and again the steel thirst that would leave her throat aching. She knew she'd be veering off the road at times, and she knew the same pasts would be with her, arguing and bickering, but as long as she took care to leave them in the passenger seats at the back, and hold her own hands firmly on the steering wheel, she'd journey on with confidence. Rosie was yet to begin her journey. This concert would be the screen-door slamming wide open, the porch, the empty seat for an exciting and wild ride. There was nothing more Wendy wished for her child than the hopes and dreams of all that would be this concert, even though it would undoubtedly be mixed with the stark loneliness of doubt, and the devastating self-loathing that echoed in some of the lyrics too. The latter was a small price to pay for the sensation of being alive.

So, when she heard the husky voice say the magic words, it took a few moments to register the fusty grey overcoat and stale deodorant. He was leaning against a dusty pick-up with his hands in his pockets. He took out a pack of cigarettes and offered one to Wendy. She shook her head. She became acutely aware of how empty this lot was. She saw a few cars nearer the exit, obviously parked there for a quick get-away after the concert, but their owners were nowhere in sight. The glare of the asphalt in the sun hurt her eyes. God, it was a hot day. He let his eyes wander all over her; he stopped at her breasts, and smirked. He clearly had not left on the next available greyhound like his haste seemed to have suggested. She fought back the impulse to shrink back from his grey nicotine breath. He took a large drag on his cigarette, and she noticed his cracked lips as they sucked in the poison.

'What do you mean?'

'That sign,' he pointed at the pizza box card that hung loosely by her side. 'You're looking for a ticket, I might happen to have gotten my hands on one or two a few weeks ago.'

'Like I'd believe they were real,' Wendy replied, annoyed at the cocksure air that clung to this spine-crawling druggie. She was not going to fall for the same mistake twice. She now knew the drill: getting a feel for the person you're dealing with; checking out the offered ticket next to a real one, looking for tell-tale signs of it being a fake: the different ink colour, the thickness of the paper, or the smoothness. Many of the scalpers she had seen around before had struck her as dodgy second-hand car dealers, or market traders, but this guy looked like a real douche. There was an ominous need to him she didn't trust. Still, this might her best and only option. 'What tickets do you have?'

'It all depends on what you've got to offer.'

That is when the one crucial flaw in the plans dawned on Wendy. She had left most of her cash at Larry's. She had with her the one $50 bill, and half a can of beer. And a credit card, but obviously this guy could not accept plastic money. She cursed her sensible self. And her impulsive self. Surely Rosie would have some cash on her, but she had forgotten to ask. 'Actually, I don't have that much cash on me, I should go back to see if my, erhm, buddie has some on them.' She was loath to let the guy in on the fact she was here with her daughter.

'You mean that juicy youngster I saw you with over at the Chevy back in lot K. Is she a cub of yours? She looks like she's ready for it. Like mother, like daughter?' He took another drag and rolled the cigarette between his pale fingers. Wendy could feel her neck hairs stand up. She had not noticed him in the train, or back at the van. Had he followed her? No, that was ridiculous. She had not gone straight here. This meeting was just a fluke. 'I like 'm young and innocent. Makes me hard just thinking of it.' He exhaled hard.

'Fuck off, you creep.'

'Okay lady, your loss.' He paused to let it sink in, then repeated, 'I thought you were looking for a spare ticket. You want to leave her out in the parking lot when the gates open?'

'I only have a $50 bill.' Wendy started to walk away from the guy. He slunk right after her, breathing in her neck. She quickened her step. She wanted to get back to a spot where there were more cars. More people, more beer, more hoagies and badly-burned burgers. He kept pace with her. Then he grabbed her ass and squeezed it hard. Wendy stopped and tried to swing a punch at him. He caught her wrist and held it inches from his face. He pulled her in.

'Money makes the world go around, lady. But seeing as you have very little of it, I might be open to other suggestions.' He drew her in close and forced her hand down to his crotch. She could feel that this power trip was exciting him. She tried to pull free, but he grabbed her by the waist and pulled her in. 'Hush now lady, not so quick. Think about it, eh?' He pushed his cock against her and sniffed behind her ears. 'Mmmm, sweet like blossom. Your pussy smell this fruity too?'

Wendy could feel the bile rise. She saw a car pull into the lot. She should scream. The guy gripped her wrist real hard now. 'Don't. Even. Think about it. Let's go for a walk. We can get to an arrangement that will leave us both satisfied.' He wrapped his arm around her shoulder a little too tight and when they got back to his pick-up, told her to get in the back of it. He unhooked the corners of the topper, and lowered the tailgate. She saw a few worn blankets and a lot of empty bottles. In the far corner on the right, she saw a heap of clothes, some workman boots, a flannel shirt with a red tartan print. Next to it was a box with some camping gear thrown into it.

'What is this? You live in this?' Stalling, she should be stalling him. 'Wow, is this your home?' Do that psychology thing on him. Make him aware she's a person, not a thing. Make him feel clever and desirable. He pushed her in, and hopped in beside her. He pulled up the tailgate. For a moment there was complete darkness. Then she heard a ripping sound and the guy had pulled off a piece of the ceiling. Light flooded in through the roof of the topper. 'I like gazing at the stars at night, without getting wet or eaten by mosquitoes,' the guy explained, as if this was a romantic date. Wendy calmed her breathing and looked the guy straight in the eye. *All this power is also part of you*, she heard Randy whisper in her ear. Sitting on her knees, she could feel her head just touching the plastic window. Her hair crackled with the static.

'It must be amazing to be free to go where you want, like this.'

'It has its advantages.' He moved in between her and the tailgate. 'So, what do you say we strike a deal? $50 and an inspection of the old gear.'

'I haven't even seen any tickets yet.' Wendy's brain was racing. 'You show the wares, I might consider a deal.' *Breathe, plant your feet firmly. Tense your muscles.*

The guy slipped off his grey overcoat. He wore one of those fisherman vests underneath. She saw the hilt top of a hunting knife from one of the pockets, but no gun. He zipped open another pocket and took out two tickets. Now these babies will get you into the sweet spot tonight.'

'I need to have a closer look, and I only need one.' He held the tickets up into the light that streamed in from the roof window. She moved closer to him, despite her revulsion. The ticket looked legit, the grass green sections, that fake typewriter font. Right ticket price, including service fees, the Ticketmaster blue and yellow, a barcode, and the same purchasing date as on her own ticket. 'So what is the deal you're looking for? I got a fifty.' She rummaged into her bum bag and pulled out the $50 bill. She could see the number shift from black to green as she tilted it. She put it on the right wheel hub. 'Now you put your ticket on the left. There's a $30 gap between the left and right wheel hub. Tell me what extras you want.'

The skinny guy laughed. 'You got a nerve making demands here.' He fingered the top of his knife. 'But then I might like 'm young, but I sure do like 'm with some attitude too. First I want to fuck you from behind, and then you suck my dick.'

'Want me to swallow? Or you wanna shoot your load all over me?' Wendy figured he'd enjoy a bit of dirt. She never thought she would, but she silently thanked Dwayne for introducing her to words she never would have said before.

She wasn't mistaken. He got that hungry look in his eyes that she'd seen in Dwayne. Desire made him careless. He leant over to put the ticket on the wheel hub. Wendy moved quickly and grabbed his crotch as she manoeuvred herself nearer to the handle of the tailback. She slowly and rhythmically massaged his balls, feeling the jeans tighten. He groaned slightly. 'Well, well, big boy. Aren't you getting a little impatient.' Instinctively, she knew she had to make him believe she'd accepted the deal. She took his hand and slid it up her shirt. He squeezed hard as she started to unbutton his fly. 'Let me suck you first. Pump you up a little. I like a firm cock in my fanny.' She was a little clumsier than she wanted to be, but she needed her right hand to be right on the handle. She knew she only had the one chance. 'Lie down baby, lemme see how well you ride. It's been a while but I am getting so wet. She moved his hand into her trousers and let him feel her. She ignored his rough jabs and moaned, 'Yes baby, getting all slippery and ready for you.' Then she took his fingers into her mouth and sucked them hard. She gently pushed him on his back, and pulled his trousers down.

It took her less than a second to grab the ticket and kick open the tailgate. She pushed herself out and fell on her knees. It stung but she wouldn't let herself think of it. She ran as fast as she could, praying the line had started to move in. She could hear the guy slam the tailgate to the car, and his heavy boots hit the tarmac. She turned the corner and saw the line.

They were checking tickets and letting the people in. 'Rosie,' she shouted and waved her hands frantically, 'Come to the front, Rosie! The front. Get to the gate! Now!!'

Rosie was talking to a young girl about her own age, but looked up from the conversation as she heard her name. She saw Wendy wave frantically. She sighed. But the shrillness of her mother's voice convinced her. She hugged the girl and mouthed later. Then she moved to the front. The people looked at her but nobody said a thing as she walked past the queue. Rosie watched her mother sprint to the front. Wendy briefly looked over her shoulder. Rosie saw a man round the corner. 'Mum, what the … what have you done?!' She sped up, ignoring the disapproving glances. Queues are a law all unto themselves. There's an unspoken etiquette, yet very few actually break rank when someone boldly breaks the "rules". The nearer to the front Rosie came, the more she felt the annoyance. A bloke with a blue leather jacket, shoved her in the ribs as she went by. Another grabbed her briefly by the arm and said he had been here a long time. Rosie ignored her embarrassment. She put her running mum and the sprinting man together. It looked like trouble.

As Wendy got nearer, Rosie spotted a manic grin on her mother's face. Trouble indeed. 'Mum, what have you done?!'

'Rosie, come!' Wendy got to the front of the queue, and squeezed in. 'I'm soooo sorry. Excuse me. She dragged Rosie beside her.

A wiry woman with sleek blonde hair and a little too much eyeliner dug her nails into Wendy's arm. 'Yeah lady, we all want to be at the front. But here we stand in line, and wait our turn. So go back to the end, why don't you.'

Wendy pleaded, 'We'll go to the back when we get in. I promise.' The man was now calmly walking towards the queue, and Wendy sensed he would not be afraid to pull her out despite all the people around. 'Just let us get through the gates.'

Security checking people's tickets looked up. 'Ma'am just go back in line. Nobody skips the line on my watch.' The wiry woman crossed her arms and tried to step in front of Wendy.

Rosie made ready to go. Wendy looked the security guy in the eye. 'Listen, I know it's illegal and all; but my daughter arrived unexpectedly from the UK. I had to get another ticket. The tout didn't like the deal he got.'

'Tout?'

'Scalper, I think you call them ticket scalpers. Anyhow, I looked for a spare, and this guy said he might help me. I didn't have enough cash.' Wendy lowered her voice but didn't take her eye off the security guy. He took obvious pride in his position of regulator. His shirt was cleanly ironed, his steel-nosed boots shone, his hair slicked back just right. 'Anyhow, he didn't like the deal I offered. I left him the money and ran. Please, please. We will wait, once we get in. I am not a cheat. Just, you know, put a gate between us and that man.' Wendy pointed to the man in the grey jacket who was now only the length of fifteen cars away.

The security guy looked at the man. Then looked at Wendy. He raised his eyebrow.

'He forced me to give him, you know …' she whispered finishing the sentence with the gesture. The security guy looked embarrassed.

The wiry woman stepped up between them. She scrutinized Wendy and asked, 'Are you saying that man forced you to give him a BJ? And is now after you? Is that why you are pushing forward?'

Wendy nodded. 'I was looking for a spare ticket. He wanted a little more than I was ready for. I mean, you gotta steal and lie sometimes in life. But this time …'

The woman looked at the man who was heading straight for the queue now, and at Wendy. 'Are you speaking the truth here?'

Wendy nodded.

The woman waved some of her friends closer. 'Girls, we have a sister in need.' She looked at Wendy and hissed, 'You'd better not go back on your word. You get in, you wait.'

Wendy and Rosie were shielded by four women. The woman with the blonde hair turned to the security guard, held up her own ticket and barked, 'Hey, we are okay with it. Let them go in. They will wait their turn.' The women locked arms to form a barrier to hold the cursing man in the filthy coat back. 'Sisters take care of their own.'

The security guard hesitated. The impatient queue behind the women was concertinaing tighter together because of the sudden bottleneck. In a low voice he spoke to Wendy. 'Okay Ma'am you and your daughter go in, and wait right there at the other end of the fence. You only move on when I tell you. If you don't do as I say, I will contact my superior. And you will get thrown out. Do not be mistaken.'

Wendy shoved her tickets in the man's direction. He just nodded and pushed the two of them through the gate.

The women followed almost immediately. They filed past them, sparing them only a brief glance. Wendy mouthed thank you. The blonde woman gave a thumbs up, then walked on. Wendy and Rosie waited where the security man had told them to stand. The guy in the grey overcoat was wildly gesticulating, but the security guy swept him aside with one arm. 'Now look here mister. Whatever deal you got, you'd be wise to take it AND leave it. Or I will call my supervisor.'

'She's a lying bitch. She stole my tickets.'

The security guy repeated, this time a little more menacing, 'Take your deal and leave it.' Then he turned away and started letting in the other people.

Rosie turned to Wendy. 'Mum, what was all that about? You are not telling me that you … ?'

'Rosie, it is nothing.'

'Mum! Did you,' Rosie lowered her voice and whispered in her mother's ear, 'really? Suck that man's dick to get a ticket? Do I know you at all? What is wrong with you?'

'I have never, ever, in my life used my sexuality to get anything. But times have changed, I have changed. These past five weeks, things have shifted. You gotta live the moment sometimes. Break the rules. I didn't have enough money …'

'Gad, mother! Look at the bloke. It's disgusting. I don't want to go to a concert knowing you … How could you?'

'Shush. I didn't, all right. I didn't. Just testing you. I'm glad I raised you well after all,' Wendy put her finger on her lips. 'It got a little hairy, but I managed to get myself out of it. So no, I did not suck his dick. There's a huge difference between enjoying sex and selling sex. I wouldn't ever. Because whatever has changed, there are certain things I won't do. I have my pride. Still. But I needed to get away from that guy. So, I told a half-truth. That I learned too.'

Rosie visibly relaxed. Her mum's new-found street-cred bemused her. The non-stop stream of excited pit people flowed by them in a controlled and orderly fashion. She arched towards the place where they were entering the stands. She could see part of the stage. A fizzy tension was building up. Somehow, the energy took on a different quality. It was like the buzz of a gig at the Tunnels when the excitement and expectations changed a room full of strip lights to the orange dim of an underground den on a sweltering midsummer night, with fly catchers fizzing at the smallest touch.

Suddenly, a voice piped up, 'Hey Rosie, cool, you got in then? Why are you waiting here?' A young girl stopped next to them. One hand in the pocket of oversized dungarees that hung loose from one shoulder, she lightly touched Rosie's arm.

'Billy, hey. Yeah, my mum found a ticket. Don't. Ask.'

The security guard asked Billy if she knew them and when she said Rosie and her had spent half an hour chatting in line, he turned to Wendy and said,' Now listen here. This was a one-time only. You got lucky, all right. Don't play with fire like this, ever again.' His gaze moved to Rosie and lingered there before moving back to Wendy.

Wendy looked him in the eye, he was younger than her. He had shaved a small pattern in his eyebrow, and had punched one small cross in his right ear. He looked stern, but Wendy felt a smile under his strong words.

'Goddamnit Ma'am, you're one heck of a mama bear.' He shook his head and whistled through his teeth. Then he got a small toothpick out and stuck it in the corner of his mouth. 'Now you all walk on in, and you'd better enjoy this show tonight, you hear?'

Hearing those words finally brought it home to Wendy. She heard Randy in the back of her mind: *this is how powerful you are. It is also part of who you are*. She realised she might be powerful, but she wasn't invincible. The reality of how close she had gotten herself to real danger momentarily took her breath away.

'Mum, are you okay?' Rosie touched Wendy's arm lightly. 'You've turned a wee bittie peely-wally.'

Wendy swallowed back the moment of panic and answered, 'I'm good Rosie. Let's go in. We came to see the Boss, and I want to see how close we can get.'

Billy didn't seem fussed. 'I'm gonna see the merch stand. Wanna come?'

Rosie hesitated but Wendy regained her composure. 'We'll walk on in first, claim our spot. Maybe later.'

Billy looked at Rosie who put up her hands defensively. Wendy put her arm through Rosie's and headed to the field. 'Later Rosie, later, I promise – trust me on this one, let's get in first.' The pit was small. And relatively empty! Obviously, Billy wasn't the only one who ventured out to the merchandise and food courts. Everywhere people had sat down on the floor. Wendy stepped past most of them, ignoring the occasional disgruntled comment, then found a spot only two rows back, near the centre and dropped on the floor. She gestured for Rosie to sit down too. 'Sorry baby, please gift me this moment. I understand going with someone of your own age is a whole lot less embarrassing. But you can only have your first Springsteen concert once.'

Rosie shrugged. She looked at the stage, and the instruments gleaming in the late afternoon sun; the sky cloudless, promising a clear full moon that night. Two enormous screens on either side of the wide stage, the American flag waving on top of all the rigging. The people around them were laid back and the proud bragging rights she'd heard in the parking lot continued here on the field. The stands were empty still, those patrons probably enjoying the last of the sunshine and BBQ burgers. Wendy grabbed Rosie's hand and squeezed.

'Your first concert. Promise, whatever we talk about now, let it all go and simply be in the moment when Bruce walks out. Have you listened to any Bruce yet?'

Rosie rolled her eyes in jest. 'Mum, you leave, out of the blue, no warning, quoting Bruce Springsteen. I find a note scribbled above the lyrics sheet for Thunder Road. Oh, and Dad tells me about how you two met. Of course, I played the albums.'

'You did!' Then immediately Wendy added, 'He did? I gotta give him that, he was at Wembley, even if it was more for the popularity credits than the music.' She smiled remembering. Rosie had her father's nose and smile. He was back in Aberdeen, on his own. Maybe even worrying about her. 'Well, today is where the fun starts, Rosie. There is only before Bruce and after Bruce. Tomorrow nothing will be the same.'

Rosie looked at Wendy sideways. 'Tomorrow you're flying home.'

Wendy paused. 'Maybe, yes. But tell me Rose, what was that you said before, about defending me?'

'It's a long story Mum. Maybe another time?'

Wendy shook her head. 'Now's as good a time as ever. You came all the way here, and then make me promise that you'll never have to defend me ever again. What is that all about? Why did you come all the way here?'

'I got scared. Dad thinks you're never coming back. He's missing you mum. Then I was confronted with your blog. I had to get to you before he did. Mum, you gotta come back.'

Wendy scooted over and took her daughter's left hand in her right. With the other, she stroked the stubble on the sides of Rosie's skull. 'What for baby? Come back for more nights in the dark, so many unspoken promises, declarations of love swallowed, like they got caught by the nets of our teeth. Dad watching the telly; you skulking in that shed of yours, playing that goddamn guitar. Listening to punk music. I can't think of a lonelier place than home Rosie. Why would I come back? Why would I come back, especially now that I somehow need defending?'

Rosie looked between her feet. 'Mum they were calling you a hoore. Now I am not saying you are. But you are married Mum. You and Dad have been together so long. It's only right you should come home. Although, after today I don't know …'

'I'm no hoore. Sleeping with a man ...'

'Men.'

'Men. When both of you are consenting adults, that is no whoring. Is this a slice of the old "a boy's a stud, a girl's a slut"? Come on Rosie, we left all that behind in the 60s surely. Sex is not a forbidden fruit only to be sampled by one person in your life. *You*'d be a trouble if that were the case.' Wendy put her finger on Rosie's mouth to stop further protest. 'I maybe was depressed a little, but I wasn't blind Rosie.'

Wendy thought about how to explain the last few weeks. She continued, 'Here's the thing Rosie: first time sex is mostly a one-off getting it over with. Fuelled by lust, excitement, the curious unknown; and if you're lucky, it's delicious. It isn't love though. When the sex between a man and woman is magical, fragility and honesty sway and move to the rhythm of the naked bodies. It is an incredible moment that you might only encounter a few times in life. It is great if that happens to be with the partner you chose to spend your days with. But there is no guarantee. Still, even this kind of magic isn't love. It is just extremely, wonderfully gratifying sex.'

Rosie snorted. 'Is that what you came here to find out? Was all of this about sexual liberation? Mum you're not a teenager anymore!'

Wendy sighed. 'I didn't set out to shag men. But I did discover sex can be a joyous act of self-expression. Of being in the moment and being alive. It wasn't all good, but when you both consent, and there is not force or violence ... ! So often the act of sex is computed with the act of faithfulness. Society likes social moulds. It brings stability. Despite the living that is lost. Yes, that is what I learned. How stuck I was in an unspoken social straightjacket.'

'What about Dad? Are you telling me you negotiated this with him? 'Cause I'm not buying it Mum. He would never agree.'

Wendy paused. 'Rosie, I gave and I received sex. I was satisfied physically. I haven't loved anyone the way I love your dad. But for too long I justified my worth through his; this time, I was faithful to myself. Were you?'

'What, was I what?'

'Faithful, to yourself. When you and Toni?' Wendy smiled. 'Baby, mums can tell. There's a new glint in a child's speech, a flitter in the eyes.'

'We kissed, that's all.'

'Did you like it? Did you want more?'

'Mum,' Rosie shrugged her shoulders, 'this is so uncomfortable, why are we talking about this, now?'

'Because not long after, you closed yourself off from me. And the house got unbearably frigid.'

'It is not normal for a teenager to discuss their sex life with their mother. It is yuck. Yes, and the other way around too. But me not discussing my sexual experiences with you is no reason to jet off to the other end of the world.'

Wendy squinted at Rosie. 'Phew, it's still hot. Gonna take my jacket off for a wee while. You must be hot too. Here, take off your sweater.'

Rosie dove into her black Ramones sweater. The old one she had found in Wendy's wardrobe, stashed in a cardboard box labelled the past.

'Didn't think you would.' Wendy stroked Rosie's hands, and slowly but resolutely stroked her wrists with her thumbs. 'If you have it all figured out, why this? Rosie? Why?'

Rosie pushed away Wendy's fingers. Pulled her sweater tightly round her fists.

Wendy took Rosie's right hand, and gently rolled up the sleeve. A tally of angry red lines, criss-crossed on the white. She touched the bumpy runes gently and then kissed them. 'I'm not angry. Just sad. That I couldn't get to you to stop it.'

Rosie looked across the people waiting patiently. She saw Billy. She had found a space about six rows back, in front of Clarence. She caught Rosie's eye, and waved enthusiastically, held up a coke whilst proudly beating her chest that now showed a tour shirt tied up to above her bellybutton. Rosie waved back. Then looked at her mum again. She didn't say anything.

'You forgot to clean out the bins one Tuesday. I went to tidy up and in my suppressed anger, was careless and accidentally tipped your bin. The razor blade caught the sun, just so. I think I died that day, just a little.

'I shave my legs.'

'Clearly more than just your legs. You shave the edge of your desk too? One hundred and fifty-three cuts I counted. Before I came here, most of the edge was ruined. What did you move onto, the inside of your thighs, the bottom of your feet?

'Mum, it's nothing. Really, just a few scratches.'

'Rosie, you are an adult. Well, almost. That doesn't mean I have ceased to exist. That you can no longer ask for help. I try to reach out. I get withdrawal. I try to ask. I get silence. And you wonder why I left?'

Rosie gently removed her mother's hand and pulled down the sweater. 'I needed to feel something. I didn't like Toni's kiss. So I tried some others.'

Wendy smiled inwardly at how Rosie had believed that had gone unnoticed. She said nothing though. It was Rosie's time to speak.

'But I didn't feel anything with them either. So I tried more sex, smoked a little here and there. Nothing. I figured there was something wrong with me. I wanted to feel. The rush of blood – it is a high-pitched rumbling like the tide rolling over the pebbles at the beach. That I could feel; the rushing trying to escape my skin.'

Wendy pulled Rosie closer to her. She rolled up Rosie's sweater and kissed the scratched wrists. Where she always talked too much, she had no words now. Was this what being a mother was all about? Sure, from the day they are born it is a long process of letting go. But is motherhood really just about failing your child? No matter how you try, always failing your child? Is that what defines motherhood in the end? 'I guess some people learn to play the guitar, write bad poetry.'

'Run away.'

'That. Too.'

Rosie leant back into her mother's arms. Wendy smelt the sweetness of the hair product that helped the Mohican stand up. She felt Rosie relax and get heavier. The stands around them were filling up. She glanced over her shoulder. She saw Billy nestle into the spot six rows back, in front of where Clarence would soon tear the air with his raw rasp. Some saxophonists had a golden-tongued honeydew to their sound. Not so with Clarence. His playing was immediate and gritty. She sat up.

'That girl! Did you say her name was Billy?'

'Yes, why?'

Wendy smiled. 'I think I might have met her granddad. I'm staying with a friend of his. Larry. What are the chances? Maybe you should go to her later? Get to know her better. Start being faithful to yourself.'

Rosie looked up. Wendy smiled, 'Like I said Rosie, not much gets past a mother…'

'You knew, how long have you known?'

'I suspected. Gut feeling.'

Rosie didn't answer. She thought about Lea back home. The way her voice had stirred something invisible. The warmth she felt even at the memory. If she closed her eyes she couldn't picture her, but she could recall the softness of her lips.

'Rosie? She seems a nice girl. Anyhow, I promised Jackson, her grandfather, I would tell her he loves her very much indeed.'

Rosie turned to face her mother. 'Mum, you are something else. You've been in Philadelphia one day and you know half the town. Jeez. Don't worry, I've got her number. But tonight, like you said, it is us two together. Wouldn't want to spend my birthday any other way.' She paused, carefully weighing up the next words. 'They called me a slut too, Mum. But I didn't care what they said about me. It didn't touch me, but when they called you a hoore, I dunno, it hurt. It wasn't me that found your stupid blog. It was that dickhead Razorboy, who shared it with the bitches in my class. They copied what you wrote, and stuck it up in the girls' toilets. Then they stuck it up in the boys' toilets too. It was so humiliating. I mean, on the internet the whole world can read it, so why would it matter that people in town should know? But it did. Somehow it made less of you. I hate that. It made less of Dad.'

'Did he read it too?'

'Not sure, he doesn't talk about it. But I know he misses you. I have to open the curtains in the morning. Turn on the heating. The Great

Western has been doing good business. Just come home, Mum. Speak to him.'

'I can't come home if nothing changes. I cannot return to love that refuses to share hurt, or a stale rut kind of love that withdraws within itself. I need a love that rattles cages. Love that throws sugar pots through the kitchen. Love that cries and howls. Love that rolls down the window. Wendy looked at the stage. It was lying in the sun, empty, but the drums, the mics and guitar racks seemed all set. She thought back to a year ago, when the band had grabbed those instruments and tore her sedated life to pieces with the first notes of The Rising.

'Rosie, the love I seek is a wild river. I want to be free to swim naked in that unpredictable stream. I want to meet your dad there. Meet you there. Laughing, trusting.'

Wendy look around her. All these faces were strangers bound to her by the one guy and his band who could make her forget the world for a while. 'Are you prepared to let the current take you? Or, as Bruce says it, get into the front seat?' Wendy paused. 'Don't answer yet, think about it carefully.'

'I know the ride isn't free Mum.' Rosie took out her purse, a simple, woven pouch with a single zipper. A colourful souvenir from a holiday to Spain back when she was seven years old. Such a tacky thing to treasure. Rosie unfolded an A4 and held it up. Wendy knew at a glance it was the lyrics she'd left Rosie. 'Mum, I'm sorry. I'm sorry I didn't come to you when I got stuck. I will next time. Just come home. Let's pull out, Mum. You and I both. To win.'

Wendy considered her daughter. The short hair suited her. Her cheekbones stood out, accentuating her eyes. Straight back, small frame, trained shoulders. A superhero in the making. But fragile still. 'What about taking some time together first Rosie? I rebook my flight. We get a car, drive to the Badlands, and live life every day for a wee while. Get reacquainted. You tell me more about your fears and dreams. And maybe about whoever it is that glazes over your eyes.' She tapped Rosie's nose lovingly. 'We'll let your father know we are safe but that we need some time.

'Mum, are you suggesting I skive school? God, I never thought I'd see the day. What about fifth year *where futures are made or broken*?'

'Rosie, you are smart, way smarter than most of your classmates. There's nothing you can't catch up with when you get back. Life isn't something you learn in school.' She laughed when Rosie rolled her eyes. 'Yeah, it sounds corny. But it is the truth and you know it. If I have learnt anything these past few weeks, it's that life throws us opportunities if we are open to them. Even if they aren't always what we thought they were going to be, or even what we wanted. You've come this far, why not run with it for a while? Think about it Rosie.'

Rosie shifted to release her left foot that had become numb. Then she took off her sweater and bound it round her waist. She leant over to hug her mother when a roar went up. All around them people shot to their feet. And sure enough, one by one the E Street band filed onto the stage to the dying notes of Fats Domino's *Blue Monday*. An almighty Bruuuuuuuce rang out as the man himself walked onto the stage with his guitar slung around his neck, blue shirt – sleeves rolled up - and waistcoat: a gentleman of rock and roll. Wendy took Rosie's hand. She stepped a bit closer to the stage, looked about her. Spotted Redheaded Woman, waved. Thumbs up came right back!

Rosie looked at her mother. She was thinner, and more drawn than five weeks ago, but radiant with excitement and life. Rosie whooped, 'Roll down that window Mum, you've lived with the sadness. Let's go find the place you really want to be.'

'Happy birthday baby!'

'I love you Mum!'

And at that, Bruce rumbled his guitar and with a giant grin on his face burst out, *'Uh one, two, three, four – one, two, three, four!'*

Acknowledgements

No book is written completely by the author alone. Life itself is the biggest driving force behind much of my writing, and I am grateful for the curveballs, the joys and lows that Life has thrown at me. At the risk of sounding like a crass Hollywood B-lister I would like to thank a few people too.

Kristin Anderson who took on the challenge of editing my manuscript and being frank, fair and eagle-eyed, without letting friendship be an obstacle for professionalism.

Peter de Koning who patiently explained the intricacies of Garage Band to me so I could produce sheet music for the songs written especially for the book. And then this once, did the job for me – all for the sake of art. I promise, next one I will create myself.

All the friends, and makers who have supported my creative outbursts over the years with attendance, support and wonderful advice. You know who you are.

The Springsteen fan community – what adventures we share. Some of you became close friends, some are mere passing ships, but all of you enriched my 40-year journey following Springsteen, whose values and words are the bedrock of this novel.

And last but not least: my family. It cannot be easy to live with a fickle, hyper-focussed, concert-going, self-doubting, affirmation-seeking, imposter-syndrome-suffering wife and mother. But you are always there, having my back. Thank you, Otto, my man-son who gives the best hugs, for your contribution to this novel in the language that comes naturally to you: music. Thank you, Noah, my concert buddy, and creative-spirit guide and inspiration, for your musical gift to this novel. Thank you, Bill, my life-long companion – I learned and appreciate that from behind that god-damn guitar, is how you speak best. And finally, Pippin, for lowering my stress … purrrrrrrrrr.

Each Chapter of this novel was inspired by words from songs. Copyright licensing had me rethink the plan to incorporate the lyrics. However, I did make a Spotify playlist of the songs, in the order of the novel. Go to: *Chasing the Heartland* playlist on spotify @poetdownhere.

Independence Day	Bruce Springsteen
Outsider	Ramones
Human Touch	Bruce Springsteen
Here Today, Gone Tomorrow	Ramones
Reason to Believe	Bruce Springsteen
Don't Go	Ramones
Night	Bruce Springsteen
Stolen Car	Bruce Springsteen
Jackson Cage	Bruce Springsteen
Lost in the Flood	Bruce Springsteen
Hungry Heart	Bruce Springsteen
I'm on Fire	Bruce Springsteen
Rosalita	Bruce Springsteen
Red headed Woman	Bruce Springsteen
Crush on You	Bruce Springsteen
Sherry Darling	Bruce Springsteen
Friday I'm in Love	The Cure
Roll of the Dice	Bruce Springsteen
Just like Heaven	The Cure
Mary Queen of Arkansas	Bruce Springsteen
Boys Don't Cry	The Cure
Does this Bus Stop at 82nd Street	Bruce Springsteen
Secret Garden	Bruce Springsteen
Da Da Da	Elastica
Streets of Philadelphia	Bruce Springsteen
From Small Things	Bruce Springsteen

For years fans have been illegally recording shows and passing these recordings on to each other for free. There is a bootleg of the concert in Philadelphia where the novel ends. Obviously, this bootleg is not endorsed by Springsteen Inc. Just saying I have it, and you have my email …